P. Asbjörnsen, G. W. Dasent

Tales from the Fjeld

A Second Series of Popular Tales

P. Asbjörnsen, G. W. Dasent

Tales from the Fjeld
A Second Series of Popular Tales

ISBN/EAN: 9783744676939

Printed in Europe, USA, Canada, Australia, Japan

Cover: Foto ©Andreas Hilbeck / pixelio.de

More available books at **www.hansebooks.com**

TALES FROM THE FJELD.

TALES FROM THE FJELD.

TALES FROM THE FJELD.

A SECOND SERIES OF POPULAR TALES,

FROM THE NORSE OF

P. Chr. ASBJÖRNSEN.

BY

G. W. DASENT, D.C.L.,

AUTHOR OF "TALES FROM THE NORSE," "ANNALS OF AN EVENTFUL LIFE," ETC.

LONDON:

CHAPMAN & HALL, 193, PICCADILLY.

1874.

[All Rights Reserved.]

PREFACE.

THE Tales contained in this volume form a second series of those " Popular Tales from the Norse," which have been received with much favour in this country, and of which a Third Edition will shortly be published. A part of them appeared some years ago in *Once a Week*, from which they are now reprinted by permission of the proprietors, the Norse originals, from which they were translated, having been communicated by the translator's friend, P. Chr. Asbjörnsen, to various Christmas books, published in Christiania. In 1871, Mr. Asbjörnsen collected those scattered Tales and added some more to them, which he published under the title " Norske Folke-Eventyr fortalte of P. Chr. Asbjörnsen, Ny Samling." It is from this new series as revised by the collector that the present version has been made. In it the translator has trodden in the path laid down in the first series of " Tales from the Norse," and tried to turn his Norse original into mother English, which any one that runs may read.

That this plan has met with favour abroad as well as at home is proved by the fact that large editions of the "Tales from the Norse" have been printed by Messrs. Appleton in New York, by which, no doubt, that appropriating firm have been great gainers, though the translator's share in their profits has amounted to nothing. It is more grateful to him to find that in Norway, the cradle of these beautiful stories, his efforts have been warmly appreciated by Messrs Asbjörnsen and Moe, who, in their preface to the Third Edition, Christiania, 1866, speak in the following terms of his version : "In France and England collections have appeared in which our Tales have not only been correctly and faultlessly translated, but even rendered with exemplary truth and care,—nay, with thorough mastery; the English translation, by George Webbe Dasent, is the best and happiest rendering of our Tales that has appeared, and it has in England been more successful and become far more widely known than the originals here at home." Then speaking of the Introduction, Messrs. Asbjörnsen and Moe go on to say, "We have here added the end of this Introduction to show how the translator has understood and grasped the relation in which these Tales stand to Norse nature and the life of the people, and how they have sprung out of both."

The title of this volume, "Tales from the Fjeld," arose out of the form in which they were published in *Once a Week*. The translator began by setting them in a frame formed by the imaginary adventures of English sportsmen on the Fjeld or Fells in Norway. "Karin and Anders," and "Edward and I," are therefore the creatures of his imagination, but the Tales are the Tales of Asbjörnsen. After a while he grew weary of the setting and framework, and when about a third of the volume had been thus framed, he resolved to let the Tales speak for themselves and stand alone as in the first series of "Popular Tales from the Norse."

With regard to the bearing of these Tales on the question of the diffusion of race and tradition, much might be said, but as he has already traversed the same ground in the Introduction to the "Tales from the Norse," he reserves what he has to say on that point till the Third Edition of those Tales shall appear. It will be enough here to mention that several of the Tales now published are variations, though very interesting ones, from some of those in the first series. Others are rather the harvest of popular experience than mythical tales, and on the whole the character of this volume is more jocose and less poetical than that of its predecessor. In a word, they are, many of them, what the Germans would call " Schwänke."

Of this kind are the Tales called " The Charcoal Burner," " Our Parish Clerk," and " The Parson and the Clerk." In " Goody 'gainst the Stream," and " Silly Men and Cunning Wives," the reader, skilled in popular fiction, will find two tales of Indian origin, both of which are wide-spread in the folk-lore of the West, and make their appearance in the Facetiæ of Poggio. The Beast Epic, in which Jacob Grimm so delighted, is largely represented, and the stories of that kind in this volume are among the best that have been collected. One of the most mythical and at the same time one of the most domestic stories of those now published, is, perhaps, " The Father of the Family," which ought rather to have been called " The Seventh, the Father of the Family," as it is not till the wayfarer has inquired seven times from as many generations of old men that he finds the real father of the family

Mr. Ralston, the accomplished writer and editor of "Russian Popular Tales," has pointed out in an article on these Norse Tales, which appeared in *Fraser's Magazine* for December, 1872, the probable antiquity of this story, which he classes with the Rigsmal of the Elder Edda. That it was known in England two centuries ago is proved by the curious fact that it has got woven into the life of "Old Jenkins," whose mythical age as well as that of "Old Parr," Mr. Thoms has recently demolished in his book on the "Longevity of Man." The story as quoted by Mr. Thoms, from Clarkson's "History and Antiquities of Richmond," in Yorkshire, is so curious that it is worth while to give it at length. There had been some legal dispute in which the evidence of Old Jenkins, as confessedly "the oldest inhabitant" was required, and the agent of Mrs. Wastell, one of the parties, went to visit the old man. "Previous to Jenkins going to York," says Mr. Clarkson, "when the agent of Mrs. Wastell went to him to find out what account he could give of the matter in dispute, he saw an old man sitting at the door, to whom he told his business. The old man said 'he could remember nothing about it, but that he would find his father in the house, who perhaps could satisfy him.' When he went in he saw another old man sitting over the fire, bowed down with years, to whom he repeated his former questions. With some difficulty he made him understand what he had said, and after a little while got the following answer, which surprised him very much : 'That he knew nothing about it, but that if he would go into the yard he would meet with his father, who perhaps could tell him.' The agent upon this thought that he had met with a race of Antediluvians. However into the yard he went, and to his no small astonishment found a venerable man with a long beard, and a broad leathern belt about him, chopping sticks. To this man he again told his business, and received such information as in the end recovered the royalty in dispute. "The fact is," adds Mr. Thoms, "that the story of Jenkins' son and grandson is only a Yorkshire version of the story as old or older than Jenkins himself, namely, of the very old man who was seen crying because his father had beaten him for throwing stones at his grandfather." On which it may be remarked, that however old Old Jenkins may have been, this story has probably out-lived as many generations as popular belief gave years to his life. Another old story is "Death and the Doctor," which centuries ago got entangled with the history of the family of Bethune, in Scotland, who were supposed to possess an hereditary gift of leechcraft, derived in the same way. "Friends in Life and Death," is a Norse variation of Rip van Winkle, which is nothing more nor less than a Dutch popular tale, while the lassie who won the prince by fulfilling his conditions of coming to him, "not driving and not riding, not walking and not carried, not fasting and not full-fed, not naked and not clad, not by daylight and not by night," has its variations in many lands. It is no little proof of the wonderful skill of Hans Christian Andersen, and at the same time of his power to enter into the spirit of popular fiction, that he has worked the tale of "The Companion" into one of his most happy stories.

In this volume, as in the former one, the translator, while striving to be as truthful as possible, has in the case of some characters adopted the English equivalent rather than a literal rendering from the Norse. Thus "Askpot" is still "Boots," the youngest of the family on whom falls all the dirty work, and not "Cinderbob" or the Scottish

"Ashiepet." "Tyrihans" he has rendered almost literally "Taper Tom," the name meaning not slender or limber Tom, but Tom who sits in the ingle and makes tapers or matchwood of resinous fir to be used instead of candles. Some of the Tales, such as "The Charcoal Burner," "Our Parish Clerk," and "The Sheep and the Pig who set up House," are filled with proverbs which it was often very difficult to render. On this and other points it must be left to others to say whether he has succeeded or not. But if his readers, young and old, will only remember that things which seem easiest are often the hardest to do, they will be as gentle readers as those he desired to find for his first volume, and so long as they are of that spirit he is sure to be well pleased.

October 18*th*, 1873.

CONTENTS.

CONTENTS.

XV

TALES FROM THE FJELD.

WE were up on the Fjeld, Edward and I and Anders our guide, in quest of reindeer. How long ago it was we will not ask ; for after all it was not so very long ago. How did we get there ? Well ; if you must know we went up to the head of the Sogne Fjord in a boat, and then we drove up the valley in carioles till we were tired, and then we took to our legs, and, now, about three P.M., we were on the Fjeld making for the *Sæter* or Shieling, where we were to pass the night. On this our first day, we did not expect to meet deer, so on we plodded over the stony soil slanting across the Fjeld which showed its long shoulder above us, while far off glared the snowy peaks, and the glaciers stooped down to meet the Fjeld, for as the Norse proverb says, if the dale won't come to the mountain, the mountain must meet the dale. On we went, Anders cheering the way by stories of *Huldror* and Trolls, and running off hither and thither to fetch us Alpine plants and flowers. All at once, in one of these flights which had brought him up to the very edge of the shoulder above us, we saw his tall form stiffen as it were against the sky, and, in another moment, he had fallen flat, beckoning us to come cautiously to him. As we reached him stooping and running, he whispered "There they are, away yonder;" and sure enough, about half a mile further on, close under the shoulder, which broke off into an immense circular valley or combe, we could make out two stags, three hinds, and some fawns, at play. It was a strange sight to see the low, thick-set stags with their heavy palmated antlers, leaping over one another and over the hinds, and the hinds and fawns in turn following their example. "A sure sign of rain and wind," said Anders. "It will blow a hurricane and pour in torrents to-morrow, mark my words. I never looked to find them so low down; let us try to get at them." We crept down then, well under cover of the shoulder, and, led by Anders, went on till he said we were opposite the spot where the deer were at play. "But, by all the powers," said he, "be sure to take good aim both of you, and bring down each a stag. I will take one of the hinds, but I will not fire before you." And now began the real stalk; we had about three hundred yards against the wind to crawl on our hands and feet over stones, and gravel, and dry grass, and brambles, and dwarf willow, before we could get to the edge of the shoulder, and look down on the deer. For nearly the whole distance all went well, our bellies clove to the dust like snakes, as we wormed our way. But, alas! when we were not ten yards from the edge, Edward uttered a cry and sprang to his feet. Anders and I did the same without the cry, only to see the deer off at full speed down the combe, followed by a volley of oaths and a billetless bullet from the old flint rifle which Anders carried. For myself I turned to Edward and felt very much as though I should like to send my bullet through him.

"Why, in the name of all that is unholy, did you utter that yell and scare them away."

"Oh, I am very sorry," he said, "but I came across this thing like a bramble, only the prickles are much sharper, and it tore me so I couldn't bear it;" and, as he spoke, he pointed to a stout trailing *Rubus arcticus* over which he had crawled, and which had taken toll both of his clothing and flesh.

Anders looked at him with unutterable scorn. "When the gentleman next goes after reindeer, he had better take Osborn's Pipe with him. Come along, no more reindeer for us to-day; no, nor to-morrow either. The peaks are going to put on their nightcaps; we must try to get to the *Sœter* before the storm comes on." After a tough walk, during which Anders said little or nothing, we got to the shieling, where two girls, a cousin of Anders and his sister, met us with bright hearty faces. They had been up there looking after the cattle since June, and it was now August, and they had made heaps of butter and cheese. There were three rooms in the *Sœter*, a living-room in the middle, and on either hand a room for the men and another for the women. There were outhouses for the butter, and cheese, and milk, and cream. We had sent up some creature comforts, and with these and the butter, cream, and cheese, we made a good supper; and now we are sitting over the fire smoking our pipes, and listening to the rain as it patters on the roof, and to the wind as it howls round the building. Under the influence of tobacco and cognac Anders was more happy, and got even reconciled to Edward, whom he regarded as a muff. Looking at him mockingly, he said again, "What a pity you had not Osborn's Pipe."

"And, pray, what was that?" asked Edward; "was it anything like this?" holding out his cutty pipe.

"God forgive us," said Anders; "there are pipes and pipes, and Osborn's Pipe was not a tobacco-pipe, but a playing pipe or whistle. At least so my grandmother said, for she said her grandmother knew a very old woman down at the head of the lake, who had known Osborn and seen his pipe. But, if you like, I'll tell you the story. The girls are gone to bed, and so they won't trouble us, though there's a good bit of kissing in the story, and, when you hear it, you'll both say we should have been lucky if we had only had Osborn's Pipe when the gentleman scared away the deer. But here goes."

OSBORN'S PIPE.

"ONCE on a time there was a poor tenant farmer who had to give up his farm to his landlord; but, if he had lost his farm, he had three sons left, and their names were Peter, Paul, and Osborn Boots. They stayed at home and sauntered about, and wouldn't do a stroke of work; that they thought was the right thing to do. They thought, too, they were too good for everything, and that nothing was good enough for them.

"At last Peter had got to hear how the king would have a keeper to watch his hares; so he said to his father that he would be off thither: the place would just suit him, for he would serve no lower man than the king; that was what he said. The old father thought there might be work for which he was better fitted than that; for he that would keep the king's hares must be light and lissom, and no lazybones, and when the hares began to skip and frisk there would be quite another dance than loitering about from house to house. Well, it was all no good: Peter would go, and must go, so he took his scrip on his back, and toddled away down the hill; and when he had gone far, and farther than far, he came to an old wife, who stood there with her nose stuck fast in a log of wood, and pulled and pulled at it; and as soon as he saw how she stood dragging and pulling to get free he burst into a loud fit of laughter.

"'Don't stand there and grin,' said the old wife, 'but come and help an old cripple; I was to have split asunder a little firewood, and I got my nose fast down here, and so I have stood and tugged and torn and not tasted a morsel of food for hundreds of years.' That was what she said.

"But for all that Peter laughed more and more. He thought it all fine fun. All he said was, as she had stood so for hundreds of years she might hold out for hundreds of years still.

"When he got to the king's grange, they took him for

keeper at once. It was not bad serving there, and he was to have good food and good pay, and maybe the princess into the bargain ; but if one of the king's hares got lost, they were to cut three red stripes out of his back and cast him into a pit of snakes.

"So long as Peter was in the byre and home-field he kept all the hares in one flock : but as the day wore on, and they got up into the wood, all the hares began to frisk, and skip, and scuttle away up and down the hillocks. Peter ran after them this way and that, and nearly burst himself with running, so long as he could make out that he had one of them left, and when the last was gone he was almost brokenwinded. And after that he saw nothing more of them.

"When it drew towards evening he sauntered along on his way home, and stood and called and called to them at each fence, but no hares came ; and when he got home to the king's grange, there stood the king all ready with his knife, and he took and cut three red stripes out of Peter's back, and then rubbed pepper and salt into them, and cast him into a pit of snakes.

"After a time, Paul was for going to the king's grange to keep the king's hares. The old gaffer said the same thing to him, and even still more ; but he must and would set off ; there was no help for it, and things went neither better nor worse with him than with Peter. The old wife stood there and tugged and tore at her nose to get it out of the log ; he laughed, and thought it fine fun, and left her standing and hacking there. He got the place at once; no one said him nay; but the hares hopped and skipped away from him down all the hillocks, while he rushed about till he blew and panted like a colley-dog in the dog-days, and when he got home at night to the king's grange, without a hare, the king stood ready with his knife in the porch, and took and cut three broad red stripes out of his back, and rubbed pepper and salt into them, and so down he went into the pit of snakes.

"Now, when a little while had passed, Osborn Boots was all for setting off to keep the king's hares, and he told his mind to the gaffer. He thought it would be just the right work for him to go into the woods and fields, and along the wild strawberry brakes, and to drag a flock of hares with him, and between whiles to lie and sleep and warm himself on the sunny hill-sides.

"The gaffer thought there might be work which suited him better; if it didn't go worse, it was sure not to go better with him than with his two brothers. The man to keep the king's hares must not dawdle about like a lazy-bones with leaden soles to his stockings, or like a fly in a tar-pot; for when they fell to frisking and skipping on the sunny slopes, it would be quite another dance to catching fleas with gloves on. No; he that would get rid of that work with a whole back had need to be more than lithe and lissom, and he must fly about faster than a bladder or a bird's-wing.

"'Well, well, it was all no good, however bad it might be,' said Osborn Boots. He would go to the king's grange and serve the king, for no lesser man would he serve, and he would soon keep the hares. They couldn't well be worse than the goat and the calf at home. So Boots threw his scrip on his shoulder, and down the hill he toddled.

"So when he had gone far, and farther than far, and had begun to get right down hungry, he too came to the old wife, who stood with her nose fast in the log, who tugged, and tore, and tried to get loose.

"' Good-day, grandmother,' said Boots. ' Are you standing there whetting your nose, poor old cripple that you are ?'

"' Now, not a soul has called me "mother" for hundreds of years,' said the old wife. 'Do come and help me to get free, and give me something to live on ; for I haven't had meat in my mouth all that time. See if I don't do you a motherly turn afterwards.'

"Yes ; he thought she might well ask for a bit of food and a drop of drink.

"So he cleft the log for her, that she might get her nose out of the split, and sat down to eat and drink with her ; and as the old wife had a good appetite, you may fancy she got the lion's share of the meal.

"When they were done, she gave Boots a pipe, which was in this wise : when he blew into one end of it, anything that he wished away was scattered to the four winds, and when he blew into the other, all things gathered themselves together again ; and if the pipe were lost or taken from him, he had only to wish for it, and it came back to him.

"'Something like a pipe, this,' said Osborn Boots.

"When he got to the king's grange, they chose him for keeper on the spot. It was no bad service there, and food and wages he should have, and, if he were man enough to keep the king's hares, he might, perhaps, get the princess too; but if one of them got away, if it were only a leveret, they were to cut three red stripes out of his back. And the king was so sure of this that he went off at once and ground his knife.

"It would be a small thing to keep these hares, thought Osborn Boots; for when they set out they were almost as tame as a flock of sheep, and so long as he was in the lane and in the home-field, he had them all easily in a flock and following; but when they got upon the hill by the wood, and it looked towards midday, and the sun began to burn and shine on the slopes and hillsides, all the hares fell to frisking and skipping about, and away over the hills.

"'Ho, ho! stop! will you all go? Go, then!' said Boots; and he blew into one end of the pipe, so that they ran off on all sides, and there was not one of them left. But as he went on, and came to an old charcoal pit, he blew into the other end of the pipe; and before he knew where he was, the hares were all there, and stood in lines and rows, so that he could take them all in at a glance, just like a troop of soldiers on parade. 'Something like a pipe, this,' said Osborn Boots; and with that he laid him down to sleep away under a sunny slope, and the hares frisked and frolicked about till eventide. Then he piped them all together again, and came down to the king's grange with them, like a flock of sheep.

"The king and the queen, and the princess, too, all stood in the porch, and wondered what sort of fellow this was who so kept the hares that he brought them home again; and the king told and reckoned them on his fingers, and counted them over and over again; but there was not one of them missing—no! not so much as a leveret.

"'Something like a lad, this,' said the princess.

"Next day he went off to the wood, and was to keep the hares again; but as he lay and rested himself on a strawberry brake, they sent the maid after him from the grange that she might find out how it was that he was man enough to keep the king's hares so well.

"So he took out the pipe and showed it her, and then he blew into one end and made them fly like the wind over all the hills and dales; and then he blew into the other end, and they all came scampering back to the brake, and all stood in row and rank again.

"'What a pretty pipe,' said the maid. She would willingly give a hundred dollars for it, if he would sell it, she said.

"'Yes! it is something like a pipe,' said Osborn Boots; 'and it was not to be had for money alone; but if she would give him the hundred dollars, and a kiss for each dollar, she should have it,' he said.

"Well! why not? of course she would; she would willingly give him two for each dollar, and thanks besides.

"So she got the pipe; but when she had got as far as the king's grange, the pipe was gone, for Osborn Boots had wished for it back, and so, when it drew towards eventide, home he came with his hares just like any other flock of sheep; and for all the king's counting or telling, there was no help,—not a hair of the hares was missing.

"The third day that he kept the hares, they sent the princess on her way to try and get the pipe from him. She made herself as blithe as a lark, and she bade him two hundred dollars if he would sell her the pipe and tell her how she was to behave to bring it safe home with her.

"'Yes! yes! it is something like a pipe,' said Osborn Boots; 'and it was not for sale,' he said, 'but all the same, he would do it for her sake, if she would give him two hundred dollars, and a kiss into the bargain for each dollar; then she might have the pipe. If she wished to keep it, she must look sharp after it. That was her look-out.'

"'This is a very high price for a hare-pipe,' thought the princess; and she made mouths at giving him the kisses; 'but, after all,' she said, 'it's far away in the wood, no one can see it or hear it—it can't be helped; for I must and will have the pipe.'

"So when Osborn Boots had got all he was to have, she got the pipe, and off she went, and held it fast with her fingers the whole way; but when she came to the grange, and was going to take it out, it slipped through her fingers and was gone!

"Next day the queen would go herself and fetch the pipe

from him.   She made sure she would bring the pipe back
with her.

"Now she was more stingy about the money, and bade
no more than fifty dollars; but she had to raise her price
till it came to three hundred.   Boots said it was something like a pipe, and it was no price at all; still for her
sake it might go, if she would give him three hundred
dollars, and a smacking kiss for each dollar into the
bargain ; then she might have it.   And he got the kisses
well paid, for on that part of the bargain she was not so
squeamish.

"So when she had got the pipe, she both bound it fast,
and looked after it well ; but she was not a hair better off
than the others, for when she was going to pull it out at
home, the pipe was gone ; and at even down came Osborn
Boots, driving the king's hares home for all the world like
a flock of tame sheep.

"'It is all stuff,' said the king ; 'I see I must set off
myself, if we are to get this wretched pipe from him ;
there's no other help for it, I can see.'   And when Osborn
Boots had got well into the woods next day with the hares,
the king stole after him, and found him lying on the same
sunny hillside, where the women had tried their hands on
him.

"Well! they were good friends and very happy; and
Osborn Boots showed him the pipe, and blew first on one
end and then on the other, and the king thought it a
pretty pipe, and wanted at last to buy it, even though he
gave a thousand dollars for it.

"'Yes! it is something like a pipe,' said Boots, 'and it's not to be had for money; but do you see that white horse yonder down there?' and he pointed away into the wood.

"'See it! of course I see it; it's my own horse Whitey,' said the king. No one had need to tell him that.

"'Well! if you will give me a thousand dollars, and then go and kiss yon white horse down in the marsh there, behind the big fir-tree, you shall have my pipe.'

"'Isn't it to be had for any other price?' asked the king.

"'No, it is not,' said Osborn.

"'Well! but I may put my silken pockethandkerchief between us?' said the king.

"Very good; he might have leave to do that. And so he got the pipe, and put it into his purse. And the purse he put into his pocket, and buttoned it up tight; and so off he strode to his home. But when he reached the grange, and was going to pull out his pipe, he fared no better than the women folk; he hadn't the pipe any more than they, and there came Osborn Boots driving home the flock of hares, and not a hair was missing.

'The king was both spiteful and wroth, to think that he had fooled them all round, and cheated him out of the pipe as well; and now he said Boots must lose his life, there was no question of it, and the queen said the same: it was best to put such a rogue out of the way red-handed.

"Osborn thought it neither fair nor right, for he had done nothing but what they told him to do; and so he had guarded his back and life as best he might.

"So the king said there was no help for it; but if he could lie the great brewing-vat so full of lies that it ran over, then he might keep his life.

"That was neither a long nor perilous piece of work : he was quite game to do that, said Osborn Boots. So he began to tell how it had all happened from the very first. He told about the old wife and her nose in the log, and then he went on to say, 'Well, but I must lie faster if the vat is to be full.' So he went on to tell of the pipe and how he got it; and of the maid, how she came to him and wanted to buy it for a hundred dollars, and of all the kisses she had to give besides, away there in the wood. Then he told of the princess how she came and kissed him so sweetly for the pipe when no one could see or hear it all away there in the wood. Then he stopped and said, 'I must lie faster if the vat is ever to be full.' So he told of the queen, how close she was about the money and how overflowing she was with her smacks. 'You know I must lie hard to get the vat full,' said Osborn.

"'For my part,' said the queen, 'I think it's pretty full already.'

"'No! no! it isn't,' said the king.

"So he fell to telling how the king came to him, and about the white horse down on the marsh, and how if the king was to have the pipe, he must—'Yes, your majesty, if the vat is ever to be full I must go on and lie hard,' said Osborn Boots.

"'Hold! hold, lad! It's full to the brim,' roared out the king; 'don't you see how it is foaming over?'

"So both the king and the queen thought it best he should have the princess to wife, and half the kingdom. There was no help for it.

"'That was something like a pipe,' said Osborn Boots.'"

That was the story of Osborn's Pipe, and when Anders stopped we all laughed, and our laughter was re-echoed by the girls, who had listened with the door ajar, and who now showed their smiling faces through the opening, and thanked Anders for telling the story so well. "Your own grandmother couldn't have told it better," said Christine, his fair-haired cousin.

THE HAUNTED MILL, AND THE HONEST PENNY.

NEXT morning we woke to find Anders' words too true; the wind still howled, and the rain still poured, deer-stalking was out of the question, nor could the girls stir out of the doors to look after the kine. There we were, all house-bound. What was to be done? After breakfast we smoked, and the girls knitted stockings. Anders, for want of something better to do, cleaned our guns and admired their make and locks. But all this was not much towards killing time on the Fjeld, and we had no books.

At last Edward, who was rather afraid of Anders and his jokes on his sportsmanship, whispered to me,

"Can't you make him tell us some more stories? I'll be bound *Osborn's Pipe* is not the only tale he has in his scrip."

Not a bad thought, but Anders was one of those free spirits who must be stalked as warily as a reindeer. I felt that if I asked him outright he might betake him to his Norse pride and say he was no story-teller. "If I wanted stories I had better ask some of the old women down in the dales." It was not the first time I had unsealed unwilling lips, and I knew the way.

"That was a good story about Osborn's Pipe, and I owe you one for it, Anders. Come listen to one of mine, and let the lassies listen to it too. It's not long."

THE HAUNTED MILL.

" ONCE on a time, there was a man who had a mill by the side of a force, and in the mill there was a brownie. Whether the man, as is the custom in most places, gave the brownie porridge and ale at Yule to bring grist to the mill, I can't say, but I don't think he did, for every time he turned the water on the mill, the brownie took hold of the spindle and stopped the mill, so that he couldn't grind a sack.

"The man knew well enough it was all the brownie's work, and at last one evening, when he went into the mill, he took a pot full of pitch and tar, and lit a fire under it. Well! when he turned the water on the wheel, it went round awhile, but soon after it made a dead stop. So he turned, and twisted, and put his shoulder to the top of the wheel, but it was all no good. By this time the pot of pitch was boiling hot, and then he opened the trap-door which opened on to the ladder that went down into the wheel, and if he didn't see the brownie standing on the steps of the ladder with his jaws all a-gape, and he gaped so wide that his mouth filled up the whole trap-door.

"'Did you ever see such a wide mouth?' said the brownie.

"But the man was handy with his pitch. He caught up the pot and threw it, pitch and all, into the gaping jaws.

"'Did you ever feel such hot pitch?'

"Then the brownie let the wheel go, and yelled and howled frightfully. Since then he has been never known to stop the wheel in that mill, and there they ground in peace."

Yes! Anders had heard a story something like that, only it was about a water kelpy, not a brownie. Brownies, he declared, never did folk much harm, except lazy maids and idle grooms, but kelpies were spiteful, and hated men. Besides, brownies hated water, they couldn't bear to cross a running stream; then how could they live in a mill? No, it was a kelpy, and his grandmother had told him so.

Then, after a pause, he went on, "But I know another story of a mill which was not canny, and I'll tell it if you like."

We were all ears, and Anders began :—

THE HAUNTED MILL.

"THIS story, too, I heard of my grandmother, who knew stories without end, and more, she believed them. This mill was not in these parts, it was somewhere up the country ; but wherever it was, north of the Fells, or south of the Fells, it was not canny. No one could grind a grain of corn in it for weeks together, when something came and haunted it. But the worst was that, besides haunting it, the trolls, or whatever they were, took to burning the mill down. Two Whitsun-eves running it had caught fire and burned to the ground.

"Well, the third year, as Whitsuntide was drawing on, the man had a tailor in his house hard by the mill, who was making Sunday clothes for the miller.

"'I wonder, now,' said the man on Whitsun-eve, 'whether the mill will burn down this Whitsuntide, too?'

"'No, it shan't,' said the tailor. 'Why should it? Give me the keys: I'll watch the mill.'

"Well, the man thought that brave, and so, as the evening drew on, he gave the tailor the keys, and showed him into the mill. It was empty, you know, for it was just new-built, and so the tailor sat down in the middle of the floor, and took out his chalk and chalked a great circle round about him, and outside the ring all round he wrote the Lord's Prayer, and when he had done that he wasn't afraid—no, not if Old Nick himself came.

"So at dead of night the door flew open with a bang, and there came in such a swarm of black cats you couldn't count them; they were as thick as ants. They were not long before they had put a big pot on the fireplace and set light under it, and the pot began to boil and bubble, and as for the broth, it was for all the world like pitch and tar.

"'Ha! ha!' thought the tailor, 'that's your game, is it!'

"And he had hardly thought this before one of the cats thrust her paw under the pot and tried to upset it.

"'Paws off, pussy,' said the tailor, 'you'll burn your whiskers.'

"'Hark to the tailor, who says "Paws off, pussy," to me,' said the cat to the other cats, and in a trice they all ran away from the fireplace, and began to dance and jump round the circle; and then all at once the same cat stole off to the fireplace and tried to upset the pot.

"'Paws off, pussy, you'll burn your whiskers,' bawled out the tailor again, and again he scared them from the fireplace.

"'Hark to the tailor, who says "Paws off, pussy"' said the cat to the others, and again they all began to dance and jump round the circle, and then all at once they were off again to the pot, trying to upset it.

"'Paws off, pussy, you'll burn your whiskers,' screamed out the tailor the third time, and this time he gave them such a fright that they tumbled head over heels on the floor, and began dancing and jumping as before.

"Then they closed round the circle, and danced faster and faster: so fast at last that the tailor's head began to turn round, and they glared at him with such big ugly eyes, as though they would swallow him up alive.

"Now just as they were at the fastest, the same cat which had tried so often to upset the pot, stuck her paw inside the circle, as though she meant to claw the tailor.

But as soon as the tailor saw that, he drew his knife out of the sheath and held it ready ; just then the cat thrust her paw in again, and in a trice the tailor chopped it off, and then, pop ! all the cats took to their heels as fast as they could, with yells and caterwauls, right out at the door.

"But the tailor lay down inside his circle, and slept till the sun shone bright in upon the floor. Then he rose, locked the mill, and went away to the miller's house.

"When he got there, both the miller and his wife were still abed, for you know it was Whitsunday morning.

"'Good morning,' said the tailor, as he went to the bedside, and held out his hand to the miller.

"'Good morning,' said the miller, who was both glad and astonished to see the tailor safe and sound, you must know.

"'Good morning, mother !' said the tailor, and held out his hand to the wife.

"'Good morning,' said she ; but she looked so wan and worried ; and as for her hand, she hid it under the quilt ; but at last she stuck out the left. Then the tailor saw plainly how things stood, but what he said to the man and what was done to the wife, I never heard."

"But I can tell you, Anders," I broke in : "she was burnt for a witch, and, do you know, over in Scotland we have the same story ; only we have the end. She tried on the Boot till her feet were crushed, and Morton's Maiden hugged her till her ribs cracked, and her fingers were fitted to the thumbscrews till they were all jelly. All this to make her own that she was a witch, and at last, when she owned it, she was burnt at Edinburgh, in the days of King James the Sixth, and seven other carlines with her."

Having unsealed Anders' lips, I was not going to let him stop, so I told the story of *Whittington and his Cat,* and I even got him and the lassies to understand the awful importance of the Lord Mayor of London. After Anders and the lassies had crossed and blessed themselves over and over again at that wonderful story, Anders said,—

"Heaven help us, we have no Lord Mayors in Norway; the sheriff is good enough for us, and trouble enough he gives us sometimes; but we have a story, the end of which is as like your Lord Mayor's story as one pea is like another, and here it is, only we call it

THE HONEST PENNY.

"ONCE on a time there was a poor woman who lived in a tumble-down hut far away in the wood. Little had she to eat, and nothing at all to burn, and so she sent a little boy she had out into the wood to gather fuel. He ran and jumped, and jumped and ran, to keep himself warm, for it was a cold gray autumn day, and every time he found a bough or a root for his billet, he had to beat his arms across his breast, for his fists were as red as the cranberries over which he walked, for very cold. So when he had got his billet of wood and was off home, he came upon a clearing of stumps on the hillside, and there he saw a white crooked stone.

"'Ah! you poor old stone,' said the boy; 'how white and wan you are! I'll be bound you are frozen to death;' and with that he took off his jacket, and laid it on the stone. So when he got home with his billet of wood his mother asked what it all meant that he walked about in wintry weather in his shirtsleeves. Then he told her how he had seen an old crooked stone which was all white and wan for frost, and how he had given it his jacket.

"'What a fool you are!' said his mother; 'do you think a stone can freeze? But even if it froze till it shook again, know this—everyone is nearest to his own self. It costs quite enough to get clothes to your back, without your going and hanging them on stones in the clearings,' and as she said that, she hunted the boy out of the house to fetch his jacket.

"So when he came where the stone stood, lo! it had turned itself and lifted itself up on one side from the ground. 'Yes! yes! this is since you got the jacket, poor old thing,' said the boy.

"But, when he looked a little closer at the stone, he saw a money-box, full of bright silver, under it.

"'This is stolen money, no doubt,' thought the boy; 'no one puts money, come by honestly, under a stone away in the wood.'

"So he took the money-box and bore it down to a tarn hard by and threw the whole hoard into the tarn; but one silver pennypiece floated on the top of the water.

" ' Ah ! ah ! that is honest,' said the lad ; ' for what is honest never sinks.'

" So he took the silver penny and went home with it and his jacket. Then he told his mother how it had all happened, how the stone had turned itself, and how he had found a money-box full of silver money, which he had thrown out into the tarn because it was stolen money, and how one silver penny floated on the top.

" ' That I took,' said the boy, ' because it was honest.'

" ' You are a born fool,' said his mother, for she was very angry ; ' were naught else honest than what floats on water, there wouldn't be much honesty in the world. And even though the money were stolen ten times over, still you had found it ; and I tell you again what I told you before, every one is nearest to his own self. Had you only taken that money we might have lived well and happily all our days. But a ne'er-do-weel thou art, and a ne'er-do-weel thou wilt be, and now I won't drag on any longer toiling and moiling for thee. Be off with thee into the world and earn thine own bread."

" So the lad had to go out into the wide world, and he went both far and long seeking a place. But wherever he came, folk thought him too little and weak, and said they could put him to no use. At last he came to a merchant, and there he got leave to be in the kitchen and carry in wood and water for the cook. Well, after he had been there a long time, the merchant had to make a journey into foreign lands, and so he asked all his servants what he should buy and bring home for each of them. So, when all had said what they would have, the turn came to the scullion, too, who brought in wood and water for the cook. Then he held out his penny.

"'Well, what shall I buy with this?' asked the merchant; 'there won't be much time lost over this bargain.'

"'Buy what I can get for it. It is honest, that I know,' said the lad.

"That his master gave his word to do, and so he sailed away.

"So when the merchant had unladed his ship and laded her again in foreign lands, and bought what he had promised his servants to buy, he came down to his ship, and was just going to shove off from the wharf. Then all at once it came into his head that the scullion had sent out a silver penny with him, that he might buy something for him.

"'Must I go all the way back to the town for the sake of a silver penny? One would then have small gain in taking such a beggar into one's house,' thought the merchant.

"Just then an old wife came walking by with a bag at her back.

"'What have you got in your bag, mother?' asked the merchant.

"'Oh! nothing else than a cat. I can't afford to feed it any longer, so I thought I would throw it into the sea, and make away with it,' answered the woman.

"Then the merchant said to himself, 'Didn't the lad say

I was to buy what I could get for his penny?' So he asked the old wife if she would take four farthings for her cat. Yes! the goody was not slow to say 'done,' and so the bargain was soon struck.

"Now when the merchant had sailed a bit, fearful weather fell on him, and such a storm, there was nothing for it but to drive and drive till he did not know whither he was going. At last he came to a land on which he had never set foot before, and so up he went into the town.

"At the inn where he turned in, the board was laid with a rod for each man who sat at it. The merchant thought it very strange, for he couldn't at all make out what they were to do with all these rods ; but he sate him down, and thought he would watch well what the others did, and do like them. Well! as soon as the meat was set on the board, he saw well enough what the rods meant ; for out swarmed mice in thousands, and each one who sate at the board had to take to his rod and flog and flap about him, and naught else could be heard than one cut of the rod harder than the one which went before it. Sometimes they whipped one another in the face, and just gave themselves time to say, 'Beg pardon,' and then at it again.

"'Hard work to dine in this land!' said the merchant. 'But don't folk keep cats here?'

"'Cats?' they all asked, for they did not know what cats were.

"So the merchant sent and fetched the cat he had bought for the scullion, and as soon as the cat got on the table, off ran the mice to their holes, and folks had never in the memory of man had such rest at their meat.

"Then they begged and prayed the merchant to sell them the cat, and at last, after a long, long time, he promised to let them have it; but he would have a hundred dollars for it; and that sum they gave and thanks besides.

"So the merchant sailed off again; but he had scarce got good sea-room before he saw the cat sitting up at the mainmast head, and all at once again came foul weather and a storm worse than the first, and he drove and drove till he got to a country where he had never been before. The merchant went up to an inn, and here, too, the board was spread with rods; but they were much bigger and longer than the first. And, to tell the truth, they had need to be; for here the mice were many more, and every mouse was twice as big as those he had before seen.

"So he sold the cat again, and this time he got two hundred dollars for it, and that without any haggling.

"So when he had sailed away from that land and got a bit out at sea, there sat Grimalkin again at the masthead; and the bad weather began at once again, and the end of it was, he was again driven to a land where he had never been before.

"He went ashore, up to the town, and turned into an inn. There, too, the board was laid with rods, but every rod was an ell and a half long, and as thick as a small broom; and the folk said that to sit at meat was the hardest trial they had, for there were thousands of big ugly rats, so that it was only with sore toil and trouble one could get a morsel into one's mouth, 'twas such hard work to keep off the rats. So the cat had to be fetched up from the ship once more, and then folks got their food in peace. Then they all begged and prayed the merchant, for heaven's sake, to sell them his cat. For a long time he said, 'No;' but at last, he gave his word to take three hundred dollars for it. That sum they paid down at once, and thanked him and blessed him for it into the bargain.

"Now, when the merchant got out to sea, he fell a-thinking how much the lad had made out of the penny he had sent out with him.

"'Yes, yes, some of the money he shall have,' said the merchant to himself; 'but not all. Me it is that he has to thank for the cat I bought; and, besides, every man is nearest to his own self.'

"But as soon as ever the merchant thought this, such a storm and gale arose that every one thought the ship must founder. So the merchant saw there was no help for it, and he had to vow that the lad should have every penny; and, no sooner had he vowed this vow, than the weather turned good, and he got a snoring breeze fair for home.

"So, when he got to land, he gave the lad the six hundred dollars, and his daughter besides; for now the little scullion was just as rich as his master, the merchant, and even richer; and, after that, the lad lived all his days in mirth and jollity; and he sent for his mother and treated her as well as or better than he treated himself; for, said the lad, 'I don't think that every one is nearest to his own self.'"

THE DEATH OF CHANTICLEER, AND THE GREEDY CAT.

ALL this time Edward and the lassies sat by and listened. It was dull work for Edward, he knew little Norse, and so could not follow the stories; sometimes he stared in a dull vacant way at the girls, and sometimes he consulted Bradshaw's Foreign Guide. Whether he solved any of the many mysteries of that most mysterious volume, I know not, let us hope he did. "Bored" is the word which best expressed his looks. But as for Christine and Karin, they knitted and knitted, and laughed and sniggered at the story, which Anders, I must say, told in a way which would have rejoiced his old grandmother's heart. But they were not to have all the fun and no work. It was now their turn to be amusing, and help to kill the ancient enemy, time.

When *The Honest Penny* was over, Anders, almost without taking breath, said,—

"Now, girls, it is my right to call for a tune. You know lots of stories, and can tell them better than I. So, Christine, do you tell *The Death of Chanticleer*; and you, Karin, *The Greedy Cat*. And mind you act them as well as tell them.　They are nursery tales meant for children, and mind you tell them well."

I am bound to say that Christine, who was a very pretty girl, now no doubt the happy mother of children, told *The Death of Chanticleer* in a way which would have gained her in China the post of Own Story-teller to the Emperor's children.　Without a blush, and without even the stereotyped "unaccustomed as I am to public story-telling," she began.　"This is the story of—

THE DEATH OF CHANTICLEER.

"ONCE on a time there were a Cock and a Hen, who walked out into the field, and scratched, and scraped, and scrabbled.　All at once, Chanticleer found a burr of hop, and Partlet found a barley-corn ; and they said they would make malt and brew Yule ale.

"'Oh ! I pluck barley, and I malt malt, and I brew ale, and the ale is good,' cackled dame Partlet.

"'Is the wort strong enough ?' crew Chanticleer ; and as he crowed he flew up on the edge of the cask, and tried to have a taste ; but, just as he bent over to drink a drop, he took to flapping his wings, and so he fell head over heels into the cask, and was drowned.

"When dame Partlet saw that, she clean lost her wits, and flew up into the chimney-corner, and fell a-screaming and screeching out.　'Harm in the house ! harm in the house !' she screeched out all in a breath, and there was no stopping her.

"'What ails you, dame Partlet, that you sit there sobbing and sighing?' said the Handquern.

"'Why not?' said dame Partlet; 'when goodman Chanticleer has fallen into the cask and drowned himself, and lies dead? That's why I sigh and sob.'

"'Well, if I can do naught else, I will grind and groan,' said the Handquern; and so it fell to grinding as fast as it could.

"When the Chair heard that, it said—

"'What ails you, Handquern, that you grind and groan so fast and oft?'

"'Why not, when goodman Chanticleer has fallen into the cask and drowned himself; and dame Partlet sits in the ingle, and sighs and sobs? That's why I grind and groan,' said the Handpuern.

"'If I can do naught else, I will crack,' said the Chair; and, with that, he fell to creaking and cracking.

"When the Door heard that, it said,—

"'What's the matter? Why do you creak and crack so, Mr. Chair?'

"'Why not?' said the Chair; 'goodman Chanticleer has fallen into the cask and drowned himself; dame Partlet sits in the ingle, sighing and sobbing; and the Handquern grinds and groans. That's why I creak and crackle, and croak and crack.'

"'Well,' said the Door, 'if I can do naught else, I can rattle and bang, and whistle and slam;' and, with that, it began to open and shut, and bang and slam, it deaved one to hear, and all one's teeth chattered.

" All this the Stove heard, and it opened its mouth and called out—

" ' Door ! Door ! why all this slamming and banging ?'

" ' Why not ?' said the Door; 'when goodman Chanticleer has fallen into the cask and drowned himself; dame Partlet sits in the ingle, sighing and sobbing ; the Hand-quern grinds and groans, and the Chair creaks and cracks. That's why I bang and slam.'

" ' Well,' said the Stove, 'if I can do naught else, I can smoulder and smoke ;' and so it fell a-smoking and steaming till the room was all in a cloud.

" The Axe saw this, as it stood outside, and peeped with its shaft through the window,—

" ' What's all this smoke about, Mrs. Stove ?' said the Axe, in a sharp voice.

" ' Why not ?' said the Stove; 'when goodman Chanticleer has fallen into the cask and drowned himself; dame Partlet sits in the ingle, sighing and sobbing ; the Hand-quern grinds and groans; the Chair creaks and cracks, and the Door bangs and slams. That's why I smoke and steam.'

" ' Well, if I can do naught else, I can rive and rend,' said the Axe ; and, with that, it fell to riving and rending all round about.

" This the Aspen stood by and saw.

" ' Why do you rive and rend everything so, Mr. Axe ?' said the Aspen.

" ' Goodman Chanticleer has fallen into the ale-cask and drowned himself,' said the Axe ; 'dame Partlet sits in the ingle, sighing and sobbing ; the Handquern grinds and groans ; the Chair creaks and cracks ; the Door slams and bangs, and the Stove smokes and steams. That's why I rive and rend all about.'

" 'Well, if I can do naught else,' said the Aspen, 'I can quiver and quake in all my leaves ;' so it grew all of a quake.

" The Birds saw this, and twittered out,—

" 'Why do you quiver and quake, Miss Aspen ?'

" 'Goodman Chanticleer has fallen into the ale-cask and drowned himself,' said the Aspen, with a trembling voice ; 'dame Partlet sits in the ingle, sighing and sobbing ; the Handquern grinds and groans ; the Chair creaks and cracks ; the Door slams and bangs ; the Stove steams and smokes ; and the Axe rives and rends. That's why I quiver and quake.'

" 'Well, if we can do naught else, we will pluck off all our feathers,' said the Birds ; and, with that, they fell a-pilling and plucking themselves till the room was full of feathers.

" This the Master stood by and saw, and, when the feathers flew about like fun, he asked the Birds,—

" 'Why do you pluck off all your feathers, you Birds ?'

" 'Oh ! goodman Chanticleer has fallen into the ale-cask and drowned himself,' twittered out the Birds ; 'dame Partlet sits sighing and sobbing in the ingle ; the Handquern grinds and groans ; the Chair creaks and cracks ; the Door slams and bangs ; the Stove smokes and steams ; the Axe rives and rends, and the Aspen quivers and quakes. That's why we are pilling and plucking all our feathers off.'

"'Well, if I can do nothing else, I can tear the brooms asunder,' said the man; and, with that, he fell tearing and tossing the brooms till the birch-twigs flew about east and west.

"The goody stood cooking porridge for supper, and saw all this.

"'Why, man!' she called out; 'what are you tearing the brooms to bits for?'

"'Oh!' said the man, 'goodman Chanticleer has fallen into the ale-vat and drowned himself; dame Partlet sits sighing and sobbing in the ingle; the Handquern grinds and groans; the Chair cracks and creaks; the Door slams and bangs; the Stove smokes and steams; the Axe rives and rends; the Aspen quivers and quakes; the Birds are pilling and plucking all their feathers off, and that's why I am tearing the besoms to bits.'

"'So, so!' said the goody; 'then I'll dash the porridge over all the walls;' and she did it; for she took one spoonful after the other and dashed it against the walls, so that no one could see what they were made of for very porridge.

"That was how they drank the burial ale after goodman Chanticleer, who fell into the brewing-vat and was drowned; and, if you don't believe it, you may set off thither and have a taste both of the ale and the porridge."

When Christine ended, I did not tell them what I could

now tell them, that this story of *The Death of Chanticleer* is, *mutatis mutandis*, the very same story as one in *Grimm's Tales*, and another in the Scotch collection of Robert Chambers. But alas! I heard *The Death of Chanticleer* up on the Fjeld long before those Scotch Stories appeared in print, and so, as some of these stories say, I could tell them nothing about it.

Karin was not so good a story-teller as Christine, but she still told her story well. Besides, it was harder to tell, and required an effort of memory, like that needed in our *This is the House that Jack built*. *The Greedy Cat* has a wildness of its own, and is full of humour. Here it is—

THE GREEDY CAT.

" ONCE on a time there was a man who had a cat, and she was so awfully big, and such a beast to eat, he couldn't keep her any longer. So she was to go down to the river with a stone round her neck, but before she started she was to have a meal of meat. So the goody set before her a bowl of porridge and a little trough of fat. That she crammed into her, and ran off and jumped through the window. Outside stood the goodman by the barn door, threshing.

" ' Good day, goodman,' said the cat.

" ' Good day, pussy,' said the goodman ; ' have you had any food to-day ? '

" ' Oh, I've had a little, but I'm 'most fasting,' said the

cat ; ' it was only a bowl of porridge and a trough of fat —and, now I think of it, I'll take you too,' and so she took the goodman and gobbled him up.

" When she had done that, she went into the byre, and there sat the goody milking.

" ' Good day, goody,' said the cat.

" ' Good day, pussy,' said the goody ; ' are you here, and have you eaten up your food yet ? '

" ' Oh, I've eaten a little to-day, but I'm 'most fasting,' said pussy ; ' it was only a bowl of porridge, and a trough of fat, and the goodman—and, now I think of it, I'll take you too,' and so she took the goody and gobbled her up.

" ' Good day, you cow at the manger,' said the cat to Daisy the cow.

" ' Good day, pussy,' said the bell-cow ; ' have you had any food to-day ? '

" ' Oh, I've had a little, but I'm 'most fasting,' said the cat ; ' I've only had a bowl of porridge, and a trough of fat, and the goodman, and the goody—and, now I think of it, I'll take you too,' and so she took the cow and gobbled her up.

" Then off she set up into the home-field, and there stood a man picking up leaves.

" ' Good day, you leaf-picker in the field,' said the cat.

" ' Good day, pussy ; have you had anything to eat to-day ? ' said the leaf-picker.

" ' Oh, I've had a little, but I'm 'most fasting,' said the

cat; 'it was only a bowl of porridge, and a trough of fat, and the goodman and the goody, and Daisy the cow —and, now I think of it, I'll take you too.' So she took the leaf-picker and gobbled him up.

"Then she came to a heap of stones, and there stood a stoat and peeped out.

"'Good day, Mr. Stoat of Stoneheap,' said the cat.

"'Good day, Mrs. Pussy; have you had anything to eat to-day?'

"'Oh, I've had a little, but I'm 'most fasting,' said the cat; 'it was only a bowl of porridge, and a trough of fat, and the goodman, and the goody, and the cow, and the leaf-picker—and, now I think of it, I'll take you too.' So she took the stoat and gobbled him up.

"When she had gone a bit farther, she came to a hazel-brake, and there sat a squirrel gathering nuts.

"'Good day, Sir Squirrel of the Brake,' said the cat.

"'Good day, Mrs. Pussy; have you had anything to eat to-day?'

"'Oh, I've had a little, but I'm 'most fasting,' said the cat; 'it was only a bowl of porridge, and a trough of fat, and the goodman, and the goody, and the cow, and the leaf-picker, and the stoat—and, now I think of it, I'll take you too.' So she took the squirrel and gobbled him up.

"When she had gone a little farther, she saw Reynard the Fox, who was prowling about by the wood-side.

"'Good day, Reynard Slyboots,' said the cat.

"'Good day, Mrs. Pussy; have you had anything to eat to-day?'

"'Oh, I've had a little, but I'm 'most fasting,' said the cat; 'it was only a bowl of porridge, and a trough of fat, and the goodman, and the goody, and the cow, and the leaf-picker, and the stoat, and the squirrel—and, now I think of it, I'll take you too.' So she took Reynard and gobbled him up.

"When she had gone a while farther she met Long Ears the Hare.

"'Good day, Mr. Hopper the Hare,' said the cat.

"'Good day, Mrs. Pussy; have you had anything to eat to-day?'

"'Oh, I've had a little, but I'm 'most fasting,' said the cat; 'it was only a bowl of porridge, and a trough of fat, and the goodman, and the goody, and the cow, and the leaf-picker, and the stoat, and the squirrel, and the fox— and, now I think of it, I'll take you too.' So she took the hare and gobbled him up.

"When she had gone a bit farther, she met a wolf.

"'Good day, you Greedy Greylegs,' said the cat.

"'Good day, Mrs. Pussy; have you had anything to eat to-day?'

"'Oh, I've had a little, but I'm 'most fasting,' said the cat; 'it was only a bowl of porridge, and a trough of fat, and the goodman, and the goody, and the cow, and the leaf-picker, and the stoat, and the squirrel, and the fox and the hare—and, now I think of it, I may as well take you too.' So she took and gobbled up Greylegs too.

"So she went on into the wood, and when she had gone far and farther than far, o'er hill and dale, she met a bear-cub.

"'Good day, you bare-breeched Bear,' said the cat.

"'Good day, Mrs. Pussy,' said the bear-cub; 'have you had anything to eat to-day?'

"'Oh, I've had a little, but I'm 'most fasting,' said the cat; 'it was only a bowl of porridge, and a trough of fat, and the goodman, and the goody, and the cow, and the leaf-picker, and the stoat, and the squirrel, and the fox, and the hare, and the wolf—and, now I think of it, I may as well take you too,' and so she took the bear-cub and gobbled him up.

"When the cat had gone a bit farther, she met a she-bear, who was tearing away at a stump till the splinters flew, so angry was she at having lost her cub.

"'Good day, you Mrs. Bruin,' said the cat.

"'Good day, Mrs. Pussy; have you had anything to eat to-day?'

"'Oh, I've had a little, but I'm 'most fasting,' said the cat; 'it was only a bowl of porridge, and a trough of fat, and the goodman, and the goody, and the cow, and the leaf-picker, and the stoat, and the squirrel, and the fox, and the hare, and the wolf, and the bear-cub—and, now I think of it, I'll take you too,' and so she took Mrs. Bruin and gobbled her up too.

"When the cat got still farther on, she met Baron Bruin himself.

" ' Good day, you Baron Bruin,' said the cat.

" ' Good day, Mrs. Pussy,' said Bruin; ' have you had anything to eat to-day ?'

" ' Oh, I've had a little, but I'm 'most fasting,' said the cat; 'it was only a bowl of porridge, and a trough of fat, and the goodman, and the goody, and the cow, and the leaf-picker, and the stoat, and the squirrel, and the fox, and the hare, and the wolf, and the bear-cub, and the she-bear—and, now I think of it, I'll take you too,' and so she took Bruin and ate him up too.

" So the cat went on and on, and farther than far, till she came to the abodes of men again, and there she met a bridal train on the road.

" ' Good day, you bridal train on the king's highway,' said she.

" ' Good day, Mrs. Pussy ; have you had anything to eat to-day ?'

" ' Oh, I've had a little, but I'm 'most fasting,' said the cat ; ' it was only a bowl of porridge, and a trough of fat, and the goodman, and the goody, and the cow, and the leaf-picker, and the stoat, and the squirrel, and the fox, and the hare, and the wolf, and the bear-cub, and the she-bear, and the he-bear—and, now I think of it, I'll take you too,' and so she rushed at them, and gobbled up both the bride and bridegroom, and the whole train, with the cook and the fiddler, and the horses, and all.

" When she had gone still farther, she came to a church, and there she met a funeral.

" ' Good day, you funeral train,' said she.

"'Good day, Mrs. Pussy; have you had anything to eat to-day?'

"'Oh, I've had a little, but I'm 'most fasting,' said the cat; 'it was only a bowl of porridge, and a trough of fat, and the goodman, and the goody, and the cow, and the leaf-picker, and the stoat, and the squirrel, and the fox, and the hare, and the wolf, and the bear-cub, and the she-bear, and the he-bear, and the bride and bridegroom and the whole train—and, now, I don't mind if I take you too,' and so she fell on the funeral train and gobbled up both the body and the bearers.

"Now when the cat had got the body in her, she was taken up to the sky, and when she had gone a long, long way, she met the moon.

"'Good day, Mrs. Moon,' said the cat.

"'Good day, Mrs. Pussy; have you had anything to eat to-day?'

"'Oh, I've had a little, but I'm 'most fasting,' said the cat; 'it was only a bowl of porridge, and a trough of fat, and the goodman, and the goody, and the cow, and the leaf-picker, and the stoat, and the squirrel, and the fox, and the hare, and the wolf, and the bear-cub, and the she-bear, and the he-bear, and the bride and bridegroom and the whole train, and the funeral train—and, now I think of it, I don't mind if I take you too,' and so she seized hold of the moon, and gobbled her up, both new and full.

"So the cat went a long way still, and then she met the sun.

"'Good day, you Sun in heaven.'

"'Good day, Mrs. Pussy,' said the sun; 'have you had anything to eat to-day?'

"'Oh, I've had a little, but I'm 'most fasting,' said the cat; 'it was only a bowl of porridge, and a trough of fat, and the goodman, and the goody, and the cow, and the leaf-picker, and the stoat, and the squirrel, and the fox, and the hare, and the wolf, and the bear-cub, and the she-bear, and the he-bear, and the bride and bridegroom, and the whole train, and the funeral train, and the moon—and, now I think of it, I don't mind if I take you too,' and so she rushed at the sun in heaven and gobbled him up.

"So the cat went far and farther than far, till she came to a bridge, and on it she met a big Billy-goat.

"'Good day, you Billy-goat on Broad-bridge,' said the cat.

"'Good day, Mrs. Pussy; have you had anything to eat to-day?' said the Billy-goat.

"'Oh, I've had a little, but I'm 'most fasting; I've only had a bowl of porridge, and a trough of fat, and the good-man, and the goody in the byre, and Daisy the cow at the manger, and the leaf-picker in the home-field, and Mr. Stoat of Stoneheap, and Sir Squirrel of the Brake, and Reynard Slyboots, and Mr. Hopper the Hare, and Greedy Greylegs the Wolf, and Bare-breech the Bear-cub, and Mrs. Bruin, and Baron Bruin, and a Bridal train on the king's highway, and a Funeral at the church, and Lady Moon in the sky, and Lord Sun in heaven, and, now I think of it, I'll take you too.'

"'That we'll fight about,' said the Billy-goat, and butted

at the cat till she fell right over the bridge into the river, and there she burst.

"So they all crept out one after the other, and went about their business, and were just as good as ever, all that the cat had gobbled up. The Goodman of the house, and the Goody in the byre, and Daisy the cow at the manger, and the Leaf-picker in the home-field, and Mr. Stoat of Stoneheap, and Sir Squirrel of the Brake, and Reynard Slyboots, and Mr. Hopper the Hare, and Greedy Greylegs the Wolf, and Bare-breech the Bear-cub, and Mrs. Bruin, and Baron Bruin, and the Bridal train on the highway, and the Funeral train at the church, and Lady Moon in the Sky, and Lord Sun in heaven."

PETER THE FORESTER AND GRUMBLEGIZZARD.

WHEN the girls had ended, we all laughed at the droll turn out of Sun, Moon, and Co. from the cat's maw; and I was just going to repay them with a Scotch story, when there came a great knock at the door.

Who could it be? said the girls. Father and mother would not come up from the dale in such weather. Who could it be? Perhaps one of the Hill folk. Perhaps a Huldra.

"Nonsense, lassies!" said Anders; "even if it were anything uncanny, we have guns enough here to fire a shot over a whole pack of them, and men enough to fire them too. Don't stand dawdling there, Karin, but open the door."

Karin did as she was bid, and drew back the wooden bolt.

"My!" she cried, "if it isn't Peter the Forester! Come in, Peter. Come in."

In strode Peter, a strapping fellow, long past youth, but still hale and hearty. His tight-fitting breeches and hose showed a well-knit frame; over his many-buttoned jacket he wore a loose cloak of russet woollen stuff, "Wadmel," as they call it in the north of Scotland, and "Vadmal," as they call it in Norway.   A broad, flapping wide-awake covered his head, which on this occasion was tied down across the top, and under the chin by a red cotton kerchief.   On his shoulder was his rifle.

"Why, Peter," said Anders, "what brought you out in such Deil's weather?"

"Well!" said Peter, "the owner of the sawmills down at the end of the dale on the other side of the Fjeld, sent me up here last night to see if I could mark down any reindeer for him: and so I came, though I told him 'twas no use. The poor, silly body fancies the deer are like a pack of barn-door fowls, that you can count morning and evening, as they go out and come home to roost.   He little thinks that the deer seen to-day here, are to-morrow fifty miles off, or more; but as I wanted to cross the Fjeld, and look at the forest on the other side down in the dale, I said I would come and tell him if I saw any deer; and to make a long story short, I came, and thought to get here last night; but just on the edge of the Fjeld it grew dark as pitch, and so I crept into a reft in the rocks, and spent the night as I best could.   Luckily I had fladbrod and gammelost, and a flask of brandy, else I should have fared badly.   But here I am, drenched to the skin, and nigh starved.   Let me have a pair of dry stockings, and a bowl of milk, and make myself comfortable.   But God's peace! I did not see you had English lords here.   Good day! Good day!   After deer, too, no doubt.   Did you see the deer yesterday?"

While Anders told him in a low voice who we were, in which story Edward's mishap was sure to find a place, Peter took off his shoes and stockings, and put on dry ones, and then draining off his bowl of milk, sate before the fire to enjoy his pipe.

But Anders was not going to let him off so lightly.

"You must often hear and see strange things in the woods, and on the Fjeld, Peter!"

"Aye! aye!" replied Peter, under a cloud of puffs, to this rather leading question. "Aye, aye, I have both heard and seen many things. Strange sounds and noises; sometimes for all the world like the sweetest music."

"And what made it?" I asked.

"What made it!" scornfully replied Peter, "why the Huldror—the fairies."

"The fairies! then you believe in the Good People?"

"Good or bad," said Peter, "and I think they are more often bad than good, by their leave be it spoken; for to tell the truth, they say this very Sæter was haunted in old days. Good or bad, why shouldn't I believe in them? Doesn't the Bible speak of evil spirits? and if I believe in the Bible I must believe in them."

I was too eager to get out of Peter what he knew about the Hill folk or Huldror or fairies, to stop to discuss his dictum as to the Bible, so I said,

"But do tell us what you saw yourself."

"Well!" said Peter, "once in August I was sitting on a knoll by the side of a path, with bushes on each side, so that I could look across the path down into a little hollow full of heath and ling. I was out calling birds, for I can call them by their notes, and just then I heard a grey hen call among the heather, and I called to her and thought, 'If I only set eyes on you, you shall have gobbled and cackled your last.' Then all at once I heard something come rustling behind me along the path, and I turned round and saw an old, old man; he was a strange looking chap altogether, but the strangest thing about him was that he had—at least so it seemed to me—three legs; and the third leg hung and dangled between the other two right down to the ground, and so he walked along the path. When I say 'walked,' it wasn't walking either, but a sliding, sloping motion, and so he went along, and I lost sight of him in one of the darkest hollows of the glen. Now if that were not a fairy I should like to know what it was?"

"Why an old gaberlunzie man, who helped himself along going down hill with his stick behind him," said I. "Come, come, Peter, you must know better stories than that. Tell us something that you have not seen, but only heard tell of. Can't you tell us 'Grumblegizzard?'" For that, you must know, was the name of a Norse tale that I had often heard of but never yet heard.

"Yes! yes," said Anders. "Peter knows it, I'll be bound."

"Well!" said Peter, "it's a queer story, but here it is. This is the story of

GRUMBLEGIZZARD.

" ONCE on a time there were five goodies, who were all reaping in a field ; they were all childless, and all wished to have a bairn. All at once they set eyes on a strangely big goose-egg, almost as big as a man's head.

" ' I saw it first,' said one.

" ' I saw it just as soon as you,' screamed another.

" ' Heaven help me, but I will have it,' swore the third ; ' I was the first to see it.'

" So they flocked round it and squabbled so much about the egg that they were tearing one another's hair. But at last they agreed that they would own it in common, all five of them, and each was to sit on it in turn like a goose, and so hatch the gosling. The first lay sitting eight days, and sat and sat, but nothing came of it ; meanwhile the others had to drag about to find food both for themselves and her. At last one of them began to scold her.

" ' Well,' said the one that sat, ' you did not chip the egg yourself before you could cry, not you ; but this egg, I think, has something in it, for it seems to me to mumble, and this is what it says, " Herrings and brose, porridge and milk, all at once." And now you may come and sit for eight days too, and we will change and change about and get food for you.'

" So when all five had sat on it eight days, the fifth heard plainly that there was a gosling in the egg, which screeched out, ' Herrings and brose, porridge and milk ; ' so she picked a hole in it, but instead of a gosling out came a man child, and awfully ugly it was, with a big head and little body. And the first thing it bawled out when it chipped the egg, was 'Herrings and brose, porridge and milk.'

"So they called it 'Grumblegizzard.'

"Ugly as it was, they were still glad to have it, at first; but it was not long before it got so greedy that it ate up all the meat in their house. When they boiled a kettle of soup or a pot of porridge, which they thought would be enough for all six, it tossed it all down its own throat. So they would not keep it any longer.

"'I've not known what it is to have a full meal since this changeling crept out of the egg-shell,' said one of them, and when Grumblegizzard heard that all the rest were of the same mind, he said he was quite willing to be off. If they did not care for him, he didn't care for them; and with that he strode off from the farm.

"After a long time he came to a farmer's house, which lay in a stone country, and there he asked for a place. Well, they wanted a labourer, and the goodman set him to pick up stones off the field. Yes! Grumblegizzard gathered the stones from the field, and he took them so big that there were many horse-loads in them, and whether they were big or little, he stuffed them all into his pocket. 'Twas not long before he was done with that work, and then he wanted to know what he was to do next.

"'I've told you to pluck out the stones from the field,'

said the goodman, 'you can't be done before you begin, I trow.'

"But Grumblegizzard turned out his pockets and threw the stones in a heap. Then the goodman saw that he had done his work, and felt he ought to keep a workman who was so strong. He had better come in and have something to eat, he said. Grumblegizzard thought so too, and he alone ate all that was ready for the master and mistress and for the servants, and after all he was not half full.

"'That was a man and a half to work, but a fearful fellow to eat, too; there was no stopping him,' said the goodman. 'Such a labourer would eat a poor farmer out of house and home before one could turn round.'

"So he told him he had no more work for him. He had best be off to the king's grange.

"Then Grumblegizzard strode on to the king, and got a place at once. In the king's grange there was enough both of work and food. He was to be odd man, and help the lasses to bring in wood and water and other small jobs. So he asked what he was to do first.

"'Oh, if you would be so good as to chop us a little firewood.'

"Yes. Grumblegizzard fell to chopping and hewing till the splinters flew about him. 'Twas not long before he had chopped up all that there was, both of firewood and timber, both planks and beams; and when he had done he came back and asked what he was to do now.

"'Go on chopping wood,' they said.

"'There's no more left to chop,' said he.

"'That couldn't be true,' said the king's grieve, and he went and looked out in the wood-yard. But it was quite true; Grumblegizzard had chopped everything up; he had made firewood both of sawn planks and hewn beams. That was bad work, the grieve said, and he told him he should not taste a morsel of food till he had gone into the forest and cut down as much timber as he had chopped up into firewood.

"Grumblegizzard went off to the smithy, and got the smith to help him to make an axe of fifteen pounds of iron; and so he went into the forest and began to clear it; down toppled tall spruces and firs fit for masts. Everything went down that he found either on the king's or his neighbour's ground; he did not stay to top or lop them, and there they lay like so many windfalls. Then he laid a good load on a sledge, and put all the horses to it, but they could not stir the load from the spot, and when he took them by the heads and wished to set them a-going, he pulled their heads off. Then he tumbled the horses out of the traces on to the ground, and drew the load home by himself.

"When he came down to the king's grange the king and his wood-grieve stood in the gallery to take him to task for having been so wasteful in the forest—the wood-grieve had been up to see what he was at—but when Grumblegizzard came along dragging back half a wood of timber, the king got both angry and afraid, and he thought he must be careful with him, since he was so strong.

"'That I call a workman, and no mistake,' said the king; 'but how much do you eat at once, for now you may well be hungry.'

"'When he was to have a good meal of porridge, he could do with twelve barrels of meal,' said Grumble-gizzard; 'but when he had got so much inside him, he could hold out for some time.'

"It took time to get the porridge boiled, and, meantime, he was to draw in a little wood for the cook; so he laid the whole pile of wood on a sledge, but when he was to get through the doorway with it, he got into a scrape again. The house was so shaken that it gave way at every joist, and he was within an ace of dragging the whole grange over on end.

"When the hour drew near for dinner, they sent him out to call home the folk from the field; he bawled and bellowed so that the rocks and hills rang again; but they did not come quick enough for him, so he fell out with them, and slew twelve of them on the spot.

"'He has slain twelve men,' said the king; 'and he eats for twelve times twelve. But for how many do you work, I should like to know?'

"'For twelve times twelve, too,' said Grumblegizzard.

"When he had eaten his dinner, he was to go out into the barn to thrash, so he took off the roof-tree and made a flail out of it; and, when the roof was just about to fall, he took a great spruce fir, branches and all, and stuck it up for a roof-tree; and then he thrashed the floor and the straw, and hay, altogether. He did great harm, for the grain and chaff and beard flew about together, and a cloud arose over the whole grange.

"When he was nearly done thrashing, enemies came into the land; and there was to be war. So the king told him to take folk with him and go on the way to meet the foe and fight them, for he thought they would put him to death. 'No! he would have no folk with him to be slain; he would fight alone, that he would,' said Grumblegizzard.

"'All the better, I shall be sooner rid of him,' said the king.

"But he must have a mighty club.

"They sent off to the smith to forge a club of fifty pounds. 'That might do very well to crack nuts,' said Grumblegizzard. So they smithied him one of a hundred pounds. 'That might do well enough to nail shoes with,' he said. Well, the smith couldn't smithy it any bigger with all his men. So Grumblegizzard went off to the smithy himself, and forged a club of fifteen tons, and it took a hundred men to turn it on the anvil. 'That might do,' said Grumblegizzard.

"Besides, he must have a scrip for food; and he made one out of fifteen oxhides, and stuffed it full of food. And so he toddled off down the hill with his scrip at his back and his club on his shoulder.

"So, when he had got so far that the enemy saw him,

they sent out a man to ask if he were coming against them.

"'Bide a bit, till I have had my dinner,' said Grumble-gizzard, as he threw himself down on the road, and fell to eating behind his great scrip.

"But they couldn't wait, and began to shoot at him at once, so that it rained and hailed rifle bullets.

"'These bilberries I don't mind a bit,' said Grumble-gizzard, and fell to eating harder than ever.

"Neither lead nor iron could touch him, and before him was his scrip, like a wall, and kept off the fire.

"So they took to throwing shells at him, and to fire cannons at him; and he just grinned a little every time they hit him.

"'Ah! ah! it's all no good,' he said. But, just then, he got a bombshell right down his throat.

"'Fie!' he said, and spat it out again; and then came a chain-shot and made its way into his butter-box, and another took the bit he was just going to eat from between his fingers. Then he got angry, and rose up, and took his club, and dashed it on the ground, and asked if they were going to snatch [the bread out of his mouth with their bilberries, which they puffed out of big peashooters. Then he gave a few more strokes, till the rocks and hills shook, and the enemy flew into the air like chaff, and so the war was over."

Having got so far, Peter said he must take breath, and called for another bowl of milk, and while he refreshed himself, we all waited open-mouthed for the rest of the story of Grumblegizzard.

" When Grumblegizzard got home again and wanted more work, the king was in a sad way, for he thought he should have been rid of him that time, and now he could think of nothing but to send him to hell.

" ' You must be off to Old Nick, and ask for my land-tax.'

" Grumblegizzard set off from the grange, with his scrip on his back and his club on his shoulder. He lost no time on the way, but, when he got there, Old Nick was gone to serve on a jury. There was no one at home but his mother, and she said she had never in her born days heard talk of any land-tax; he had better come again another day.

" ' Yes, yes! come to me to-morrow,' said Grumble-gizzard. ' That's all stuff and nonsense, for to-morrow never comes.' Now he was there, he would stay there. He must and would have the land-tax, and he had lots of time to wait.

" But when he had eaten up all his food, the time hung heavy, and so he went and asked the old dame to give him the land-tax. She must pay it down.

" ' No,' she said, ' she couldn't do it. That stood as fast as the old fir-tree,' she said, ' that grew outside the gate of hell, and was so big that fifteen men could scarcely span it when they held hands.'

" But Grumblegizzard climbed up to the top of it, and twisted and turned it about like an osier; and then he asked if she were ready with the land-tax.

" Yes, she dared not do anything else, and found so many pence as he thought he could carry in his scrip.

" And now he started for home with the land-tax; but, as soon as he was off, Old Nick came back. When he heard that Grumblegizzard had stridden off from his house with his big scrip full of money, he first of all beat and banged his mother, and then ran after him to catch him on the way.

" And he caught him up, too, for he ran light, and used his wings, while Grumblegizzard had to keep to the ground under the weight of the big scrip; but, just as Old Nick was at his heels, he began to run and jump as fast as he could; and he held his club behind him to keep Old Nick off.

" And so they went along, Grumblegizzard holding the haft, and Old Nick clawing at the head, till they came to a deep dale; there Grumblegizzard leapt from one hill-top to the other, and Old Nick was so hot to follow, that he tripped over the club and fell down into the dale, and broke his leg, and so there he lay.

" ' Here you have the land-tax,' said Grumblegizzard, as he came to the king's grange, and dashed down the scripful of money before the king, so that the whole gallery creaked and cracked.

" The king thanked him, and put a good face on it, and promised him good pay and a safe pass home if he cared to have it; but all Grumblegizzard wanted was more work.

"'What shall I do now?' he asked. Well, when the king had thought about it, he said he had better travel to the Hill Troll, who had carried off his grandfather's sword to that castle he had by the lake, whither no one dared to go.

"So Grumblegizzard got several loads of food into his big scrip, and set off again; and he fared both far and long, over wood and fell, and wild wastes, till he came to some high hills, where the Troll was said to dwell, who had taken the king's grandfather's sword.

"But the Troll was not to be seen under bare sky, and the hill was fast shut, so that even Grumblegizzard was not man enough to get in.

"So he joined fellowship with some quarrymen, who were living at a hill farm, and who lay up there quarrying stone in those hills. Such help they never yet had, for he beat and battered the fell till the rocks were rent, and great stones were rolled down as big as houses; but when he was to rest at noon, and take out one load of food, the whole scrip was clean eaten out.

"'I'm a pretty good trencherman myself,' said Grumblegizzard; 'but whoever has been here, has a sharper tooth, for he has eaten up bones and all.'

"That was how things went the first day, and it was no better the next. The third day he set off to quarry stones again, and took with him the third meal of food; but he laid down behind it, and shammed sleep.

"Just then there came out of the hill a Troll with seven heads, and began to munch and eat his food.

"'Now the board is laid, and I will eat,' said the Troll.

"'That we'll have a tussle for,' said Grumblegizzard; and gave him a blow with his club, and knocked off all his seven heads at once.

"So he went into the hill, out of which the Troll had come, and in there stood a horse, which ate out of a tub of glowing coals, and at its heels stood a tub of oats.

"'Why don't you eat out of the tub of oats?' said Grumblegizzard.

"'Because I am not able to turn round,' said the horse.

"'I'll soon turn you,' said he.

"'Rather strike off my head,' said the horse.

"So he struck it off, and then the horse was turned into a handsome man. He said he had been taken into the hill by the Troll, and turned into a horse, and then he helped him to find the sword, which the Troll had hidden at the bottom of his bed, and upon the bed lay the Troll's old mother, asleep and snoring.

"Home again they went by water, and when they had got well out, the old witch came after them; as she could not catch them, she fell to drinking the lake dry, and she drank and drank, till the water in the lake fell; but she could not drink the sea dry, and so she burst.

"When they came to shore, Grumblegizzard sent a message to the king, to come and fetch his sword. He sent four horses. No! they could not stir it; he sent eight, and he sent twelve; but the sword stayed where it was, they could not move it an inch. But Grumblegizzard took it up alone, and bore it along.

"The king could not believe his eyes, when he saw Grumblegizzard again ; but he put a good face on it, and promised him gold, and green woods ; and when Grumblegizzard wanted more work, he said he had better set off for a haunted castle he had, where no one dared to be, and there he must sleep till he had built a bridge over the Sound, so that folk could pass over. If he were good to do that he would pay him well ; nay, he would be glad to give him his daughter to wife.

"'Yes! yes! I am good to do that,' said Grumblegizzard.

"No man had ever left that castle alive ; those who reached it lay there slain and torn to bits, and the king thought he should never see him more, if he only got him to go thither.

"But Grumblegizzard set off ; and he took with him his scrip of food, a very tough and twisted stump of a fir-tree, an axe, a wedge, and a few matches, and besides, he took the workhouse boy from the king's grange.

"When they got to the Sound, the river ran full of ice, and was as headlong as a force ; but he stuck his legs fast at the bottom, and waded on till he got over at last.

"When he had lighted a fire and warmed himself, and got a bit of food, he tried to sleep ; but it was not long before there was such a noise and din, as though the whole castle was turned topsy-turvy. The door blew back against the wall, and he saw nothing but a gaping jaw, from the threshold up to the lintel.

"'There, you have a bit, taste that!' said Grumblegizzard, as he threw the workhouse boy into the gaping maw.

"'Now let me see you, what kind you are. May be we are old friends.'

"So it was, for it was Old Nick, who was outside. Then they took to playing cards, for the Old One wanted to try and win back some of the land-tax, which Grumblegizzard had squeezed out of his mother, when he went to ask it for the king; but whichever way they cut the cards, Grumblegizzard won, for he put a cross on all the court cards, and when he had won all his ready money, Old Nick was forced to give Grumblegizzard some of the gold and silver that was in the castle.

"Just as they were hard at it the fire went out, so that they could not tell one card from another.

"'Now we must chop wood,' said Grumblegizzard, and with that he drove his axe into the fir stump, and thrust the wedge in; but the gnarled root was tough, and would not split at once, however much he twisted and turned his axe.

"'They say you are very strong,' he said to Old Nick; 'spit in your fists and bear a hand with your claws, and rive and rend, and let me see the stuff you are made of.'

"Old Nick did so, and put both his fists into the split, and strove to rend it with might and main, but, at the same time, Grumblegizzard struck the wedge out, and Old

Nick was caught in a trap; and then Grumblegizzard tried his back with his axe. Old Nick begged and prayed so prettily to be let go, but Grumblegizzard was hard of hearing on that side till he gave his word never to come there again, and make a noise. And so, he too, had to promise to build a bridge over the Sound, so that folks could pass over it at all times of the year, and it was to be ready when the ice was gone.

"'This is a hard bargain,' said Old Nick. But there was no help for it, if he wished to get out. He had to give his word; only, he bargained, he was to have the first soul that passed over the bridge. That was to be the Sound due.

"'That he should have,' said Grumblegizzard. So he got loose, and went home; but Grumblegizzard lay down to sleep, and slept till far on next day.

"So, when the king came to see if he was hacked to pieces, or torn to bits, he had to wade through heaps of money before he could get to the bed. It lay in piles and sacks high up the wall: but Grumblegizzard lay in the bed asleep and snoring.

"'God help both me and my daughter,' said the king when he saw that Grumblegizzard was alive and rich. Yes, all was good and well done; there was no gainsaying that. But it was not worth while talking of the wedding till the bridge was ready.

"So, one day, the bridge stood ready, and Old Nick stood on it to take the toll he had bargained for.

"Now Grumblegizzard wanted to take the king with him

to try the bridge, but he had no mind to do that. So he got up himself on a horse, and threw the fat milkmaid from the king's grange upon the pommel before him ;—she looked for all the world like a big fir-stump—and then he rode over till the bridge thundered under him.

"'Where is the Sound due? Where have you put the soul?' screamed Old Nick.

"'It sits inside this stump. If you want it, spit in your fists and take it,' said Grumblegizzard.

"'Nay, nay! many thanks,' said Old Nick. 'If she doesn't take me, I'll not take her. You caught me once, and you shan't catch me again in a cleft stick ;' and, with that, he flew off straight home to his old mother ; and, since then, he has never been seen or heard in those parts.

"But Grumblegizzard went home to the king's grange, and wanted the wages the king had promised him ; and when the king tried to wriggle out of it, and would not keep his word, Grumblegizzard said he had better pack up a good scrip of food, for he was going to take his wages himself. Yes, the king did that : and, when all was ready, Grumblegizzard took the king out before the door, and gave him a good push and sent him flying up into the air. As for the scrip, he threw it after him, that he might have something to eat. And, if he hasn't come down again, there he is still hanging, with his scrip, between Heaven and Earth, to this very day that now is."

PETER'S THREE TALES.

WHEN *Grumblegizzard* was over, we all laughed so that Peter was quite in good humour. At first he had not liked the doubt thrown on his vision of the old fairy man, but our applause soothed his ruffled spirit.

"As you like stories," he said, "I'll tell you three short ones right off, and then I'll call on Anders to tell one. The first is *Father Bruin in the Corner*, and it shows too what tongues old wives have, and how there's no stopping them even in a pitfall. Many's the time I've trapped Bruin, and Graylegs, and Reynard, in a pit; but I never yet trapped an old woman, and I hope I never shall. It would be like shearing a pig, 'all cry and no wool.' But here is the story."

FATHER BRUIN IN THE CORNER.

"ONCE on a time there was a man who lived far, far away in the wood. He had many, many goats and sheep, but never a one could he keep for fear of Graylegs, the wolf.

"At last he said, 'I'll soon trap Grayboots,' and so he

set to work digging a pitfall. When he had dug it deep enough, he put a pole down in the midst of the pit, and on the top of the pole he set a board, and on the board he put a little dog. Over the pit itself he spread boughs and branches and leaves, and other rubbish, and a-top of all he strewed snow, so that Graylegs might not see there was a pit underneath.

"So when it got on in the night, the little dog grew weary of sitting there : 'Bow-wow, bow-wow,' it said, and bayed at the moon. Just then up came a fox, slouching and sneaking, and thought here was a fine time for marketing, and with that gave a jump—head over heels down into the pitfall.

"And when it got a little farther on in the night, the little dog got so weary and so hungry, and it fell to yelping and howling : 'Bow-wow, bow-wow,' it cried out. Just at that very moment up came Graylegs, trotting and trotting. He, too, thought he should get a fat steak, and he too made a spring—head over heels down into the pitfall.

"When it was getting on towards gray dawn in the morning, down fell snow, with a north wind, and it grew so cold that the little dog stood and froze, and shivered and shook ; it was so weary and hungry, 'Bow-wow, bow-wow, bow-wow,' it called out, and barked and yelled and howled. Then up came a bear, tramping and tramping along, and thought to himself how he could get a morsel for breakfast at the very top of the morning, and so he thought and thought among the boughs and branches till he too went bump—head over heels down into the pitfall.

"So when it got a little further on in the morning, an old beggar wife came walking by, who toddled from farm to farm with a bag on her back. When she set eyes on the little dog that stood there and howled, she couldn't help going near to look and see if any wild beasts had fallen into the pit during the night. So she crawled up on her knees and peeped down into it.

"' Art thou come into the pit at last, Reynard ?' she said to the fox, for he was the first she saw; 'a very good place, too, for such a hen-roost robber as thou : and thou, too, Graypaw,' she said to the wolf; 'many a goat and sheep hast thou torn and rent, and now thou shalt be plagued and punished to death. Bless my heart ! Thou, too, Bruin ! art thou, too, sitting in this room, thou mare-flayer ? Thee, too, will we strip, and thee shall we flay, and thy skull shall be nailed up on the wall.' All this the old lass screeched out as she bent over towards the bear. But just then her bag fell over her ears, and dragged her down, and slap ! down went the old crone— head over heels into the pitfall.

"So there they all four sat and glared at one another, each in a corner. The fox in one, Graylegs in another, Bruin in a third, and the old crone in a fourth.

"But as soon as it was broad daylight, Reynard began to peep and peer, and to twist and turn about, for he thought he might as well try to get out. But the old lass cried out,—

" ' Canst thou not sit still, thou whirligig thief, and not go twisting and turning ? Only look at Father Bruin himself in the corner, how he sits as grave as a judge,' for now she thought she might as well make friends with the bear. But just then up came the man who owned the pitfall. First he drew up the old wife, and after that he slew all the beasts, and neither spared Father Bruin himself in the corner, nor Graylegs, nor Reynard, the whirligig thief. That night, at least, he thought he had made a good haul."

" The next story," said Peter, " is also out of the wood. It isn't often that Reynard gets cheated, but even the wisest folk sometimes get the worst of it, and so it was with Reynard in this story."

REYNARD AND CHANTICLEER.

" ONCE on a time there was a Cock who stood on a dung-heap, and crew, and flapped his wings. Then the Fox came by.

" ' Good day,' said Reynard, ' I heard you crowing so nicely ; but can you stand on one leg and crow, and wink your eyes ? '

" ' Oh, yes,' said Chanticleer. ' I can do that very well.' So he stood on one leg and crew ; but he winked only with one eye, and when he had done that he made himself big and flapped his wings, as though he had done a great thing.

"'Very pretty, to be sure,' said Reynard. 'Almost as pretty as when the parson preaches in church; but can you stand on one leg and wink both your eyes at once? I hardly think you can.'

"'Can't I though!' said Chanticleer, and stood on one leg, and winked both his eyes, and crew. But Reynard caught hold of him, took him by the throat, and threw him over his back, so that he was off to the wood before he had crowed his crow out, as fast as Reynard could lay legs to the ground.

"When they had come under an old spruce fir, Reynard threw Chanticleer on the ground, set his paw on his breast, and was going to take a bite!

"'You are a heathen, Reynard!' said Chanticleer. 'Good Christians say grace, and ask a blessing before they eat.'

"But Reynard would be no heathen. God forbid it! So he let go his hold, and was about to fold his paws over his breast and say grace—but pop! up flew Chanticleer into a tree.

"'You sha'n't get off for all that,' said Reynard to himself. So he went away, and came again with a few chips, which the woodcutters had left. Chanticleer peeped and peered to see what they could be.

"'Whatever have you got there?' he asked.

"'These are letters I have just got,' said Reynard,' 'won't you help me to read them, for I don't know how to read writing.'

"'I'd be so happy, but I dare not read them now;

said Chanticleer; 'for here comes a hunter, I see him, I see him, as I sit by the tree trunk.'

"When Reynard heard Chanticleer chattering about a hunter, he took to his heels as quick as he could.

"This time it was Reynard who was made game of.

"The third story," said Peter, "is about an old fellow who was as deaf as a post, and who had a goody who was no better than she should have been. Where he lived I'm sure I don't know, but I've heard it said he lived in different parts of the country, both north of Stad and south of Stad; but at any rate this is the story."

GOODMAN AXEHAFT.

"THERE was once a ferryman who was so hard of hearing he could neither hear nor catch anything that any one said to him. He had a goody and a daughter, and they did not care a pin for the goodman, but lived in mirth and jollity so long as there was aught to live on, and then they took to running up a bill with the inn-keeper, and gave parties, and had feasts every day.

"So when no one would trust them any longer, the sheriff was to come and seize for what they owed and had wasted. Then the goody and her child set off for her kinsfolk, and left the deaf husband behind, all alone, to see the sheriff and the bailiff.

"Well, there stood the man and pottered about and

wondered what the sheriff wanted to ask, and what he should say when he came.

"'If I take to doing something,' he said to himself, 'he'll be sure to ask me something about it. I'll just begin to cut out an axehaft, so when he asks me what that is to be, I shall answer, "Axehaft." Then he'll ask how long it is to be, and I'll say, "Up as far as this twig that sticks out." Then he'll ask, "What's become of the ferry-boat?" and I'll say, "I am going to tar her; and yonder she lies on the strand, split at both ends." Then he'll ask, "Where's your grey mare?" and I'll answer, "She is standing in the stable, big with foal." Then he'll ask, "Whereabouts is your sheepcote and shieling?" and I'll say, "Not far off; when you get a bit up the hill you'll soon see them."'

"All this he thought well-planned.

"A little while after in came the sheriff; he was true to time, but as for his man, he had gone another way round by an inn, and there he sat still drinking.

"'Good-day, sir,' he said.

"'Axehaft,' said the ferryman.

"'So, so,' said the sheriff. 'How far off is it to the inn?'

"'Right up to this twig,' said the man, and pointed a little way up the piece of timber.

"The sheriff shook his head and stared at him open-mouthed.

"'Where is your mistress, pray?'

"'I am just going to tar her,' said the ferryman, 'for

yonder she lies on the strand, split open at both ends.'

"'Where is your daughter?'

"'Oh, she stands in the stable, big with foal,' answered the man, who thought he answered very much to the purpose.

"'Oh, go to hell with you,' said the sheriff.

"'Very good; 'tis not so far off; when you get a bit up the hill, you'll soon get there,' said the man.

"So the sheriff was floored, and went away."

THE COMPANION.

WE all thought Peter's three stories first rate, but he was not going to be put off with praise, and asked Anders if he knew *The Companion.*

"Yes," was the answer, "but it's a long story, though a very good one."

"If it's long, the sooner you begin it the better," said Peter; "and then it will be sooner over."

Anders made no more mouths about it, but began:

THE COMPANION.

"ONCE on a time there was a farmer's son who dreamt that he was to marry a princess far, far out in the world. She was as red and white as milk and blood, and so rich there was no end to her riches. When he awoke he seemed to see her still standing bright and living before him, and he thought her so sweet and lovely that his life was not worth having unless he had her too. So he sold all he had, and set off into the world to find her out. Well, he went far, and farther than far, and about winter he came to a land where all the high-roads lay right straight on end; there wasn't a bend in any of them.

When he had wandered on and on for a quarter of a year he came to a town, and outside the church-door lay a big block of ice, in which there stood a dead body, and the whole parish spat on it as they passed by to church. The lad wondered at this, and when the priest came out of church he asked him what it all meant.

" ' It is a great wrong-doer,' said the priest. 'He has been executed for his ungodliness, and set up there to be mocked and spat upon.'

" ' But what was his wrong-doing ? ' asked the lad.

" ' When he was alive here he was a vintner,' said the priest, ' and he mixed water with his wine.'

" The lad thought that no such dreadful sin.

" ' Well,' he said, ' after he had atoned for it with his life, you might as well have let him have Christian burial and peace after death.'

" But the priest said that could not be in any wise, for there must be folk to break him out of the ice, and money to buy a grave from the church ; then the grave-digger must be paid for digging the grave, and the sexton for tolling the bell, and the clerk for singing the hymns, and the priest for sprinkling dust over him.

" ' Do you think now there would be any one who would be willing to pay all this for an executed sinner ? '

" ' Yes,' said the lad. ' If he could only get him buried in Christian earth, he would be sure to pay for his funeral ale out of his scanty means.'

" Even after that the priest hemmed and hawed ; but when the lad came with two witnesses, and asked him right out in their hearing if he could refuse to sprinkle dust over the corpse, he was forced to answer that he could not.

"So they broke the vintner out of the block of ice, and laid him in Christian earth, and they tolled the bell and sang hymns over him, and the priest sprinkled dust over him, and they drank his funeral ale till they wept and laughed by turns; but when the lad had paid for the ale he hadn't many pence left in his pocket.

" He set off on his way again, but he hadn't got far ere a man overtook him who asked if he did not think it dull work walking on all alone.

"No; the lad did not think it dull. 'I have always something to think about,' he said.

"Then the man asked if he wouldn't like to have a servant.

" 'No,' said the lad; 'I am wont to be my own servant, therefore I have need of none ; and even if I wanted one ever so much, I have no means to get one, for I have no money to pay for his food and wages.'

" 'You do need a servant, that I know better than you,' said the man, 'and you have need of one whom you can trust in life and death. If you won't have me as a servant, you may take me as your companion ; I give you my word I will stand you in good stead, and it shan't cost you a penny. I will pay my own fare, and as for food and clothing, you shall have no trouble about them.'

" Well, on those terms he was willing enough to have him as his companion ; so after that they travelled together, and the man for the most part went on ahead and showed the lad the way.

"So after they had travelled on and on from land to land, over hill and wood, they came to a crossfell that stopped the way. There the companion went up and knocked, and bade them open the door; and the rock opened sure enough, and when they got inside the hill up came an old witch with a chair, and asked them, 'Be so good as to sit down. No doubt ye are weary.'

"'Sit on it yourself,' said the man. So she was forced to take her seat, and as soon as she sat down she stuck fast, for the chair was such that it let no one loose that came near it. Meanwhile they went about inside the hill, and the companion looked round till he saw a sword hanging over the door. That he would have, and if he got it he gave his word to the old witch that he would let her loose out of the chair.

"'Nay, nay,' she screeched out; 'ask me anything else. Anything else you may have, but not that, for it is my Three-Sister Sword; we are three sisters who own it together.'

"'Very well; then you may sit there till the end of the world,' said the man. But when she heard that, she said he might have it if he would set her free.

"So he took the sword and went off with it, and left her still sitting there.

"When they had gone far, far away over naked fells and wide wastes, they came to another crossfell. There, too, the companion knocked and bade them open the door, and the same thing happened as happened before; the rock opened, and when they had got a good way into the hill another old witch came up to them with a chair and begged them to sit down. 'Ye may well be weary,' she said.

"'Sit down yourself,' said the companion. And so she fared as her sister had fared, she did not dare to say nay, and as soon as she came on the chair she stuck fast. Meanwhile the lad and his companion went about in the hill, and the man broke open all the chests and drawers till he found what he sought, and that was a golden ball of yarn. That he set his heart on, and he promised the old witch to set her free if she would give him the golden ball. She said he might take all she had, but that she could not part with; it was her Three-Sister Ball. But when she heard that she should sit there till Doomsday unless he got it, she said he might take it all the same if he would only set her free. So the companion took the golden ball, but he left her sitting where she sat.

"So on they went for many days, over waste and wood, till they came to a third crossfell. There all went as it had gone twice before. The companion knocked, the rock opened, and inside the hill an old witch came up, and asked them to sit on her chair, they must be tired. But the companion said again, 'Sit on it yourself,' and there she sat. They had not gone through many rooms before they saw an old hat which hung on a peg behind the door. That the companion must and would have; but the old witch couldn't part with it. It was her Three-Sister

Hat, and if she gave it away, all her luck would be lost. But when she heard that she would have to sit there till the end of the world unless he got it, she said he might take it if he would only let her loose. When the companion had got well hold of the hat, he went off, and bade her sit there still, like the rest of her sisters.

"After a long, long time, they came to a Sound; then the companion took the ball of yarn, and threw it so hard against the rock on the other side of the stream that it bounded back, and after he had thrown it backwards and forwards a few times it became a bridge. On that bridge they went over the Sound, and when they reached the other side, the man bade the lad to be quick and wind up the yarn again as soon as he could, for, said he :—

"'If we don't wind it up quick, all those witches will come after us, and tear us to bits.'

"So the lad wound and wound with all his might and main, and when there was no more to wind than the very last thread, up came the old witches on the wings of the wind. They flew to the water, so that the spray rose before them, and snatched at the end of the thread; but they could not quite get hold of it, and so they were drowned in the Sound.

"When they had gone on a few days further, the companion said, 'Now we are soon coming to the castle where she is, the princess of whom you dreamt, and when we get there, you must go in and tell the king what you dreamt, and what it is you are seeking.'

"So when they reached it he did what the man told him,

and was very heartily welcomed. He had a room for him-self, and another for his companion, which they were to live in, and when dinner-time drew near, he was bidden to dine at the king's own board. As soon as ever he set eyes on the princess he knew her at once, and saw it was she of whom he had dreamt as his bride. Then he told her his business, and she answered that she liked him well enough, and would gladly have him; but first he must undergo three trials. So when they had dined she gave him a pair of golden scissors, and said,—

"'The first proof is that you must take these scissors and keep them, and give them to me at mid-day to-mor-row. It is not so very great a trial, I fancy,' she said, and made a face; 'but if you can't stand it, you lose your life; it is the law, and so you will be drawn and quartered, and your body will be stuck on stakes, and your head over the gate, just like those lovers of mine, whose skulls and skeletons you see outside the king's castle.'

"'That is no such great art,' thought the lad.

"But the princess was so merry and mad, and flirted so much with him, that he forgot all about the scissors and himself, and so while they played and sported, she stole the scissors away from him without his knowing it. When he went up to his room at night, and told how he had fared, and what she had said to him, and about the scissors she gave him to keep, the companion said,—

"'Of course you have the scissors safe and sure.'

"Then he searched in all his pockets; but there were no

scissors, and the lad was in a sad way when he found them wanting.

" ' Well ! well ! ' said the companion ; ' I'll see if I can't get you them again.'

" With that he went down into the stable, and there stood a big, fat Billygoat, which belonged to the princess, and it was of that breed that it could fly many times faster through the air than it could run on land.   So he took the Three-Sister Sword, and gave it a stroke between the horns, and said,—

" 'When rides the princess to see her lover to-night ?'

" The Billygoat baaed, and said it dared not say, but when it had another stroke, it said the princess was coming at eleven o'clock.   Then the companion put on the Three-Sister Hat, and all at once he became invisible, and so he waited for her.   When she came, she took and rubbed the Billygoat with an ointment which she had in a great horn, and said,—

" ' Away, away, o'er roof tree and steeple, o'er land, o'er sea, o'er hill, o'er dale, to my true love who awaits me in fell this night.'

" At the very moment that the goat set off, the companion threw himself on behind, and away they went like a blast through the air.   They were not long on the way, and in a trice they came to a crossfell.   There she knocked, and so the goat passed through the fell to the Troll, who was her lover.

" ' Now, my dear,' she said, ' a new lover is come, whose heart is set on having me.   He is young and handsome but I will have no other than you,' and so she coaxed and petted the Troll.

"'So I set him a trial, and here are the scissors he was to watch and keep; now do you keep them,' she said.

"So the two laughed heartily, just as though they had the lad already on wheel and stake.

"'Yes! yes!' said the Troll; 'I'll keep them safe enough.

> And I shall sleep on the bride's white arm,
> While ravens round his skeleton swarm.'

"And so he laid the scissors in an iron chest with three locks; but just as he dropped them into the chest, the companion snapped them up. Neither of them could see him, for he had on the Three-Sister Hat; and so the Troll locked up the chest for naught, and he hid the keys he had in the hollow eye-tooth in which he had the toothache. There it would be hard work for any one to find them, the Troll thought.

"So when midnight was passed she set off home again. The companion got up behind the goat, and they lost no time on the way back.

"Next day, about noon, the lad was asked down to the king's board; but then the princess gave herself such airs, and was so high and mighty, she would scarce look towards the side where the lad sat. After they had dined, she dressed her face in holiday garb, and said, as if butter wouldn't melt in her mouth,—

"'May be you have those scissors which I begged you to keep, yesterday?'

"'Oh, yes, I have;' said the lad, 'and here they are,' and with that he pulled them out, and drove them into the board, till it jumped again. The princess could not have been more vexed had he driven the scissors into her face; but for all that she made herself soft and gentle, and said,—

"'Since you have kept the scissors so well, it won't be any trouble to you to keep my golden ball of yarn, and take care you give it me to-morrow at noon; but if you have lost it, you shall lose your life on the scaffold. It is the law.'

"The lad thought that an easy thing, so he took and put the golden ball into his pocket. But she fell a-playing and flirting with him again, so that he forgot both himself and the golden ball, and while they were at the height of their games and pranks, she stole it from him, and sent him off to bed.

"Then when he came up to his bed-room, and told what they had said and done, his companion asked,—

"'Of course you have the golden ball she gave you?'

"'Yes! yes!' said the lad, and felt in his pocket where he had put it; but no, there was no ball to be found, and he fell again into such an ill mood, and knew not which way to turn.

"'Well! well! bear up a bit,' said the companion. 'I'll see if I can't lay hands on it;' and with that he took the sword and hat and strode off to a smith, and got twelve pounds of iron welded on to the back of the sword-blade. Then he went down to the stable, and gave 'the Billygoat a stroke between his horns, so that the brute went head over heels, and he asked,—

"'When rides the princess to see her lover to-night?'

"'At twelve o'clock,' baaed the Billygoat.

"So the companion put on the Three-Sister Hat again, and waited till she came, tearing along with her horn of ointment, and greased the Billygoat. Then she said, as she had said the first time,—

"'Away, away, o'er rooftree and steeple, o'er land, o'er sea, o'er hill, o'er dale, to my true love who awaits me in the fell this night.'

"In a trice they were off, and the companion threw himself on behind the Billygoat, and away they went like a blast through the air. In the twinkling of an eye they came to the Troll's hill; and, when she had knocked three times, they passed through the rock to the Troll, who was her lover.

"'Where was it you hid the golden scissors I gave you yesterday, my darling?' cried out the princess. 'My wooer had it and gave it back to me.'

"'That was quite impossible,' said the Troll; 'for he had locked it up in a chest with three locks and hidden the keys in the hollow of his eye-tooth;' but, when they unlocked the chest, and looked for it, the Troll had no scissors in his chest.

"So the princess told him how she had given her suitor her golden ball.

"'And here it is,' she said; 'for I took it from him again without his knowing it. But what shall we hit upon now, since he is master of such craft!'

"Well, the Troll hardly knew; but, after they had thought a bit, they made up their minds to light a large fire and burn the golden ball; and so they would be cock-sure that he could not get at it. But, just as she tossed it into the fire, the companion stood ready and caught it; and neither of them saw him, for he had on the Three-Sister Hat.

"When the princess had been with the Troll a little while, and it began to grow towards dawn, she set off home again, and the companion got up behind her on the goat, and they got back fast and safe.

" Next day, when the lad was bidden down to dinner, the companion gave him the ball. The princess was even more high and haughty than the day before, and, after they had dined, she perked up her mouth, and said, in a dainty voice,—

"'Perhaps it is too much to look for that you should give me back my golden ball, which I gave you to keep yesterday?'

"'Is it?' said the lad. 'You shall soon have it. Here it is, safe enough;' and, as he said that, he threw it down on the board so hard, that it shook again; and, as for the king, he gave a jump high up into the air.

"The princess got as pale as a corpse, but she soon came to herself again, and said, in a sweet, small voice,—

" ' Well done, well done ! ' Now he had only one more trial left, and it was this :

" ' If you are so clever as to bring me what I am now thinking of by dinner-time to-morrow, you shall win me, and have me to wife.'

" That was what she said.

" The lad felt like one doomed to death, for he thought it quite impossible to know what she was thinking about, and still harder to bring it to her; and so, when he went up to his bed-room, it was hard work to comfort him at all. His companion told him to be easy, he would see if he could not get the right end of the stick this time too, as he had done twice before. So the lad at last took heart, and lay down to sleep.

" Meanwhile, the companion went to the smith and got twenty-four pounds of iron welded on to his sword ; and, when that was done, he went down to the stable and let fly at the Billygoat between the horns with such a blow, that he went right head over heels against the wall.

" ' When rides the princess to her lover to-night ?' he asked.

" ' At one o'clock,' baaed the Billygoat.

" So, when the hour drew near, the companion stood in the stable with his Three-Sister Hat on ; and, when she had greased the goat, and uttered the same words that they were to fly through the air to her true love, who was waiting for her in the fell, off they went again, on the wings of the wind ; and, all the while, the companion sat behind.

"But he was not light-handed this time; for, every now and then, he gave the princess a slap, so that he almost beat the breath out of her body.

" And when they came to the wall of rock, she knocked at the door, and it opened, and they passed on into the fell to her lover.

" As soon as she got there, she fell to bewailing, and was very cross, and said she never knew the air could deal such buffets; she almost thought, indeed, that some one sat behind, who beat both the Billygoat and herself; she was sure she was black and blue all over her body, such a hard flight had she had through the air.

" Then she went on to tell how her lover had brought her the golden ball too; how it happened, neither she nor the Troll could tell.

" ' But now do you know what I have hit upon ? '

" No; the Troll did not.

" ' Well,' she went on; ' I have told him to bring me what I was then thinking of by dinner-time to-morrow, and what I thought of was your head. Do you think he can get that, my darling ? ' said the princess, and began to fondle the Troll.

" ' No, I don't think he can,' said the Troll. ' He would take his oath he couldn't ;' and then the Troll burst out laughing, and scunnered worse than any ghost, and both the princess and the Troll thought the lad would be drawn and quartered, and that the crows would peck out his eyes, before he could get the Troll's head.

" So when it turned towards dawn, she had to set off

home again ; but she was afraid, she said, for she thought
there was some one behind her, and so she was afraid to
ride home alone. The Troll must go with her on the
way. Yes; the Troll would go with her, and he led out
his Billygoat (for he had one that matched the princess's),
and he smeared it and greased it between the horns. And
when the Troll got up, the companion crept on behind,
and so off they set through the air to the king's grange.
But all the way the companion thrashed the Troll and his
Billygoat, and gave them cut and thrust and thrust and
cut with his sword, till they got weaker and weaker, and
at last were well on the way to sink down into the sea
over which they passed. Now the Troll thought the
weather was so wild, he went right home with the princess
up to the king's grange, and stood outside to see that she
got home safe and well. But just as she shut the door
behind her, the companion struck off the Troll's head and
ran up with it to the lad's bedroom.

"'Here is what the princess thought of,' said he.

"Well, they were merry and joyful, one may think, and
when the lad was bidden down to dinner, and they had
dined, the princess was as lively as a lark.

"'No doubt you have got what I thought of?' said she.

"'Aye; aye; I have it,' said the lad, and he tore it out
from under his coat, and threw it down on the board with
such a thump that the board, trestles and all, was upset.
As for the princess, she was as though she had been dead
and buried ; but she could not say that this was not what
she was thinking of, and so now he was to have her to

wife as she had given her word. So they made a bridal
feast, and there was drinking and gladness all over the
kingdom.

"But the companion took the lad on one side, and told
him that he might just shut his eyes and sham sleep on
the bridal night; but if he held his life dear, and would
listen to him, he wouldn't let a wink come over them
till he had stripped her of her troll-skin, which had
been thrown over her, but he must flog it off her with
a rod made of nine new birch twigs, and he must tear
it off her in three tubs of milk: first he was to scrub
her in a tub of year-old whey, and then he was to scour
her in the tub of buttermilk, and lastly, he was to rub
her in a tub of new milk. The birch twigs lay under
the bed, and the tubs he had set in the corner of the
room. Everything was ready to his hand. Yes; the lad
gave his word to do as he was bid and to listen to him.
So when they got into the bridal bed at even, the lad
shammed as though he had given himself up to sleep.
Then the princess raised herself up on her elbow and
looked at him to see if he slept, and tickled him under
the nose; but the lad slept on still. Then she tugged
his hair and his beard; but he lay like a log, as she
thought. After that she drew out a big butcher's knife
from under the bolster, and was just going to hack off his
head; but the lad jumped up, dashed the knife out of her
hand, and caught her by the hair. Then he flogged her
with the birchrods, and wore them out upon her till there
was not a twig left. When that was over he tumbled her

into the tub of whey, and then he got to see what sort of beast she was: she was black as a raven all over her body; but when he scrubbed her well in the whey, and scoured her with butter-milk, and rubbed her well in new milk, her troll-skin dropped off her, and she was fair and lovely and gentle; so lovely she had never looked before.

"Next day the companion said they must set off home. Yes; the lad was ready enough, and the princess too, for her dower had been long waiting. In the night the companion fetched to the king's grange all the gold and silver and precious things which the Troll had left behind him in the Fell, and when they were ready to start in the morning the whole grange was so full of silver, and gold, and jewels, there was no walking without treading on them. That dower was worth more than all the king's land and realm, and they were at their wits' end to know how to carry it with them. But the companion knew a way out of every strait. The Troll left behind him six billygoats, who could all fly through the air. Those he so laded with silver and gold that they were forced to walk along the ground, and had no strength to mount aloft and fly, and what the billygoats could not carry had to stay behind in the king's grange. So they travelled far, and farther than far, but at last the billygoats got so footsore and tired they could not go another step. The lad and the princess knew not what to do; but when the companion saw they could not get on, he took the whole dower on his back, and the billygoats atop of it, and bore it all so far on that there was only half a mile left to the lad's home.

"Then the companion said : 'Now we must part. I can't stay with you any longer.'

"But the lad would not part from him, he would not lose him for much or little. Well, he went with them a quarter of a mile more; but farther he could not go, and when the lad begged and prayed him to go home and stay with him altogether, or at least as long as they had drunk his home-coming ale in his father's house, the companion said, 'No. That could not be. Now he must part, for he heard heaven's bells ringing for him.' He was the vintner who had stood in the block of ice outside the church door, whom all spat upon; and he had been his companion and helped him because he had given all he had to get him peace and rest in Christian earth.

"'I had leave,' he said, 'to follow you a year, and now the year is out.'

"When he was gone the lad laid together all his wealth in a safe place, and went home without any baggage. Then they drank his home-coming ale, till the news spread far and wide, over seven kingdoms, and when they had got to the end of the feast, they had carting and carrying all the winter both with the billygoats and the twelve horses which his father had before they got all that gold and silver safely carted home."

THE SHOPBOY AND HIS CHEESE, AND PEIK.

WHEN Anders had ended *The Companion*, that strangely wild story, we all admired it, but he too had his call, and, turning to Karin, he said,

"Now do you tell *The Shopboy and his Cheese*. I know you know it, for I heard you telling it to the children last winter over the stove."

So Karin began

THE SHOPBOY AND HIS CHEESE.

"ONCE on a time there was a shopboy who was so well liked by all who knew him, that they thought him too good to stand behind the counter with a yard measure, and weights and scales. So they made up their minds to send him out with a venture to foreign parts, and they let him choose what he would take out. He chose old cheese, and set off with it to Turkey. There he sold his cheeses very well; but as he was on his way home, he met two who had slain a man, and it was not enough that they had slain him in this life, but they ill-treated his body after he was dead. This the shopboy could not bear to see, how wickedly they behaved ; so he bought the body of them and got a grave with his money, and buried it, and then he had spent all he had.

"After a long, long time, he got safe home, and was both illcome and welcome. Some of those who had helped and fitted him out thought he had done a good deed ; but others were ill-pleased that he should have so thrown away his money. But for all that they were ready to try if he could not do better another time, so they let him choose his lading again. He chose the same freight, and took the same way, and sold his cheese even better than before. But, as he was on his way home, he met two who had stolen a king's daughter, and they had put harness on her, and had got so far as to drive her; they had stripped off her clothes to the waist, and one went on either side of her and whipped her. The lad's heart melted at this, for she was a lovely lass. So he asked if they would sell her. Yes, if he would pay down her weight in silver he might have her, and there was no long bargaining : he paid all they asked.

"After a long, long time, he got safe home ; but those who had fitted him out were one and all so ill-pleased at his dealing, that they banished him the land. So he had to set off to England. There he stayed for four years with his sweetheart, and the way they got their living was by her weaving ribbons, which she wove so well that he sold two shillings' worth a-day.

"One day he met two who were foes, and one wished to thrash the other because he owed him eighteen-pence.

That seemed to the lad wrong, and he paid the debt for him. Another day he met two travellers, who began to talk with him, and asked if he had anything to sell. ‘Nothing but ribbons,’ he said. Well, they would have three shillings’ worth, and asked him where he lived, and fixed a day to come and fetch them; and when the day came, they came too, and lo! when they came, if one of them was not the princess’s brother, and the other an emperor’s son, to whom she was betrothed. So they got the ribbons for which they had bargained, and wanted to take her home with them. But she wouldn’t go unless they would let him go with them, and take care of him ; for she would not forsake the man who had freed her, so long as she had breath in her body. So they had to give way to her if they were to take her at all. But when they were to go on board ship, the brother and sister went first into the boat, and when the emperor’s son was to get into her, he shoved her off, and jumped into her himself, and so the lad was left standing on the shore. The ship lay ready for sea, and they sailed as soon as ever they came on board. But then up came the man for whom the lad had paid eighteen-pence, in a boat and put him on board. Then the princess was so glad, and took a gold ring off her finger and gave it to him, and made him go down into the cabin where she lay.

“ Well ! they sailed many days, till they came to a desert island, where they landed to look for game, and they settled things so that the brother, and the Norseman who had saved the princess’s life, were to go each on his side of the island, and the emperor's son in the middle, and when the lad was well gone, so that they could neither see him, nor he them, they got on board, and he was left to walk about the island alone. Then he saw there was no help for it but to stay there; and there he stayed seven years. He got his food from a fruit-bearing tree which he found, and when the seven years were up, an old, old man came to him and said,—

" 'To-day your true-love is to be married. They have not got a kind word out of her these seven years, since you parted; but for all that the emperor's son wants to marry her, for that he knows she is wise and witty, and for that she is so rich.'

" After that, the man asked if he had not a mind to be at the wedding. So he said : well ! what he said any one can guess, but he saw no way of getting there. But lo ! in a little while there he stood in the palace where the wedding was to be. Then he wanted to know what kind of man that was who had brought him thither. He was no man, he said; but a spirit. He it was whose body he had bought and buried in Turkey.

" After that, he gave him a glass and a bottle, with wine in it, and told him to send some one in with a message to the cook to come out to him.

" 'When he comes, you must first pour out a glass and drink it yourself; and then another, and give it to the cook ; and then you must pour out a third, and send it to the bride ; but first of all you must take the ring off your finger, and put it into the glass which you send her.'

"So when the cook came in with the glass, they all cried out, 'She mustn't drink.' But the cook said, 'First he drank, and then I drank, so she may very safely drink the wine.'

"And when she drank the glass out, she saw the ring that lay at the bottom, and ran out, and as soon as she got outside she knew him again, and fell on his neck and kissed him, all shaggy as he was, for you may fancy, he had neither lather nor razor on his beard for seven years.

"But now the king came after, and wanted to know the meaning of all this fondling between them. So they were brought into a room, and told the whole story from first to last. Then the king bade them go and fetch a barber, and scrape the bristles off him, and trim him ; and a tailor with a new court dress ; and then the king went into the bridal hall, and asked the bridegroom, that emperor's son, what doom should be passed on one who had robbed a man both of life and honour. He answered,—

"'Such a scoundrel should be first hanged on a gallows and then his body should be burnt quick.'

"So he was taken at his word and suffered the doom that he uttered over himself, and the shopboy was wedded to the king's daughter, and lived both long and luckily.

"After that I was no longer with them, and I don't know how they fared ; but this I know, that he who last told this Tale is alive this very day, and he is Ole Olsen, of Hitli, in Roldale."

When *The Shopboy and his Cheese* was over, Anders, who ordered about his cousins like a Turk, called on Christina for *Peik*; but nothing could get the story out of her. There was something in it she did not like. It was not a girl's story. He had better tell it himself.

"Well, I will," said Anders; "I'm sure there's no harm in it; but judge for yourselves."

PEIK.

"ONCE on a time there was a man, and he had a wife; they had a son and a daughter who were twins, and they were so like, no one could tell the one from the other by anything else than their clothing. The boy they called Peik. He was of little good while his father and mother lived, for he had no mood to do aught else than to befool folk, and he was so full of tricks and pranks that no one could be at peace for him; but when they were dead it got worse and worse, he wouldn't turn his hand to anything; all he would do was to squander what they left behind them, and as for his neighbours he fell out with all of them. His sister toiled and moiled all she could, but it helped little; so at last she said to him how silly this was that he would do naught for her house, and ended by asking him,

"'What shall we have to live on when you have wasted everything?'

"'Oh, I'll go out and befool somebody,' said Peik.

"'Yes, Peik, I'll be bound you'll do that soon enough,' said his sister.

"'Well, I'll try,' said Peik.

"So at last they had nothing more, for there was an end of everything; and Peik trotted off, and walked and walked till he came to the king's grange. There stood the King in the porch, and as soon as he set eyes on the lad, he said,—

"'Whither away to day, Peik?'

"'Oh, I was going out to see if I could befool anybody,' said Peik.

"'Can't you befool me, now?' said the King.

"'No, I'm sure I can't,' said Peik, 'for I've forgotten my fooling rods at home.'

"'Can't you go and fetch them?' said the King, 'for I should be very glad to see if you are such a trickster as folks say.'

"'I've no strength to walk,' said Peik.

"'I'll lend you a horse and saddle,' said the King.

"'But I can't ride either,' said Peik.

"'Then we'll lift you up,' said the King, 'then you'll be able to stick on.'

"Well, Peik stood and clawed and scratched his head, as though he would pull the hair off, and let them lift him up into the saddle, and there he sat swinging this side and that so long as the King could see him, and the King laughed till the tears came into his eyes, for such a tailor on horseback he had never before seen. But when Peik was come well into the wood behind the hill, so that he was out of the King's sight, he sat as though he were nailed to the horse, and off he rode as though he had stolen both steed and bridle, and when he got to the town, he sold both horse and saddle.

"All the while the King walked up and down, and loitered and waited for Peik to come tottering back again with his fooling rods; and every now and then he laughed when he called to mind how wretched he looked as he sat swinging about on the horse like a sack of corn, not knowing on which side to fall off; but this lasted for seven lengths and seven breadths, and no Peik came, and so at last the King saw that he was fooled and cheated out of his horse and saddle, even though Peik had not his fooling rods with him. And so there was another story, for the King got wroth, and was all for setting off to kill Peik.

"But Peik had found out the day he was coming, and told his sister she must put on the big boiler with a drop of water in it. But just as the King came in Peik dragged the boiler off the fire and ran off with it to the chopping-block, and so boiled the porridge on the block.

"The King wondered at that, and wondered on and on so much that he clean forgot what brought him there.

"'What do you want for that pot?' said he.

"'I can't spare it,' said Peik.

"'Why not?' said the King, 'I'll pay what you ask.'

"'No, no!' said Peik. 'It saves me time and money, woodhire and choppinghire, carting and carrying.'

"'Never mind,' said the King, 'I'll give you a hundred dollars. It's true you've fooled me out of a horse and saddle, and bridle besides, but all that shall go for nothing if I can only get the pot.'

"'Well! if you must have it you must,' said Peik.

"When the King got home he asked guests and made a feast, but the meat was to be boiled in the new pot, and so he took it up and set it in the middle of the floor. The guests thought the King had lost his wits, and went about elbowing one another, and laughing at him. But he walked round and round the pot, and cackled and chattered, saying all in a breath—

"'Well, well! bide a bit, bide a bit! 'twill boil in a minute.'

"But there was no boiling. So he saw that Peik had been out again with his fooling rods and cheated him, and now he would set off at once and slay him.

"When the King came Peik stood out by the barn door. 'Wouldn't it boil?' he asked.

"'No! it would not,' said the King; 'but now you shall smart for it,' and so he was just going to unsheath his knife.

"'I can well believe that,' said Peik, 'for you did not take the block too.'

"'I wish I thought,' said the King, 'you weren't telling me a pack of lies.'

"'I tell you it's all because of the block it stands on; it won't boil without it,' said Peik.

"'Well; what did he want for it?' It was well worth

three hundred dollars; but for the King's sake it should go for two. So he got the block and travelled home with it, and bade guests again, and made a feast, and set the pot on the chopping-block in the middle of the room. The guests thought he was both daft and mad, and they went about making game of him, while he cackled and chattered round the pot, calling out 'Bide a bit, now it boils! now it boils in a trice.'

"But it wouldn't boil a bit more on the block than on the bare floor. So he saw again that Peik had been out with his fooling rods this time too. Then he fell a-tearing his hair, and swore he would set off at once and slay him. He wouldn't spare him this time, whether he put a good or a bad face on it.

"But Peik had taken steps to meet him again. He slaughtered a wether and caught the blood in the bladder, and stuffed it into his sister's bosom, and told her what to say and do.

"'Where's Peik!' screeched out the King. He was in such a rage that his tongue faltered.

"'He is so poorly that he can't stir hand or foot,' she said, 'and now he's trying to get a nap.'

"'Wake him up,' said the King.

"'Nay, I daren't; he is so hasty,' said the sister.

"'Well! I'm hastier still,' said the King, 'and if you don't wake him, I will,' and with that he tapped his side where his knife hung.

"Well! she would go and wake him; but Peik turned hastily in his bed, drew out a little knife, and ripped open the bladder in her bosom, so that a stream of blood gushed out, and down she fell on the floor, as though she were dead.

"'What a dare devil you are, Peik,' said the King, 'if you haven't stabbed your sister to death, and here I stood by and saw it with my own eyes.'

"'There's no risk with her body so long as there's breath in my nostrils;' and with that he pulled out a ramshorn, and began to toot upon it, and when he had tooted a bridal tune, he put the end to her body, and blew life into her again, and up she rose as though there was naught the matter with her.

"'Bless me, Peik! can you kill folk and blow life into them again? Can you do that?' said the King.

"'Why!' said Peik, 'how could I get on at all if I couldn't? I'm always killing everyone I come near; don't you know I'm very hasty.'

"'So am I hot-tempered,' said the King, 'and that horn I must have; I'll give you a hundred dollars for it, and besides I'll forgive you for cheating me out of my horse, and for fooling me about the pot and the block, and all else.'

" Peik was very loth to part with it, but for his sake he would let him have it, and so the King went off home with it, and he had hardly got back before he must try it. So he fell a-wrangling and quarrelling with the Queen and his eldest daughter, and they paid him back in the same coin; but before they knew a word about it he whipped out his knife and cut their throats, so that they fell down stone dead, and everyone else ran out of the room, they were so afraid.

"The King walked and paced about the floor for a while, and kept chattering that there was no harm done, so long as there was breath in him, and a pack of such stuff which had flowed out of Peik's mouth, and then he pulled out the horn and began to blow 'Toot-i-too, Toot-i-too,' but though he blew and tooted as hard as he could all that day and the next too, he couldn't blow life into them again. Dead they were, and dead they stayed, both the Queen and his daughter, and he was forced to buy graves for them in the churchyard, and to spend money on their funeral ale into the bargain.

"So he must and would go and cut Peik off; but Peik had his spies out, and knew when the King was coming, and then he said to his sister,—

"'Now you must change clothes with me and set off. If you will do that you may have all we have got.'

"Well! she changed clothes with him, and packed up and started off as fast as she could; but Peik sat all alone in his sister's clothes.

"'Where is that Peik?' said the King, as he came in a towering rage through the door.

"'He has run away,' said Peik.

"'Ah! had he been at home,' said the King, 'I'd have slain him on the spot. It's no good sparing the life of such a rogue.'

"'Yes! he knew by his spies that your Majesty was

coming, and was going to take his life for his wicked
tricks; but he has left me all alone without a morsel of
bread or a penny in my purse,' said Peik, who made himself as soft and mealy-mouthed as a young lady.

"'Come along then to the King's Grange, and you
shall have enough to live on. There's no good sitting
here and starving in this cabin by yourself,' said the King.

"Yes! he was glad to do that; so the King took him
with him, and had him taught everything, and treated
him as his own daughter, and it was almost as if the King
had his three daughters again, for Miss Peik sewed and
stitched, and sung and played with the others, and was
with them early and late.

"After a time a king's son came to look for a wife.

"'Yes! I have three daughters,' said the King; 'it
rests with you which you will have?'

"So he got leave to go up to their bower to make friends
with them, and the end was that he liked Miss Peik best,
and threw a silk kerchief into her lap as a love token. So
they set to work to get ready the bridal feast, and in a
little while his kinsfolk came, and the King's men, and
they all fell to feasting and drinking on the bridal eve;
but as night was falling Miss Peik daren't stay longer, but
ran away from the King's Grange, out into the wide world,
and the bride was lost; but there was worse behind, for
just then both the other princesses felt very queer, and all
at once two little princes came travelling into the world,
and folk had to break up and go home just as the fun and
feasting were highest.

" The King got both wroth and sorrowful, and began to wonder if it wasn't Peik again that had a finger in this pie.

"So he mounted his horse and rode out, for he thought it dull work staying at home; but when he got out among the ploughed fields, there sat Peik on a stone playing on a Jews' harp.

"'What! are you sitting there, Peik?' said the King.

"'Here I sit, sure enough,' said Peik. 'Where else should I sit?'"

"'Now you have cheated me foully, time after time,' said the King; 'but now you must come along home with me, and I'll kill you.'

"'Well, well,' said Peik, 'if it can't be helped it can't; I suppose I must go along with you.'

"When they got home to the King's Grange, they got ready a cask which Peik was to be put in, and when it was ready they carted it up to a high fell; there he was to lie three days thinking on all the evil he had done, then they were to roll him down the fell into the firth.

"The third day a rich man passed by, but Peik sat inside the cask and sang,—

> 'To heaven's bliss and Paradise,
> To heaven's bliss and Paradise.

"'I'd sooner far stay here and not be made an angel.'

"When the man heard that, he asked what he would take to change places with him.

"'It ought to be a good sum,' said Peik, 'for there wasn't a coach ready to start for Paradise every day.'

"So the man said he would give all he had, and so he knocked out the head of the cask and crept into it instead of Peik.

"'A happy journey,' said the King, when he came to roll him down; 'now you'll go faster to the firth than if you were in a sledge with reindeer; and now it's all over with you and your fooling rods.'

"Before the cask was half-way down the fell, there wasn't a whole stave of it left, nor a limb of him who was inside. But when the King came back to the Grange, Peik was there before him, and sat in the courtyard playing on the Jews' harp.

"'What! you sitting here, you Peik?'

"'Yes! here I sit, sure enough; where else should I sit?' said Peik. 'Maybe I can get house-room here for all my horses and sheep and money.'

"'But whither was it that I rolled you that you got all this wealth?' asked the King.

"'Oh, you rolled me into the firth,' said Peik, 'and when I got to the bottom there was more than enough and to spare, both of horses and sheep and of gold and silver. The cattle went about in great flocks, and the gold and silver lay in large heaps as big as houses.'

"'What will you take to roll me down the same way?' asked the King.

"'Oh,' said Peik, 'it costs little or nothing to do it.

Besides, you took nothing from me, and so I'll take nothing from you either.'

"So he stuffed the King into a cask and rolled him over, and when he had given him a ride down to the firth for nothing, he went home to the King's Grange. Then he began to hold his bridal feast with the youngest princess, and afterwards he ruled both land and realm, but he kept his fooling rods to himself, and kept them so well that nothing was ever afterwards heard of Peik and his tricks, but only of OURSELF THE KING."

KARIN'S THREE STORIES.

"Now," said Karin, "as you have told *Peik*, which I did not want to tell, I'll tell you three stories all of a row, *Death and the Doctor, The Way of the World*, and *The Pancake.*" So she began with the first.

DEATH AND THE DOCTOR.

"ONCE on a time there was a lad, who had lived as a servant a long time with a man of the North Country. This man was a master at ale-brewing; it was so out-of-the-way good the like of it was not to be found. So, when the lad was to leave his place and the man was to pay him the wages he had earned, he would take no other pay than a keg of yule-ale. Well! he got it and set off with it, and he carried it both far and long, but the longer he carried the keg the heavier it got, and so he began to look about to see if anyone were coming with whom he might have a drink, that the ale might lessen, and the keg lighten. And after a long, long time, he met an old man with a big beard.

"'Good-day,' said the man.

" 'Good-day to you,' said the lad.

" 'Whither away?' asked the man.

" 'I'm looking after some one to drink with, and get my keg lightened,' said the lad.

" 'Can't you drink as well with me as with anyone else?' said the man. 'I have fared both far and wide, and I am both tired and thirsty.'

" 'Well! why shouldn't I?' said the lad; 'but tell me, whence do you come, and what sort of man are you?'

" 'I am "Our Lord," and come from Heaven,' said the man.

" 'Thee will I not drink with,' said the lad; 'for thou makest such distinction between persons here in the world, and sharest rights so unevenly that some get so rich and some so poor. No! with thee I will not drink,' and as he said this he trotted off with his keg again.

" So, when he had gone a bit farther the keg grew too heavy again; he thought he never could carry it any longer unless some one came with whom he might drink, and so lessen the ale in the keg. Yes! he met an ugly scrawny man who came along fast and furious.

" 'Good-day,' said the man.

" 'Good-day to you,' said the lad.

" 'Whither away?' asked the man.

" 'Oh! I'm looking for some one to drink with, and get my keg lightened,' said the lad.

" 'Can't you drink with me as well as with any one else?' said the man; 'I have fared both far and wide, and I am tired and thirsty.'

" ' Well! why not?' said the lad; 'but who are you, and whence do you come?'

" ' Who am I? I am the De'il, and I come from Hell; that's where I come from,' said the man.

" ' No!' said the lad; 'thou only pinest and plaguest poor folk, and if there is any unhappiness a-stir, they always say it is thy fault. Thee I will not drink with.'

" So he went far and farther than far again with his ale-keg on his back, till he thought it grew so heavy there was no carrying it any farther. He began to look round again if any one were coming with whom he could drink and lighten his keg. So after a long, long time, another man came, and he was so dry and lean 'twas a wonder his bones hung together.

" ' Good-day,' said the man.

" ' Good-day to you,' said the lad.

" ' Whither away?' asked the man.

" ' Oh, I was only looking about to see if I could find some one to drink with, that my keg might be lightened a little, it is so heavy to carry.'

" ' Can't you drink as well with me as with anyone else?' said the man.

" ' Yes; why not?' said the lad. 'But what sort of man are you?'

" ' They call me Death,' said the man.

" ' The very man for my money,' said the lad. 'Thee I am glad to drink with,' and as he said this he put down his keg, and began to tap the ale into a bowl. 'Thou art an honest, trustworthy man, for thou treatest all alike, both rich and poor.'

"So he drank his health, and Death drank his health, and Death said he had never tasted such drink, and as the lad was fond of him, they drank bowl and bowl about, till the ale was lessened, and the keg grew light.

"At last, Death said, 'I have never known drink which smacked better, or did me so much good as this ale that you have given me, and I scarce know what to give you in return.' But after he had thought a while, he said the keg should never get empty, however much they drank out of it, and the ale that was in it should become a healing drink, by which the lad could make the sick whole again better than any doctor. And he also said that when the lad came into the sick man's room Death would always be there, and show himself to him, and it should be to him for a sure token if he saw Death at the foot of the bed that he could cure the sick with a draught from the keg; but if he sate by the pillow, there was no healing nor medicine, for then the sick belonged to Death.

"Well, the lad soon grew famous, and was called in far and near, and he helped many to health again, who had been given over. When he came in and saw how Death sate by the sick man's bed, he foretold either life or death, and his foretelling was never wrong. He got both a rich and powerful man, and at last he was called in to a king's daughter far, far away in the world. She was so dangerously ill no doctor thought he could do her any good, and

so they promised him all that he cared either to ask or
have if he would only save her life.

"Now, when he came into the princess's room, there sate
Death at her pillow ; but as he sate he dozed and nodded,
and while he did this she felt herself better.

"'Now, life or death is at stake,' said the doctor; 'and
I fear, from what I see, there is no hope.'

"But they said he *must* save her, if it cost land and
realm. So he looked at Death, and while he sate there
and dozed again, he made a sign to the servants to turn
the bed round so quickly that Death was left sitting at the
foot, and at the very moment they turned the bed, the
doctor gave her the draught, and her life was saved.

"'Now you have cheated me,' said Death, 'and we are
quits.'

"'I was forced to do it,' said the doctor, 'unless I
wished to lose land and realm.'

"'That shan't help you much,' said Death; 'your time
is up, for now you belong to me.'

"'Well,' said the lad, 'what must be, must be; but
you'll let me have time to read the Lord's Prayer first.'

"Yes, he might have leave to do that; but he took very
good care not to read the Lord's Prayer; everything else
he read; but the Lord's Prayer never crossed his lips, and
at last he thought he had cheated Death for good and all.
But when Death thought he had really waited too long, he
went to the lad's house one night, and hung up a great tablet
with the Lord's Prayer painted on it over against his bed.
So when the lad woke in the morning he began to read

the tablet, and did not quite see what he was about till he
came to AMEN; but then it was just too late, and Death
had him."

THE WAY OF THE WORLD.

"ONCE on a time, there was a man who went into the
wood to cut hop-poles, but he could find no trees so
long and straight, and slender, as he wanted, till he came
high up under a great heap of stones. There he heard
groans and moans as though some one were at Death's
door. So he went up to see who it was that needed help,
and then he heard that the noise came from under a great
flat stone which lay upon the heap. It was so heavy it
would have taken many a man to lift it. But the man
went down again into the wood and cut down a tree,
which he turned into a lever, and with that he tilted up
the stone, and lo! out from under it crawled a Dragon,
and made at the man to swallow him up. But the man
said he had saved the Dragon's life, and it was shameful
thanklessness in him to want to eat him up.

"'May be,' said the Dragon; 'but you might very well
know I must be starved when I have been here hundreds
of years and never tasted meat. Besides, it's the way of
the world,—that's how it pays its debts.'

"The man pleaded his cause stoutly, and begged prettily
for his life; and at last they agreed to take the first living
thing that came for a daysman, and if his doom went the

other way the man should not lose his life, but if he said the same as the Dragon, the Dragon should eat the man.

"The first thing that came was an old hound, who ran along the road down below under the hillside. Him they spoke to, and begged him to be judge.

"'God knows,' said the hound, 'I have served my master truly ever since I was a little whelp. I have watched and watched many and many a night through, while he lay warm asleep on his ear, and I have saved house and home from fire and thieves more than once; but now I can neither see nor hear any more, and he wants to shoot me. And so I must run away, and slink from house to house, and beg for my living till I die of hunger. No! it's the way of the world,' said the hound; 'that's how it pays its debts.'

"'Now I am coming to eat you up,' said the Dragon, and tried to swallow the man again. But the man begged and prayed hard for his life, till they agreed to take the next comer for a judge; and if he said the same as the Dragon and the Hound, the Dragon was to eat him, and get a meal of man's meat; but if he did not say so, the man was to get off with his life.

"So there came an old horse limping down along the road which ran under the hill. Him they called out to come and settle the dispute. Yes; he was quite ready to do that.

"'Now, I have served my master,' said the horse, 'as long as I could draw or carry. I have slaved and striven for him till the sweat trickled from every hair, and I have worked till I have grown lame, and halt, and worn out with toil and age; now I am fit for nothing. I am not worth my food, and so I am to have a bullet through me, he says. Nay! nay! It's the way of the world. That's how the world pays its debts.'

"'Well, now I'm coming to eat you,' said the Dragon, who gaped wide, and wanted to swallow the man. But he begged again hard for his life.

" But the Dragon said he must have a mouthful of man's meat; he was so hungry, he couldn't bear it any longer.

"'See, yonder comes one who looks as if he was sent to be a judge between us,' said the man, as he pointed to Reynard the fox, who came stealing between the stones of the heap.

"' All good things are three,' said the man; 'let me ask him, too, and if he gives doom like the others, eat me up on the spot.'

"'Very well,' said the Dragon. He, too, had heard that all good things were three, and so it should be a bargain. So the man talked to the fox as he had talked to the others.

"'Yes, yes,' said Reynard; 'I see how it all is;' but as he said this he took the man a little on one side.

"'What will you give me if I free you from the Dragon?' he whispered into the man's ear.

"'You shall be free to come to my house, and to be lord and master over my hens and geese, every Thursday night,' said the man.

"' Well, my dear Dragon,' said Reynard, 'this is a very

hard nut to crack. I can't get it into my head how you, who are so big and mighty a beast, could find room to lie under yon stone.'

"'Can't you,' said the Dragon; 'well, I lay under the hill-side, and sunned myself, and down came a landslip, and hurled the stone over me.'

"'All very likely, I dare say,' said Reynard; 'but still I can't understand it, and what's more, I won't believe it till I see it.'

"So the man said they had better prove it, and the Dragon crawled down into the hole again; but in the twinkling of an eye they whipped out the lever, and down the stone crashed again on the Dragon.

"'Lie now there till Doomsday,' said the fox. 'You would eat the man, would you, who saved your life?'

"The Dragon groaned, and moaned, and begged hard to come out; but the two went their way, and left him alone.

"The very first Thursday night Reynard came to be lord and master over the hen-roost, and hid himself behind a great pile of wood hard by. When the maid went to feed the fowls, in stole Reynard. She neither saw nor heard anything of him; but her back was scarce turned before he had sucked blood enough for a week, and stuffed himself so that he couldn't stir. So when she came again in the morning, there Reynard lay and snored, and slept in the morning sun, with all four legs stretched straight; and he was as sleek and round as a German sausage.

"Away ran the lassie for the goody, and she came, and all the lassies with her, with sticks and brooms to beat

Reynard; and, to tell the truth, they nearly banged the life out of him; but, just as it was almost all over with him, and he thought his last hour was come, he found a hole in the floor, and so he crept out, and limped and hobbled off to the wood.

"'Oh, oh,' said Reynard; 'how true it is. 'Tis the way of the world; and this is how it pays its debts.'"

THE PANCAKE.

"ONCE on a time there was a goody who had seven hungry bairns, and she was frying a pancake for them. It was a sweet-milk pancake, and there it lay in the pan bubbling and frizzling so thick and good, it was a sight for sore eyes to look at. And the bairns stood round about, and the goodman sat by and looked on.

"'Oh, give me a bit of pancake, mother, dear; I am so hungry,' said one bairn.

"'Oh, darling mother,' said the second.

"'Oh, darling good mother,' said the third.

"'Oh, darling, good, nice mother,' said the fourth.

"'Oh, darling, pretty, good, nice mother,' said the fifth.

"'Oh, darling, pretty, good, nice, clever mother,' said the sixth.

"'Oh, darling, pretty, good, nice, clever, sweet mother,' said the seventh.

"So they begged for the pancake all round, the one more

prettily than the other; for they were so hungry and so good.

"'Yes, yes, bairns, only bide a bit till it turns itself,'—she ought to have said 'till I can get it turned,'—'and then you shall all have some—a lovely sweet-milk pancake; only look how fat and happy it lies there.'

"When the pancake heard that, it got afraid, and in a trice it turned itself all of itself, and tried to jump out of the pan; but it fell back into it again t'other side up, and so when it had been fried a little on the other side too, till it got firmer in its flesh, it sprang out on the floor, and rolled off like a wheel through the door and down the hill.

"'Holloa! Stop, pancake!' and away went the goody after it, with the frying-pan in one hand, and the ladle in the other, as fast as she could, and her bairns behind her, while the goodman limped after them last of all.

"'Hi! won't you stop? Seize it. Stop, pancake, they all screamed out, one after the other, and tried to catch it on the run and hold it; but the pancake rolled on and on, and in the twinkling of an eye it was so far ahead that they couldn't see it, for the pancake was faster on its feet than any of them.

"So when it had rolled awhile it met a man.

"'Good-day, pancake,' said the man.

"'God bless you, Manny Panny!' said the pancake.

"'Dear pancake,' said the man, 'don't roll so fast; stop a little and let me eat you.'

"'When I have given the slip to Goody Poody, and the

goodman, and seven squalling children, I may well slip through your fingers, Manny Panny,' said the pancake, and rolled on and on till it met a hen.

" ' Good-day, pancake,' said the hen.

" ' The same to you, Henny Penny,' said the pancake.

" ' Pancake, dear, don't roll so fast, bide a bit and let me eat you up,' said the hen.

" ' When I have given the slip to Goody Poody, and the goodman, and seven squalling children, and Manny Panny, I may well slip through your claws, Henny Penny,' said the pancake, and so it rolled on like a wheel down the road.

" Just then it met a cock.

" ' Good-day, pancake,' said the cock.

" ' The same to you, Cocky Locky,' said the pancake.

" ' Pancake, dear, don't roll so fast, but bide a bit and let me eat you up.'

" ' When I have given the slip to Goody Poody, and the goodman, and seven squalling children, and to Manny Panny, and Henny Penny, I may well slip through your claws, Cocky Locky,' said the pancake, and off it set rolling away as fast as it could; and when it had rolled a long way it met a duck.

" ' Good-day, pancake,' said the duck.

" ' The same to you, Ducky Lucky.'

" ' Pancake, dear, don't roll away so fast; bide a bit and let me eat you up.'

" ' When I have given the slip to Goody Poody, and the goodman, and seven squalling children, and Manny

Panny, and Henny Penny, and Cocky Locky, I may well slip through your fingers, Ducky Lucky,' said the pancake, and with that it took to rolling and rolling faster than ever; and when it had rolled a long, long while, it met a goose.

" 'Good-day, pancake,' said the goose.

" 'The same to you, Goosey Poosey.'

" 'Pancake, dear, don't roll so fast ; bide a bit and let me eat you up.'

" 'When I have given the slip to Goody Poody, and the goodman, and seven squalling children, and Manny Panny, and Henny Penny, and Cocky Locky, and Ducky Lucky, I can well slip through your feet, Goosey Poosey,' said the pancake, and off it rolled.

" So when it had rolled a long, long way farther, it met a gander.

" 'Good-day, pancake,' said the gander.

" 'The same to you, Gander Pander,' said the pancake.

" 'Pancake, dear, don't roll so fast : bide a bit and let me eat you up.'

" 'When I have given the slip to Goody Poody, and the goodman, and seven squalling children, and Manny Panny, and Henny Penny, and Cocky Locky, and Ducky Lucky, and Goosey Poosey, I may well slip through your feet, Gander Pander,' said the pancake, which rolled off as fast as ever.

" So when it had rolled a long, long time, it met a pig.

" 'Good-day, pancake,' said the pig.

" 'The same to you, Piggy Wiggy,' said the pancake,

which, without a word more, began to roll and roll like mad.

" ' Nay, nay,' said the pig, ' you needn't be in such a hurry ; we two can then go side by side and see one another over the wood ; they say it is not too safe in there.'

" The pancake thought there might be something in that, and so they kept company. But when they had gone awhile, they came to a brook. As for piggy, he was so fat he swam safe across, it was nothing to him ; but the poor pancake couldn't get over.

" ' Seat yourself on my snout,' said the pig, ' and I'll carry you over.'

" So the pancake did that.

" ' Ouf, ouf,' said the pig, and swallowed the pancake at one gulp ; and then, as the poor pancake could go no farther, why—this story can go no farther either."

PETER'S BEAST STORIES.

"Now," said Peter, "I'll tell you another lot of stories right out of the wood, as fresh as a spruce fir or a juniper. Here they are :—

PORK AND HONEY.

"AT dawn the other day, when Bruin came tramping over the bog with a fat pig, Reynard sat up on a stone by the moorside.

"'Good day, grandsire,' said the fox, 'what's that so nice that you have there?'

"'Pork,' said Bruin.

"'Well! I have got a dainty bit, too,' said Reynard

"'What is that?' asked the bear.

"'The biggest wild bees-comb I ever saw in my life,' said Reynard.

"'Indeed, you don't say so,' said Bruin, who grinned and licked his lips. He thought it would be so nice to taste a little honey. At last he said, 'Shall we swop our fare?'

"'Nay, nay!' said Reynard, 'I can't do that.'

"The end was that they made a bet, and agreed to name three trees. If the fox could say them off faster than the bear he was to have leave to take one bite off the bacon; but if the bear could say them faster he was to have leave to take one sup out of the comb. Greedy Bruin thought he was sure to sup out all the honey at one breath.

"'Well,' said Reynard, it's all fair and right no doubt, but all I say is, if I win, you shall be bound "to tear" off the bristles where I am to bite.'

"'Of course,' said Bruin, 'I'll help you as you can't help yourself.'

"So they were to begin and name the trees.

"'FIR, SCOTCH FIR, SPRUCE,' growled out Bruin, for he was gruff in his tongue, that he was. But for all that he only named two trees, for Fir and Scotch Fir are both the same.

"'*Ash, Aspen, Oak*,' screamed Reynard, so that the wood rang again!

"So he had won the wager, and down he ran and took the heart out of the pig at one bite, and was just running off with it. But Bruin was angry because he had taken the best bit out of the whole pig, and so he laid hold of his tail and held him fast.

"'Stop a bit, stop a bit,' he said, and was wild with rage.

"'Never mind,' said the fox, 'it's all right; let me go, grandsire, and I'll give you a taste of my honey.'

"When Bruin heard that, he let go his hold, and away went Reynard after the honey.

" 'Here, on this honeycomb,' said Reynard, ' lies a leaf, and under this leaf is a hole, and that hole you are to suck.'

"As he said this he held up the comb under the Bear's nose, took off the leaf, jumped up on a stone, and began to gibber and laugh, for there was neither honey nor honeycomb, but a wasp's nest, as big as a man's head, full of wasps, and out swarmed the wasps and settled on Bruin's head, and stung him in his eyes and ears, and mouth and snout. And he had such hard work to rid himself of them that he had no time to think of Reynard.

" And that's why, ever since that day, Bruin is so afraid of wasps."

THE HARE AND THE HEIRESS.

" ONCE on a time there was a hare, who was frisking up and down under the greenwood tree.

" ' Oh ! hurrah ! hip, hip, hurrah !' he cried, and leapt and sprang, and all at once he threw a somersault, and stood upon his hind legs. Just then a fox came slouching by.

" ' Good-day, good-day,' said the hare; ' I'm *so* merry to-day, for you must know I was married this morning.'

" ' Lucky fellow you,' said the fox.

" 'Ah, no ! not so lucky after all,' said the hare, ' for she was very heavy handed, and it was an old witch I got to wife.

" ' Then you were an unlucky fellow,' said the fox.

"'Oh, not so unlucky either,' said the hare, 'for she was an heiress. She had a cottage of her own.'

"'Then you were lucky after all,' said the fox.

"'No, no! not so lucky either,' said the hare, 'for the cottage caught fire and was burnt, and all we had with it.'

"'That I call downright unlucky,' said the fox.

"'Oh, no; not so very unlucky after all,' said the hare, 'for my witch of a wife was burnt along with her cottage.'"

SLIP ROOT, CATCH REYNARD'S FOOT.

"ONCE on a time there was a bear, who sat on a hillside in the sun and slept. Just then Reynard came slouching by and caught sight of him.

"'There you sit taking your ease, grandsire,' said the fox. 'Now see if I don't play you a trick.' So he went and caught three field mice and laid them on a stump close under Bruin's nose, and then he bawled out, into his ear, 'Bo! Bruin, here's Peter the Hunter, just behind this stump;' and as he bawled this out he ran off through the wood as fast as ever he could.

"Bruin woke up with a start, and when he saw the three little mice, he was as mad as a March hare, and was going to lift up his paw and crush them, for he thought it was they who had bellowed in his ear.

"But just as he lifted it he caught sight of Reynard's tail among the bushes by the woodside, and away he set after him, so that the underwood crackled as he went, and, to tell the truth, Bruin was so close upon Reynard, that he caught hold of his off-hind foot just as he was crawling into an earth under a pine-root. So there was Reynard in a pinch, but for all that he had his wits about him, for he screeched out, 'SLIP THE PINE-ROOT AND CATCH REYNARD'S FOOT,' and so the silly bear let his foot slip and laid hold of the root instead. But by that time Reynard was safe inside the earth, and called out—

"'I cheated you that time, too, didn't I, grandsire!'

"'Out of sight isn't out of mind,' growled Bruin down the earth, and was wild with rage."

BRUIN GOODFELLOW.

"ONCE on a time there was a husbandman who travelled ever so far up to the Fells to fetch a load of leaves for litter for his cattle in winter. So when he got to where the litter lay he backed the sledge close up to the heap, and began to roll down the leaves on to the sledge. But under the heap lay a bear who had made his winter lair there, and when he felt the man trampling about he jumped out right down on to the sledge.

"As soon as the horse got wind of Bruin, he was afraid, and ran off as though he had stolen both bear and sledge, and he went back faster by many times than he had come up.

"Bruin, they say, is a brave fellow, but even he was not quite pleased with his drive this time. So there he sat, holding fast, as well as he could, and he glared and grinned on all sides, and he thought of throwing himself off, but he was not used to sledge travelling, and so he made up his mind to sit still where he was.

"So when he had driven a good bit, he met a pedlar.

"'Whither in heaven's name is the sheriff bound to-day? He has surely little time, and a long way; he drives so fast.'

"But Bruin said never a word, for all he could do was to stick fast.

"A little further on a beggar-woman met him. She nodded to him and greeted him, and begged for a penny, in God's name. But Bruin said never a word, but stuck fast and drove on faster than ever.

"So when he had gone a bit further, Reynard the fox met him.

"'Ho! ho!' said Reynard, 'are you out taking a drive. Stop a bit, and let me get up behind and be your post-boy.'

"But still Bruin said never a word, but held on like grim death, and drove on as fast as the horse could lay legs to the ground.

"'Well, well,' screamed Reynard, after him, 'if you won't take me with you I'll spae your fortune; and that is, though you drive like a dare-devil to-day, you'll be hanging up to-morrow with the hide off your back.'

"But Bruin never heard a word that Reynard said. On and on he drove just as fast; but when the horse got to the farm, he galloped into the open stable door at full speed, so that he tore off both sledge and harness, and as for poor Bruin, he knocked his skull against the lintel, and there he lay dead on the spot.

"All this time the man knew nothing of what had happened. He rolled down bundle after bundle of leaves, and when he thought he had enough to load his sledge, and went down to bind on the bundles, he could find neither horse nor sledge.

"So he had to tramp along the road to find his horse again, and, after a while, he met the pedlar.

"'Have you met my horse and sledge?' he asked.

"'No,' said the pedlar; 'but lower down along the road I met the sheriff; he drove so fast, he was surely going to lay some one by the heels.'

"A while after he met the beggar-woman.

"'Have you seen my horse and sledge?' said the man.

"'No,' said the beggar-woman, 'but I met the parson lower down yonder; he was surely going to a parish meeting, he drove so fast, and he had a borrowed horse.'

"A while after, the man met the fox.

"'Have you seen my horse and sledge?'

"'Yes! I have,' said the fox, 'and Bruin Goodfellow sat on it and drove just as though he had stolen both horse and harness.'

"'Deil take him,' said the man, 'Ill be bound he'll drive my horse to death.'

"'If he does, flay him,' said Reynard, 'and roast him before the fire! But if you get your horse again you may give me a lift over the Fell, for I can ride well, and besides, I have a fancy to see how it feels when one has four legs before one.'

" ' What will you give for the lift ? ' said the man.

" ' You can have what you like,' said Reynard ; ' either wet or dry. You may be sure you'll always get more out of me than out of Bruin Goodfellow, for he is a rough carle to pay off when he takes a fancy to riding and hangs on a horse's back.'

" ' Well ! you shall have a lift over the Fell,' said the man, ' if you will only meet me at this spot to-morrow.'

" But he knew that Reynard was only playing off some of his tricks upon him, and so he took with him a loaded gun on the sledge, and when Reynard came, thinking to get a lift for nothing, he got, instead, a charge of shot in his body, and so the husbandman flayed the coat off him too, and then he had gotten both Bruin's hide and Reynard's skin."

BRUIN AND REYNARD PARTNERS.

" ONCE on a time Bruin and Reynard were to own a field in common. They had a little clearing up in the wood, and the first year they sowed rye.

" ' Now we must share the crop as is fair and right,' said Reynard. ' If you like to have the root, I'll take the top.'

" Yes, Bruin was ready to do that ; but when they had

threshed out the crop, Reynard got all the corn, but Bruin got nothing but roots and rubbish. He did not like that at all; but Reynard said it was how they had agreed to share it.

"'This year I have the gain,' said Reynard; 'next year it will be your turn. Then you shall have the top, and I shall have to put up with the root.'

"But when spring came, and it was time to sow, Reynard asked Bruin what he thought of turnips.

"'Aye, aye!' said Bruin, 'that's better food than corn;' and so Reynard thought also. But when harvest came Reynard got the roots, while Bruin got the turnip-tops. And then Bruin was so angry with Reynard that he put an end at once to his partnership with him."

REYNARD WANTS TO TASTE HORSE-FLESH.

"ONE day as Bruin lay by a horse which he had slain, and was hard at work eating it, Reynard was out that day too, and came up spying about and licking his lips, if he might get a taste of the horse-flesh. So he doubled and turned till he got just behind Bruin's back, and then he jumped on the other side of the carcass and snapped a mouthful as he ran by. Bruin was not slow either, for he made a grab at Reynard and caught the tip of his red brush in his paw; and ever since then Reynard's brush is white at the tip, as any one may see.

"But that day Bruin was merry, and called out,

" ' Bide a bit, Reynard; and come hither, and I'll tell you how to catch a horse for yourself.'

" Yes, Reynard was ready enough to learn, but he did not for all that trust himself to go very close to Bruin.

" ' Listen,' said Bruin, ' when you see a horse asleep, sunning himself in the sunshine, you must mind and bind yourself fast by the hair of his tail to your brush, and then you must make your teeth meet in the flesh of his thigh.'

" As you may fancy, it was not long before Reynard found out a horse that lay asleep in the sunshine, and then he did as Bruin had told him; for he knotted and bound himself well into the hair of his tail, and made his teeth meet in the horse's thigh.

" Up sprang the horse, and began to kick and rear and gallop, so that Reynard was dashed against stock and stone, and got battered black and blue, so that he was not far off losing both wit and sense. And while the horse galloped, they passed Jack Longears, the Hare.

" ' Whither away so fast, Reynard ? ' cried Jack Longears.

" ' Post haste,' on business of life and death, dear Jack,' cried Reynard.

" And with that Jack stood up on his hind legs, and laughed till his sides ached and his jaws split right up to his ears. It was so funny to see Reynard ride post haste.

" But you must know, since that ride Reynard has never thought of catching a horse for himself. For that once at least it was Bruin who had the best of it in wit, though they do say he is most often as simple-minded as the Trolls."

Many other stories Edward and I heard that season up on the Fjeld, either from the girls, or Peter, or Anders; and here some of them follow standing by themselves, and not set in a frame.

MASTER TOBACCO.

"ONCE on a time there was a poor woman who went about begging with her son ; for at home she had neither a morsel to eat nor a stick to burn. First she tried the country, and went from parish to parish ; but it was poor work, and so she came into the town. There she went about from house to house for a while, and at last she came to the lord mayor. He was both open-hearted and open-handed, and he was married to the daughter of the richest merchant in the town, and they had one little daughter. As they had no more children, you may fancy she was sugar and spice and all that's nice, and in a word there was nothing too good for her. This little girl soon came to know the beggar boy as he went about with his mother ; and as the lord mayor was a wise man, as soon as he saw what friends the two were, he took the boy into his house, that he might be his daughter's playmate. Yes, they played and read and went to school together, and never had so much as one quarrel.

" One day the lady mayoress stood at the window, and watched the children as they were trudging off to school. There had been a shower of rain, and the street was flooded, and she saw how the boy first carried the basket with their dinner over the stream, and then he went back and lifted the little girl over, and when he set her down he gave her a kiss.

"When the lady mayoress saw this, she got very angry. 'To think of such a ragamuffin kissing our daughter— we, who are the best people in the place!' That was what she said. Her husband did his best to stop her tongue. 'No one knew,' he said, 'how children would turn out in life, or what might befall his own: the boy was a clever, handy lad, and often and often a great tree sprang from a slender plant.'

"But no! it was all the same whatever he said, and whichever way he put it. The lady mayoress held her own, and said, beggars on horseback always rode their cattle to death, and that no one had ever heard of a silk purse being made out of a sow's ear; adding, that a penny would never turn into a shilling, even though it glittered like a guinea. The end of it all was that the poor lad was turned out of the house, and had to pack up his rags and be off.

"When the lord mayor saw there was no help for it, he sent him away with a trader who had come thither with a ship, and he was to be cabin-boy on board her. He told his wife he had sold the boy for a roll of tobacco.

"But before he went the lord mayor's daughter broke her ring into two bits, and gave the boy one bit, that it might be a token to know him by if they ever met again; and so the ship sailed away, and the lad came to a town, far, far

off in the world, and to that town a priest had just come
who was so good a preacher that every one went to church
to hear him, and the crew of the ship went with the rest
the Sunday after to hear the sermon. As for the lad, he
was left behind to mind the ship and to cook the dinner.
So while he was hard at work he heard some one calling
out across the water on an island. So he took the boat
and rowed across, and there he saw an old hag, who called
and roared.

"'Aye,' she said, 'you have come at last! Here have I
stood a hundred years calling and bawling, and thinking
how I should ever get over this water; but no one has
ever heard or heeded but you, and you shall be well paid,
if you will put me over to the other side.'

"So the lad had to row her to her sister's house, who
lived on a hill on the other side, close by; and when they
got there, she·told him to beg for the old table-cloth
which lay on the dresser. Yes! he begged for it, and
when the old witch who lived there knew that he had
helped her sister over the water, she said he might have
whatever he chose to ask.

"'Oh,' said the boy, 'then I won't have anything else
than that old table-cloth on the dresser yonder.'

"'Oh,' said the old witch, 'that you never asked out of
your own wits.'

"'Now I must be off,' said the lad, 'to cook the
Sunday dinner for the church-goers.'

"'Never mind that,' said the first old hag; 'it will cook
itself while you are away. Stop with me, and I will pay

you better still. Here have I stood and called and bawled for a hundred years, but no one has ever heeded me but you.'

"The end was he had to go with her to another sister, and when he got there the old hag said he was to be sure and ask for the old sword, which was such that he could put it into his pocket and it became a knife, and when he drew it out it was a long sword again. One edge was black and the other white; and if he smote with the black edge everything fell dead, and if with the white everything came to life again. So when they came over, and the second old witch heard how he had helped her sister across, she said he might have anything he chose to ask for her fare.

"'Oh,' said the lad, 'then I will have nothing else but that old sword which hangs up over the cupboard.'

"'That you never asked out of your own wits,' said the old witch; but for all that he got the sword.

"Then the old hag said again, 'Come on with me to my third sister. Here have I stood and called and bawled for a hundred years, and no one has heeded me but you. Come on to my third sister, and you shall have better pay still.'

"So he went with her, and on the way she told him he was to ask for the old hymn-book; and that was such a book that when any one was sick and the nurse sang one of the hymns, the sickness passed away, and they were well again. Well! when they got across, and the third old witch heard he had helped her sister across, she said he was to have whatever he chose to ask for his fare.

" ' Oh,' said the lad, ' then I won't have anything else but granny's old hymn-book.'

" ' That,' said the old hag, ' you never asked out of your own wits.'

" When he got back to the ship the crew were still at church, so he tried his table-cloth, and spread just a little bit of it out, for he wanted to see what good it was before he laid it on the table. Yes! in a trice, it was covered with good food and strong drink; enough, and to spare. So he just took a little snack, and then he gave the ship's dog as much as it could eat.

" When the church-goers came on board, the captain said, ' Wherever did you get all that food for the dog? Why, he's as round as a sausage, and as lazy as a snail.'

" ' Oh, if you must know,' said the lad, ' I gave him the bones.'

" ' Good boy,' said the captain, ' to think of the dog.'

" So he spread out the cloth, and at once the whole table was covered all over with such brave meat and drink as they had never before seen in all their born days.

" Now when the boy was again alone with the dog, he wanted to try the sword, so he smote at the dog with the black edge, and it fell dead on the deck; but when he turned the blade and smote with the white edge, the dog came to life again and wagged his tail and fawned on his playmate. But the book,—that he could not get tried just then.

"Then they sailed well and far till a storm overtook them, which lasted many days; so they lay to and drove till they were quite out of their course, and could not tell where they were. At last the wind fell, and then they came to a country far, far off, that none of them knew; but they could easily see there was great grief there, as well there might be, for the king's daughter was a leper. The king came down to the shore, and asked was there any one on board who could cure her and make her well again.

"'No, there was not.' That was what they all said who were on deck.

"'Is there no one else on board the ship than those I see?' asked the king.

"'Yes; there's a little beggar boy.'

"'Well,' said the king, 'let him come on deck.'

"So when he came, and heard what the king wanted, he said he thought he might cure her; and then the captain got so wrath and mad with rage that he ran round and round like a squirrel in a cage, for he thought the boy was only putting himself forward to do something in which he was sure to fail, and he told the king not to listen to such childish chatter.

" But the king only said that wit came as children grew, and that there was the making of a man in every bairn. The boy had said he could do it, and he might as well try. After all, there were many who had tried and failed before him. So he took him home to his daughter, and the lad sang an hymn once. Then the princess could lift her arm. Once again he sang it, and she could sit up in bed. And when he had sung it thrice the king's daughter was as well as you and I are.

"The king was so glad, he wanted to give him half his kingdom and the princess to wife.

"'Yes,' said the lad, 'land and power were fine things to have half of, and was very grateful; but as for the princess, he was betrothed to another,' he said, 'and he could not take her to wife.'

"So he stayed there awhile, and got half the kingdom; and when he had not been very long there, war broke out, and the lad went out to battle with the rest, and you may fancy he did not spare the black edge of his sword. The enemy's soldiers fell before him like flies, and the king won the day. But when they had conquered, he turned the white edge, and they all rose up alive and became the king's soldiers, who had granted them their lives. But then there were so many of them that they were badly off for food, though the king wished to send them away full, both of meat and drink. So the lad had to bring out his table-cloth, and then there was not a man that lacked anything.

"Now when he had lived a little longer with the king, he began to long to see the lord mayor's daughter. So he fitted out four ships of war and set sail; and when he came off the town where the lord mayor lived, he fired off his cannon like thunder, till half the panes of glass in the town were shivered. On board those ships everything was as grand as in a king's palace; and as

for himself, he had gold on every seam of his coat, so
fine he was. It was not long before the lord mayor
came down to the shore and asked if the foreign lord
would not be so good as to come up and dine with him.
'Yes, he would go,' he said; and so he went up to
the mansion-house where the lord mayor lived, and there
he took his seat between the lady mayoress and her
daughter.

"So as they sat there in the greatest state, and ate and
drank and were merry, he threw the half of the ring
into the daughter's glass, and no one saw it; but she
was not slow to find out what he meant, and excused
herself from the feast and went out and fitted his half
to her half. Her mother saw there was something in
the wind and hurried after her as fast as she could.

"'Do you know who that is in there, mother?' said
the daughter.

"'No!' said the lady mayoress.

"'He whom papa sold for a roll of tobacco,' said the
daughter.

"At these words the lady mayoress fainted, and fell
down flat on the floor.

"In a little while the lord mayor came out to see what
was the matter, and when he heard how things stood he
was almost as uneasy as his wife.

"'There is nothing to make a fuss about,' said Master
Tobacco. 'I have only come to claim the little girl I
kissed as we were going to school.'

"But to the lady mayoress, he said,

" ' You should never despise the children of the poor and needy, for none can tell how they may turn out ; for there is the making of a man in every child of man, and wit and wisdom come with growth and strength.' "

THE CHARCOAL-BURNER.

"ONCE on a time there was a charcoal-burner, who had a son, who was a charcoal-burner too. When the father was dead, the son took him a wife; but he was lazy and would turn his hand to nothing. He was careless in minding his pits too, and the end was no one would have him to burn charcoal for them.

"It so fell out that one day he had burned a pit full for himself, and set off to the town with a few loads and sold them; and when he had done selling, he loitered in the street and looked about him. On his way home he fell in with townsmen and neighbours, and made merry, and drank, and chattered of all he had seen in the town. 'The prettiest thing I saw,' he said, 'was a great crowd of priests, and all the folks greeted them and took off their hats to them. I only wish I were a priest myself; then maybe they would take off their hats to me too. As it was they looked as though they did not even see me at all.'

"'Well, well!' said his friends, 'if you are nothing else, you can't say you're not as black as a priest. And now we are about it, we can go to the sale of the old priest, who is dead, and have a glass, and meanwhile you can buy his gown and hood.' That was what the neighbours said; and what they said he did, and when he got home he had not so much as a penny left.

"'Now you have both means and money, I dare say,' said his goody, when she heard he had sold his charcoal.

"'I should think so. Means, indeed!' said the charcoal-burner, 'for you must know I have been ordained priest. Here you see both gown and hood.'

"'Nay, I'll never believe that,' said the goody, 'strong ale makes big words. You are just as bad, whichever end of you turns up. That you are,' she said.

"'You shall neither scold nor sorrow for the pit, for its last coal is quenched and cold,' said the charcoal-burner.

"It fell out one day that many people in priests' robes passed by the charcoal-burner's cottage on their way to the king's palace, so that it was easy to see there was something in the wind there. Yes! the charcoal-burner would go to, and so he put on his gown and hood.

"His goody thought it would be far better to stay at home; for even if he chanced to hold a horse for some great man, the drink-money he got would only go down his throat like so many before it.

"'There are many, mother, who talk of drink,' said the man, 'who never think of thirst. All I know is, the more one drinks the more one thirsts;' and with that he set off for the palace. When he got there, all the strangers were bidden to come in, and the charcoal-burner followed with the rest So the king made them a speech, and said he had lost his costliest ring, and was quite sure it had been stolen. That was why he had summoned all the learned priests in the land, to see if there were one of them who could tell him who the thief was. And he made a vow there and then, and said what reward he would give to the man who found out the thief. If he were a curate, he should have a living; if he was a rector, he should be made a dean; if he were a dean, he should be made a bishop; and if he were a bishop, he should become the first man in the kingdom after the king.

"So the king went round and round among them all, from one to the other, asking them if they could find the thief; and when he came to the charcoal-burner, he said,

"'Who are you?'

"'I am the wise priest and the true prophet,' said the charcoal-burner.

"'Then you can tell me,' said the king, 'who has taken my ring?'

"'Yes!' said the charcoal-burner; 'it isn't so right against rhyme and reason that what has happened in darkness should come to light; but it isn't every year that salmon spawn in fir-tree tops. Here have I been a curate for seven years, trying to feed myself and my children, and I havn't got a living yet. If that thief is to be found out, I must have lots of time and reams of paper; for I must write and reckon, and track him out through many lands.'

"'Yes! he should have as much time and paper as he chose, if he would only lay his finger on the thief.'

"So they shut him up by himself in a room in the king's palace, and it was not long before they found out that he must know much more than his Lord's Prayer; for he scribbled over so much paper that it lay in great heaps and rolls, and yet there was not a man who could make out a word of what he wrote, for it looked like nothing else than pot-hooks and hangers. But, as he did this, time went on, and still there was not a trace of the thief. At last the king got weary, and so he said, if the priest couldn't find the thief in three days he should lose his life.

" 'More haste, worse speed. You can't cart coal till the pit is cool,' said the charcoal-burner. But the king stuck to his word—that he did; and the charcoal-burner felt his life wasn't worth much.

"Now there were three of the king's servants who waited on the charcoal-burner day by day, in turn, and these three fellows had stolen the ring between them. So when one of these servants came into the room and cleared the table when he had eaten his supper, and was going out again, the charcoal-burner heaved a deep sigh as he looked after him, and said,

" 'THERE GOES THE FIRST OF THEM!' but he only meant the first of the three days he had still to live.

" 'That priest knows more than how to fill his mouth,' said the servant, when he was alone with his fellows; for he said, I was the first of them.'

"The next day, the second servant was to mark what the prisoner said when he waited on him, and sure enough when he went out, after clearing the table, the charcoal-burner stared him full in the face and fetched a deep sigh, and said,

"'THERE GOES THE SECOND OF THEM!'

"So the third was to take heed to what the charcoal-burner said on the third day, and it was all worse and no better; for when the servant had his hand on the door as he went out with the plates and dishes, the charcoal-burner clasped his hands together, and said, with a sigh as though his heart would break,

"'THERE GOES THE THIRD OF THEM!'

"So the man went down to his fellows with his heart in his throat, and said it was clear as day the priest knew all about it; and so they all three went into his room and fell on their knees before him, and begged and prayed he would not say it was they who had stolen the ring. If he would do this, they were ready to give him, each of them, a hundred dollars, if he would not bring them into trouble.

"Well, he gave his word, like a man, to do that and keep them harmless, if they would only give him the money and the ring and a great bowl of porridge. And what do you think he did with the ring when he got it? Why, he stuffed it well down into the porridge, and bade them go and give it to the biggest pig in the king's stye.

"Next morning the king came, and was in no mood for jokes, and said he must know all about the thief.

"'Well! well! now I have written and reckoned all the world round,' said the charcoal-burner, 'but it is no child of man that stole your majesty's ring.'

"'Pooh! said the king; 'who was it, then?'

"'It was the biggest pig in your stye,' said the charcoal-burner.

"Yes! they killed the pig, and there the ring was inside it; there was no mistake about that; and so the charcoal-burner got a living, and the king was so glad he gave him a farm and a horse, and a hundred dollars into the bargain.

"You may fancy the charcoal-burner was not slow in flitting to the living, and the first Sunday after he got there he was going to church to read himself in; but before he left his house he was to have his breakfast, and so he took the king's letter and laid it on a bit of dry toast and then, by mistake, he dipped both toast and letter into his brose, and when he found it tough to chew, he gave the whole morsel to his dog Tray, and Tray gobbled up both toast and letter.

"And now he scarce knew what to do, or how to turn. To church he must, for the people were waiting; and when he got there, he went straight up into the pulpit. In the pulpit he put on such a grave face that all thought he was a grand priest; but as the service went on, it was not so good after all. This was how he began :

"'The words, my brethren, which you should have heard this day have gone, alas! to the dogs; but come next Sunday, dear parishioners, and you shall hear something else; and so this sermon comes to an end. Amen!'

"All the parish thought they had got a strange priest,

for they had never heard such a funny sermon before; but still they said to themselves, 'He'll be better perhaps by-and-by, and if he isn't better we shall know how to deal with him.'

"Next Sunday, when there was service again, the church was so crowded full with folk who wished to hear the new priest that there was scarce standing-room. Well, he came again, and went straight up into the pulpit, and there he stood awhile and said never a word. But all at once he burst out, and bawled at the top of his voice—

"'Hearken to me, old Nannygoat Bridget! Why in the world do you sit so far back in the church?'

"'Oh, your reverence,' said she, 'if you must know, it's because my shoes are all in holes.'

"'That's no reason; for you might take an old bit of pig-skin and stitch yourself new shoes, and then you could also come far forward in the church, like the other fine ladies. For the rest, you all ought to bethink yourselves of the way you are going; for I see when ye come to church, some of you come from the north and some from the south, and it is the same when you go from church again. But sometimes ye stand and loiter on the way, and then it may well be asked, What will become of you? Yea! who can tell what will become of every one of us? By the way, I have to give notice of a black mare which has strayed from the old priest's widow. She has hair on her fetlocks and a falling mane, and other marks which I will not name in this place. Besides, I may tell you, I have a hole in my old breeches-pocket, and I know it, but you do not know it; and another thing you do not know, and which I do not know, is whether any of you has a bit of cloth to patch that hole. Amen.'

"Some few of the hearers were very well pleased with this sermon. They thought it sure he would make a brave priest in time; but, to tell the truth, most of them thought it too bad, and when the dean came they complained of the priest, and said no one had ever heard such sermons before, and there was even one of them who knew the last by heart, and wrote it down and read it to the dean.

"'I call it a very good sermon,' said the dean, 'for it was likely that he spoke in parables as to seeking light and shunning darkness and its deeds, and as to those who were walking either on the broad or the strait path; but most of all,' he said, 'that was a grand parable when he gave that notice about the priest's black mare, and how it would fare with us all at the last. The pocket with the hole in it was to show the need of the church, and the piece of cloth to patch it was the gifts and offerings of the congregation.' That was what the dean said.

"As for the parish, what they said was, 'Ay! ay!' so much we could understand that it was to go into the priest's pocket.

"The end was, the dean said, he thought the parish had got such a good and understanding priest, there was no fault to find with him, and so they had to make the best of him; but after a while, as he got worse instead of better, they complained of him to the bishop.

"Well! sooner or later the bishop came, and there was to be a visitation. But, the day before, the priest had gone into the church, unbeknown to anybody, and sawed the props of the pulpit all but in two, so that it would only just hang together if one went up into it very carefully. So when the people were gathered together and he was to preach before the bishop, he crept up into the pulpit and began to expound, as he was wont; and when he had gone on a while, he got more in earnest, threw his arms about and bawled out,

"'If there be any here who is wicked or given to ill deeds, it were better he left this place; for this very day there shall be a fall, such as hath not been seen since the world began.'

"With that he struck the reading-desk like thunder, and lo! the desk and the priest and the whole pulpit tumbled down on the floor of the church with such a crash that the whole congregation ran out of church, as if Doomsday were at their heels.

"But then the bishop told the fault-finders he was amazed that they dared to complain of a priest who had such gifts in the pulpit, and so much wisdom that he could foresee things about to happen. For his part, he thought he ought to be a dean at least, and it was not long either before he was a dean. So there was no help for it; they had to put up with him.

"Now it so happened that the king and queen had no children; but when the king heard that, perhaps, there was one coming, he was eager to know if it would be an heir to his crown and realm, or if it would only be a princess. So all the wise men in the land were gathered to the palace, that they might say beforehand what it would be. But when there was not a man of them that could say that, both the king and the bishop thought of the charcoal-burner, and it was not long before they got him between them, and asked him about it. 'No!' he said, 'that was past his power, for it was not good to guess at what no man alive could know.'

"'All very fine, I dare say,' said the king. 'It's all the same to me, of course, if you know it or if you don't know it; but, you know, you are the wise priest and the true prophet who can foretell things to come; and all I can say is if you don't tell it me, you shall lose your gown. And now I think of it, I'll try you first.'

"So he took the biggest silver tankard he had and went down to the sea-shore, and, in a little while, called the priest.

"'If you can tell me now what there is in this tankard,' said the king, 'you will be able to tell me the other also;' and as he said this, he held the lid of the tankard tight.

"The charcoal-burner only wrung his hands and bemoaned himself.

"'Oh! you most wretched crab and cripple on this earth,' he cried out, "this is what all your backslidings and sidelong tricks have brought on you.'

"'Ah!' cried out the king, 'how could you say you did not know?' for you must know he had a crab in the tankard. So the charcoal-burner had to go into the parlour to the queen. He took a chair and sat down in the middle of the floor, while the queen walked up and down in the room.

"'One should never count one's chickens before they are hatched, and never quarrel about a baby's name before it is born,' said the charcoal-burner; 'but I never heard or saw such a thing before! When the queen comes toward me, I almost think it will be a prince, and when she goes away from me it looks as if it would be a princess.'

"Lo! when the time came, it was both a prince and a princess, for twins were born; and so the charcoal-burner had hit the mark that time too. And because he could tell that which no man could know, he got money in carts full, and was the next man to the king in the realm.

> "Trip, trap, trill,
> A man is often more than he will.'

THE BOX WITH SOMETHING PRETTY IN IT.

"ONCE on a time there was a little boy who was out walking on the road, and when he had walked a bit he found a box.

"'I am sure there must be something pretty in this box,' he said to himself; but however much he turned it, and however much he twisted it, he was not able to get it open.

"But when he had walked a bit farther, he found a little tiny key. Then he got tired and sat down, and all at once he thought what fun it would be if the key fitted the box, for it had a little key-hole in it. So he took the little key out of his pocket, and then he blew first into the pipe of the key, and afterwards into the key-hole, and then he put the key into the key-hole and turned it. 'Snap' it went within the lock; and when he tried the hasp, the box was open.

"But can you guess what there was in the box?" Why a cow's tail; and if the cow's tail had been longer, this story would have been longer too."

THE THREE LEMONS.

"ONCE on a time there were three brothers, who had lost their parents; and as they had left nothing behind them on which the lads could live, they had to go out into the world to try their luck. The two elder fitted themselves out as well as they could; but the youngest, whom they called Taper Tom, because he always sat in the chimney-corner and held tapers of pine wood, him they would not have with them.

"The two set out early in the grey dawn; but, however fast they went, or did not go, Taper Tom came just as soon as the others to the king's palace. So when they got there, they asked for work. The king said he had nothing for them to do; but as they were so pressing, he'd see if he could not find them something,—there must be always something to do in such a big house. Yes! they might drive nails into the wall; and when they had done driving them in, they might pull them out again. When they had done that, they might carry wood and water into the kitchen.

"Taper Tom was the handiest in driving nails into the wall and in pulling them out again and he was the handiest also in carrying wood and water. So his brothers were jealous of him, and said he had given out that he was good enough to get the king the prettiest princess who was to be found in twelve kingdoms; for you must know the king had lost his old dame, and was a widower. When the king heard that, he told Taper Tom he must do what he had said, or else he would make them lay him on the block and chop his head off.

"Taper Tom answered, he had never said nor thought anything of the kind; but, as the king was so stern, he would try what he could do. So he got him a scrip of food over his shoulders, and set off from the palace; but he had not gone far on the road before he grew hungry, and wanted to taste the food they had given him when he set out. So when he had seated himself to rest at his ease, under a spruce by the roadside, up came an old hag hobbling, who asked what he had in his scrip.

"'Salt meat and fresh meat,' said the lad. 'If you are hungry, granny, come and take a snack with me.'

"Yes! She thanked him, and then she said, might be she would do him a good turn herself; and away she hobbled through the wood. So when Taper Tom had eaten his full, and had rested, he threw his scrip over his shoulder and set off again; but he had not gone far before he found a pipe. That, he thought, would be nice to have with him and play on by the way; and it was not long before he brought the sound out of it, you may fancy. But then there came about him such a swarm of little Trolls, and each asked the other in full cry,—

"'What has my lord to order? What has my lord to order?'

"Taper Tom said he never knew he was lord over them; but if he was to order anything, he wished they would fetch him the prettiest princess to be found in twelve kingdoms. Yes! that was no great thing, the little Trolls thought; they knew well enough where she was, and they could show him the way, and then he might go and get her for himself, for they had no power to touch her.

"Then they showed him the way, and he got to the end of his journey well and happily. There was not anyone who laid so much as two sticks across in his way. It was a Troll's castle, and in it sat three lovely princesses; but as soon as ever Taper Tom came in, they all lost their wits for fear, and ran about like scared lambs, and all at once they were turned into three lemons that lay in the window. Taper Tom was so sorry and unhappy at that, he scarce knew which way to turn. But when he had thought a little, he took and put the lemons into his pocket, for he thought they would be good to have if he got thirsty by the way, for he had heard say lemons were sour.

"So when he had gone a bit of the way, he got so hot and thirsty; water was not to be had, and he did not know what he should do to quench his thirst. So he fell to thinking of the lemons, and took one of them out and bit a hole in it. But, lo! inside sat the princess as far as her armpits, and screamed out—

"'Water!—water!' Unless she got water, she must die, she said.

"Yes! the lad ran about looking for water as though he were a mad thing; but there was no water to be got, and all at once the princess was dead.

"So when he had gone a bit further, he got still hotter and thirstier; and as he could find nothing to quench his thirst, he pulled out the second lemon and bit a hole in it. Inside it was also a princess, sitting as far as her armpits, and she was still lovelier than the first. She, too, screamed for water, and said, if she could not get it she must die outright. So Taper Tom hunted under stone and moss, but he could find no water; and so the end was the second Princess died too.

"Taper Tom thought things got worse and worse, and so it was, for the farther he went the hotter it got. The earth was so dry and burnt up, there was not a drop of water to be found, and he was not far off being half dead of thirst. He kept himself as long as he could from biting a hole in the lemon he still had, but at last there was no help for it. So when he had bitten the hole, there sat a princess inside it also; she was the loveliest in twelve kingdoms, and she screamed out if she could not get water she must die at once. So Taper Tom ran about hunting for water; and this time he fell upon the king's miller, and he showed him the way to the mill-dam. So when he came to the dam with her and gave her some water, she came quite out of the lemon, and was stark naked. So Taper Tom had to let her have the wrap he had to throw over her, and then she hid herself up a tree while he went up to the king's palace to fetch her clothes, and tell the king how he had got her, and, in a word, told him the whole story.

"But while this was going on, the cook came down to the mill-dam to fetch water; and when she saw the lovely face which played on the water, she thought it was her own, and grew so glad she fell a-dancing and jumping because she had grown so pretty.

"'The deil carry water,' she cried, 'since I am so pretty;' and away she threw the water-buckets. But in a little while she got to see that the face in the mill-dam belonged to the princess who sat up in the tree; and then she got so cross, that she tore her down from the tree, and threw her out into the dam. But she herself put on Taper Tom's cloak, and crept up into the tree.

"So when the king came and set eyes on the ugly swarthy kitchen-maid, he turned white and red; but when he heard how they said she was the loveliest in twelve kingdoms, he thought he could not help believing there must be something in it; and besides he felt for poor Taper Tom, who had taken so much pains to get her for him.

"'She'll get better, perhaps, as time goes on,' he thought, 'when she is dressed smartly, and wears fine clothes;' and so he took her home with him.

"Then they sent for all the wig-makers and needlewomen, and she was dressed and clad like a princess; but for all they washed and dressed her, she was still as ugly and black as ever.

"After a while the kitchen-maid was to go to the dam to fetch water, and then she caught a great silver fish in her bucket. She bore it up to the palace, and showed it to the king, and he thought it grand and fine; but the ugly princess said it was some witchcraft, and they must burn it, for she soon saw what it was. Well! the fish was burnt, and next morning they found a lump of silver in the ashes. So the cook came and told it to the king, and he thought it passing strange; but the princess said it was all witchcraft, and bade them bury it in the dung-heap. The king was much against it; but she left him neither rest nor peace, and so he said at last they might do it.

"But lo! next day stood a tall lovely linden tree on the spot where they had buried the lump of silver, and that linden had leaves which gleamed like silver. So when they told the king that, he thought it passing strange; but the princess said it was nothing but witchcraft, and they must cut down the linden at once. The king was against that; but the princess plagued him so long that at last he had to give way to her in this also.

"But lo! when the lasses went out to gather the chips of the linden to light the fires, they were pure silver.

"'It isn't worth while,' one of them said, 'to say anything about this to the king or the princess, or else they, too, will be burnt and melted. It is better to hide them in our drawers. They will be good to have when a lover comes, and we are going to marry.'

"Yes! They were all of one mind as to that; but when

they had borne the chips a while, they grew so fearfully heavy that they could not help looking to see what it was; and then they found the chips had been changed into a child, and it was not long before it grew into the loveliest princess you ever set eyes on.

"The lasses could see very well that something wrong lay under all this. So they got her clothes, and flew off to find the lad, who was to fetch the loveliest princess in twelve kingdoms, and told him their story.

"So when Taper Tom came, the princess told him her story, and how the cook had come and torn her from the tree and thrown her into the dam; and how she had been the silver fish, and the silver lump, and the linden, and the chips, and how she was the true princess.

"It was not so easy to get the king's ear, for the ugly black cook hung over him early and late; but at last they made out a story, and said that a challenge had come from a neighbour king, and so they got him out; and when he came to see the lovely princess, he was so taken with her, he was for holding the bridal feast on the spot; and when he heard how badly the ugly black cook had behaved to her, he said they should take her and roll her down hill in a cask full of nails. Then they kept the bridal feast at such a rate that it was heard and talked of over twelve kingdoms."

THE PRIEST AND THE CLERK.

" ONCE on a time there was a priest, who was such a
bully, that he bawled out, ever so far off, whenever
he met anyone driving on the king's highway,—

"'Out of the way, out of the way! Here comes the
priest!'

"One day when he was driving along and behaving so,
he met the king himself.

"'Out of the way, out of the way,' he bawled a long
way off. But the king drove on and kept his own; so
that time it was the priest who had to turn his horse
aside, and when the king came alongside him, he said,
"To-morrow you shall come to me to the palace, and if
you can't answer three questions which I will set you, you
shall lose hood and gown for your pride's sake.'

"This was something else than the priest was wont to
hear. He could bawl and bully, shout, and behave worse
than badly. All THAT he could do, but question and
answer was out of his power. So he set off to the clerk
who was said to be better in a gown than the priest himself, and told him he had no mind to go to the king.

"'For one fool can ask more than ten wise men can

answer;' and the end was, he got the clerk to go in his stead.

"Yes! The clerk set off, and came to the palace in the priest's gown and hood. There the king met him out in the porch with crown and sceptre, and was so grand it glittered and gleamed from him.

"'Well! Are you there?' said the king.

"Yes; he was there, sure enough.

"'Tell me first,' said the king; 'how far the east is from the west?'

"'Just a day's journey,' said the clerk.

"'How is that?' asked the king.

"'Don't you know,' said the clerk, 'that the sun rises in the east and sets in the west, and he does it just nicely in one day.'

"'Very well!' said the king; 'but tell me now what you think I am worth, as you see me stand here?'

"'Well,' said the clerk; 'Our Lord was valued at thirty pieces of silver, so I don't think I can set your price higher than twenty-nine.'

"'All very fine!' said the king; 'but as you are so wise, perhaps you can tell me what I am thinking about now?'

"'Oh!' said the clerk; 'you are thinking it's the priest who stands before you, but so help me, if you don't think wrong, for I am the clerk.'

"'Be off home with you,' said the king, 'and be you priest, and let him be clerk,' and so it was."

FRIENDS IN LIFE AND DEATH.

"ONCE on a time there were two young men who were such great friends that they swore to one another they would never part, either in life or death. One of them died before he was at all old, and a little while after the other wooed a farmer's daughter, and was to be married to her. So when they were bidding guests to the wedding the bridegroom went himself to the churchyard where his friend lay, and knocked at his grave, and called him by name. No! he neither answered nor came. He knocked again, and he called again, but no one came. A third time he knocked louder and called louder to him, to come that he might talk to him. So, after a long, long time, he heard a rustling, and at last the dead man came up out of the grave.

"'It was well you came at last,' said the bridegroom, 'for I have been standing here ever so long, knocking and calling for you.'

"'I was a long way off,' said the dead man, 'so that I did not quite hear you till the last time you called.'

"'All right,' said the bridegroom; 'but I am going to stand bridegroom to-day, and you mind well, I dare say, what we used to talk about, and how we were to stand by each other at our weddings as best man.'

"'I mind it well,' said the dead man, 'but you must wait a bit till I have made myself a little smart ; and, after all, no one can say I have on a wedding garment.'

"The lad was hard put to it for time, for he was overdue at home to meet the guests, and it was all but time to go to church ; but still he had to wait awhile and let the dead man go into a room by himself, as he begged, so that he might brush himself up a bit, and come smart to church like the rest, for, of course, he was to go with the bridal train to church.

"Yes! the dead man went with him both to church and from church, but when they had got so far on with the wedding that they had taken off the bride's crown, he said he must go. So, for old friendship's sake, the bridegroom said he would go with him to the grave again. And as they walked to the churchyard the bridegroom asked his friend if he had seen much that was wonderful, or heard anything that was pleasant to know.

"'Yes! that I have,' said the dead man. 'I have seen much, and heard many strange things.'

"'That must be fine to see,' said the bridegroom. 'Do you know I have a mind to go along with you, and see all that with my own eyes.'

"'You are quite welcome,' said the dead man ;' but it may chance that you may be away some time.'

"'So it might,' said the bridegroom ; but for all that he would go down into the grave.

"But before they went down the dead man took and cut up a turf out of the graveyard and put it on the young man's head. Down and down they went, far and far away, through dark, silent wastes, across wood, and moor, and bog, till they came to a great, heavy gate, which opened to them as soon as the dead man touched it. Inside it began to grow lighter, first as though it were moonshine, and the further they went the lighter it got. At last they got to a spot where there were such green hills, knee-deep in grass, and on them fed a large herd of kine, who grazed as they went; but for all they ate those kine looked poor, and thin, and wretched.

"'What's all this?' said the lad who had been bridegroom; 'why are they so thin, and in such bad case, though they eat, every one of them, as though they were well paid to eat?'

"'This is a likeness of those who never can have enough, though they rake and scrape it together ever so much,' said the dead man.

"So they journeyed on far and farther than far, till they came to some hill pastures, where there was naught but bare rocks and stones, with here and there a blade of grass. Here was grazing another herd of kine, which were so sleek, and fat, and smooth that their coats shone again.

"'What are these,' asked the bridegroom, 'who have so little to live on, and yet are in such good plight? I wonder what they can be.'

"'This,' said the dead man, 'is a likeness of those who are content with the little they have, however poor it be.'

"So they went farther and farther on till they came to a great lake, and it and all about it was so bright and shining that the bridegroom could scarce bear to look at it—it was so dazzling.

"'Now, you must sit down here,' said the dead man, 'till I come back. I shall be away a little while.'

"With that he set off, and the bridegroom sat down, and as he sat sleep fell on him, and he forgot everything in sweet deep slumber. After a while the dead man came back.

"'It was good of you to sit still here, so that I cóuld find you again.'

"But when the bridegroom tried to get up he was all overgrown with moss and bushes, so that he found himself sitting in a thicket of thorns and brambles.

"So when he had made his way out of it they journeyed back again, and the dead man led him by the same way to the brink of the grave. There they parted and said fare-well, and as soon as the bridegroom got out of the grave he went straight home tó the house where the wedding was.

"But when he got where he thought the house stood, he could not find his way. Then he looked about on all sides, and asked every one he met, but he could neither hear nor learn anything of the bride, or the wedding, or his kindred, or his father and mother; nay, he could not so much as find any one whom he knew. And all he met wondered at the strange shape, who went about and looked for all the world like a scarecrow.

"Well! as he could find no one he knew, he made his

way to the priest, and told him of his kinsmen and all that had happened up to the time he stood bridegroom, and how he had gone away in the midst of his wedding. But the priest knew nothing at all about it at first ; but when he had hunted in his old registers he found out that the marriage he spoke of had happened a long, long time ago, and that all the folk he talked of had lived four hundred years before.

"In that time there had grown up a great stout oak in the priest's yard, and when he saw it he clambered up into it, that he might look about him.   But the grey-beard who had sat in Heaven and slumbered for four hundred years, and had now at last come back, did not come down from the oak as well as he went up.   He was stiff and gouty, as was likely enough ; and so when he was coming down he made a false step, fell down, broke his neck, and that was the end of him."

THE FATHER OF THE FAMILY.

—

" ONCE on a time there was a man who was out on a
journey; so at last he came to a big and a fine
farm, and there was a house so grand that it might well
have been a little palace.

" ' Here it would be good to get leave to spend the
night,' said the man to himself, as he went inside the
gate.   Hard by stood an old man with grey hair and
beard, who was hewing wood.

" ' Good evening, father,' said the wayfarer.   ' Can I
have house-room here to-night ?'

" ' I'm not father in the house,' said the grey-beard.
' Go into the kitchen, and talk to my father.'

" The wayfarer went into the kitchen, and there he met
a man who was still older, and he lay on his knees before
the hearth, and was blowing up the fire.

" ' Good evening, father,' said the wayfarer.   ' Can I
get house-room to-night ?'

" ' I'm not father in the house,' said the old man : ' but
go in and talk to my father.   You'll find him sitting at
the table in the parlour.'

" So the wayfarer went into the parlour, and talked to

him who sat at the table. He was much older than
either of the other two, and there he sat, with his teeth
chattering, and shivered and shook, and read out of a big
book, almost like a little child.

"'Good evening, father,' said the man. 'Will you let
me have house-room here to-night?'

"'I'm not father in the house,' said the man who sat
at the table, whose teeth chattered, and who shivered and
shook; 'but speak to my father yonder—he who sits on
the bench.'

"So the wayfarer went to him who sat on the bench,
and he was trying to fill himself a pipe of tobacco; but he
was so withered up and his hands shook so with the palsy
that he could scarce hold the pipe.

"'Good evening, father,' said the wayfarer again.
'Can I get house-room here to-night?'

"'I'm not father in the house,' said the old withered
fellow; 'but speak to my father, who lies in bed yonder.'

"So the wayfarer went to the bed, and there lay an
old, old man, who but for his pair of big staring eyes
scarcely looked alive.

"'Good evening, father,' said the wayfarer. 'Can I
get house-room here to-night?"

"'I'm not father in the house,' said the old carle with
the big eyes; 'but go and speak to my father, who lies
yonder in the cradle.'

"Yes, the wayfarer went to the cradle, and there lay a
carle as old as the hills, so withered and shrivelled he
was no bigger than a baby, and it was hard to tell that

there was any life in him, except that there was a sound of breathing every now and then in his throat.

"'Good evening, father," said the wayfarer. "May I have house-room here to-night?'

"It was long before he got an answer, and still longer before the carle brought it out; but the end was he said, as all the rest, that he was not father in the house. 'But go,' said he, 'and speak to my father—you'll find him hanging up in the horn yonder against the wall.'

"So the wayfarer stared about round the walls, and at last he caught sight of the horn; but when he looked for him who hung in it he looked more like a film of ashes that had the likeness of a man's face. Then he was so frightened that he screamed out,—

"'Good evening, father! will you let me have house-room here to-night?'

"Then a chirping came out of the horn like a little tom-tit, and it was all he could do to make out that the chirping meant, ' YES, MY CHILD.'

"And now a table came in which was covered with the costliest dishes, and with ale and brandy; and when he had eaten and drank there came in a good bed, with reindeer skins; and the wayfarer was so very glad because he had at last found the right father in the house."

"ONCE on a time there was a poor householder, who had an only son, but he was so lazy and unhandy, this son, that he would neither mix with folk nor turn his hand to anything in the world. So the father said:

"'If I'm not to go on for ever feeding this long lazy fellow, I must pack him off a long way, where no one knows him. If he runs away then it won't be so easy for him to come home.'

"Yes! the man took his son with him, and went about far and wide offering him as a serving man; but there was no one who would have him.

"So last of all they came to a rich man, of whom the story went that he turned a penny over seven times before he let it go. He was to take the lad as a ploughboy, and there he was to serve three years without wages. But when the three years were over the man was to go to the town two mornings, and buy the first thing he met that was for sale, but the third morning the lad was to go himself to the town, and buy the first thing he met, and these three things he was to have instead of wages.

"Well! the lad served his three years out, and behaved

better than any one would have believed. He was not the best ploughboy in the world, sure enough ; but then his master was not of the best sort either, for he let him go the whole time with the same clothes he had when he came, so that at last they were nothing else but patch on patch and mend on mend. Now, when the man was to set off and buy he was up and away at cockcrow, long before dawn.

" 'Dear wares must be seen by daylight,' he said ; ' they are not to be found on the road to town so early. Still, they may be dear enough, for after all it's all risk and chance what I find.'

" Well ! the first person he found in the street was an old hag, and she carried a basket with a cover.

" ' Good day, granny,' said the man.

" ' Good day to you, father,' said the old hag.

" ' What have you got in your basket ?' asked the man.

" ' Do you mean business ?' said the old hag.

" ' Yes, I do, for I was to buy the first thing I met.'

" ' Well, if you want to know you had better buy it,' said the old hag.

" ' But what does it cost ?' asked the man.

" Yes ! she must have fourpence.

" The man thought that no such very high price after all. He couldn't do better, and lifted the lid, and it was a puppy that lay in the basket.

" When the man came home from his trip to town the lad stood out in the yard, and wondered what he should get for his wages for the first year.

" ' So soon home, master ?' said the lad.

" Yes, he was.

" ' What was it you bought ?' he asked.

" ' What I bought,' said the man, ' was not worth much. I scarcely know if I ought to show it ; but I bought the first thing that was to be had, and it was a puppy.'

" ' Now, thank you so much,' said the lad. ' I have always been so fond of dogs.'

" Next morning things went no better. The man was up at dawn again, and he had not got well into the town before he saw the old hag with her basket.

" ' Good day, granny,' he said.

" ' Good day to you, sir,' she said.

" ' What have you got in your basket to-day ?' asked the man.

" ' If you wish to know you had better buy it,' said the old hag.

" ' What does it cost ?' asked the man.

" ' Yes ! she must have fourpence ; she never had more than one price,' she said.

" So the man said he would take it ; it would be hard to find anything cheaper. When he lifted the lid this time there lay a kitten in it.

" When he got home the lad stood out in the yard, waiting and wondering what he should get for his wages the second year.

" ' Is that you, master ?' he said.

" Yes, there he was.

" ' What did you buy to-day now ?' asked the lad.

"'Oh! it was worse, and no better,' said the man; 'but it was just as we bargained. I bought the first thing I met, and it was nothing else than this kitten.'

"'You could not have met anything better,' said the lad; 'I have been as fond of cats all my life as of dogs.'

"'Well,' thought the man, 'I did not get so badly out of that after all; but there's another day to come, when he is to go to town himself.'

"The third morning the lad set off, and just as he got into the town he met the same old hag with her basket on her arm.

"'Good morning, granny!' said the lad.

"'Good morning to you, my son,' said the old hag.

"'What have you got in your basket?'

"'If you want to know you had better buy it,' said the old hag.

"'Will you sell it then?' asked the lad.

"Yes, she would; and fourpence was her price.

"'That was cheap enough,' said the lad, 'and he would have it, for he was to buy the first thing he met.'

"'Now you may take it, basket and all,' said the old hag; 'but mind you don't look inside it before you get home. Do you hear what I say?'

"'Nay, nay, never fear, he wouldn't look inside it; was it likely?' But for all that he walked and wondered what there could be inside the basket, and whether he would or no he could not help just lifting the lid and peeping in. In the twinkling of an eye out popped a little lizard, and ran away so fast along the street that the air whistled after it.   There was nothing else in the basket.

"'Nay! nay!' cried the lad, 'stop a bit, and don't run off so.   You know I have bought you.'

"'Stick me in the tail—stick me in the tail!' bawled the lizard.

"Well, the lad was not slow in running after it and sticking his knife into its tail just as it was crawling into a hole in the wall, and that very minute it was turned into a young man as fine and handsome as the grandest prince, and a prince he was indeed.

"'Now you have saved me,' said the prince, 'for that old hag with whom you and your master have dealt is a witch, and me she has changed into a lizard, and my brother and sister into a puppy and kitten.'

"'A pretty story!' said the lad.

"'Yes,' said the prince; 'and now she was on her way to cast us into the fjord and kill us; but if any one came and wanted to buy us she must sell us for fourpence each; that was settled, and that was all my father could do.   Now you must come home to him and get the meed for what you have done.'

"'I dare say,' said the lad, 'it's a long way off?'

"'Oh,' said the prince, 'not so far after all.   There it is yonder,' he said, as he pointed to a great hill in the distance.

"So they set off as fast as they could, but as was to be weened it was farther off than it looked, and so they did not reach the hill till far on in the night.

"Then the prince began to knock and knock.

"'WHO IS THAT,' said some one inside the hill, 'that knocks at my door, and spoils my rest?' and that some one was so loud of speech that the earth quaked.

"'Oh! open the door, father, there's a dear,' said the prince. 'It is your son who has come home again.'

"Yes! he opened the door fast and well.

"'I almost thought you lay at the bottom of the sea,' said the grey-beard. 'But you are not alone, I see,' he said.

"'This is the lad who saved me,' said the prince. 'I have asked him hither that you may give him his meed.'

"Yes, he would see to that, said the old fellow.

"'But now you must step in,' he said; 'I am sure you have need of rest.'

"Yes! they went in and sat down, and the old man threw on the fire an armful of dry fuel and one or two logs, so that the fire blazed up and shone as clear as the day in every corner, and whichever way they looked it was grander than grand. Anything like it the lad had never seen before, and such meat and drink as the grey-beard set before them he had never tasted either; and all the plates, and cups, and stoops, and tankards were all of pure silver or real gold.

"It was not easy to stop the lads. They ate and drank and were merry, and afterwards they slept till far on next morning. But the lad was scarcely awake before the grey-beard came with a morning draught in a tumbler of gold.

"So when he had huddled on his clothes and broken his fast, the old man took him round with him and showed him everything that he might choose something that he would like to have as his meed for saving his son. There was much to see and to choose from you, may fancy.

"'Now what will you have?' said the king; 'you see there is plenty of choice, you can have what you please.'

"But the lad said, he would think it over and ask the prince. Yes! the king was willing he should do that.

"'Well!' said the prince, 'you have seen many grand things.'

"'Yes, I have, as was likely,' said the lad; 'but tell me, what shall I choose of all the wealth. Do tell me, for your father says I may choose what I please.'

"'Do not take anything of all you have seen,' said the prince; 'but he has a little ring on his finger, that you must ask for.'

"Yes! he did so, and begged for the little ring which he had on his finger.

"'Why! it is the dearest thing I have,' said the king; 'but, after all, my son is just as dear and so you shall have it all the same. Do you know now what it is good for?'

"No! he knew nothing about it.

"'When you have this ring on your finger,' said the king, 'you can have anything you wish for."

"So the lad thanked the king, and the king and the

prince bade him God speed home, and told him to be sure and take care of the ring.

"So he had not gone far on his way before he thought he would prove what the ring was worth, and so he wished himself a new suit of clothes, and he had scarce wished for them before he had them on him. And now he was as grand and bright as a new-struck penny. So he thought it would be fine fun to play his father a trick.

'He was not so very nice all the time I was at home;' and so he wished he was standing before his father's door, just as ragged as he was of old, and in a second he stood at the door.

"'Good day, father, and thank you for our last meal,' said the lad.

"But when the father saw that he had come back still more ragged and tattered than when he set out, he began to bellow and to bemoan himself.

"'There's no helping you,' he said. 'You have not so much as earned clothes to your back all the time you have been away.'

"'Don't be in such a way, father,' said the lad, 'you ought never to judge a man by his clothes; and now you shall be my spokesman, and go up to the palace and woo the king's daughter for me.' That was what the lad said.

"'Oh, fie, fie,' said the father, 'this is only gibing and jeering.'

"But the lad said it was the right down earnest, and so he took a birch cudgel and drove his father up to the gate of the palace, and there he came hobbling right up to the king with his eyes full of tears.

"'Now, now!' said the king, 'what's the matter my man. If you have suffered wrong, I will see you righted.'

"No, it wasn't that, he said, but he had a son who had brought him great sorrow, for he could never make a man of him, and now he must say he had gone clean out of the little wit he had before, and then he went on,—

"'For now he has hunted me up to the palace gate with a big birch cudgel, and forced me to ask for the king's daughter to wife.'

"'Hold your tongue, my man,' said the king; 'and as for this son of yours, go and ask him to come here indoors to me, and then we will see what to make of him.'

"So the lad ran in before the king till his rags fluttered behind him.

"'Am I to have your daughter?'

"'That was just what we were to talk about,' said the king; 'perhaps she mayn't suit you, and perhaps you mayn't suit her either.'

"'That was very likely!' said the lad.

"Now you must know there had just come a big ship from over the sea, and she could be seen from the palace windows.

"'All the same!" said the King. 'If you are good to make a ship in an hour or two like that lying yonder in the fjord and looking so brave, you may perhaps have her.' That was what the king said.

"'Nothing worse than that!' said the lad.

"So he went down to the strand and sat down on a sandhill, and when he had sat there long enough, he wished that a ship might be out on the fjord fully furnished with masts, and sails and rigging, the very match of that which lay there already. And as he wished for it there it lay, and when the king saw there were two ships for one, he came down to the strand to see the rights of it, and there he saw the lad standing out in a boat with a brush in his hand as though he were painting out spots and making blisters in the paint good—but as soon as he saw the king down on the shore he threw away the brush and said,—

" 'Now the ship is ready, may I have your daughter ? '

" 'This is all very well,' said the king, 'but you try your hand at another masterpiece first. If you can build a palace, a match to my palace in one or two hours, we will see about it.' That was what the king said.

" 'Nothing worse than that,' bawled out the lad and strode off. So when he had sauntered about so long, that the time was nearly up, he wished that a palace might stand there the very match of that which stood there already. It was not long, I trow, before it stood there, and it was not long either before the king came, both with queen and princess to look about him in the new palace. There stood the lad again with his broom and swept.

" 'Here's the palace right and ready,' he called out 'may I have her now ? '

" 'Very well, very well,' said the king, 'you may come

x

in and we will talk it over,' for he saw clearly the lad could do more than eat his meat, and so he walked up and down, and thought and thought how he might be rid of him. Yes! there they walked, the king first and foremost, and after him the queen, and then the princess next before the lad. So as they walked along, all at once the lad wished that he might become the handsomest man in all the world, and so he was in a trice. When the princess saw how handsome he had grown in no time, she gave the queen a nudge, and the queen passed it on to the king, and when they had all stared their full, they saw still more plainly, the lad was more than he seemed to be when he first came in all tattered and torn. So they settled it among them, that the princess should go daintily to work till she had found out all about him. Yes! the princess made herself as sweet and as soft as a whole firkin of butter, and coaxed and hoaxed the lad, telling him she could not bear him out of her eyes, day or night. So when the first evening was coming to an end, she said,—

"'As we are to have one another, you and I, you must keep nothing back from me, dearest, and so you will tell me, I am sure, how you came to make all these grand things.'

"'Aye, aye,' then said the lad, 'all that you'll come to know in good time. Only let us be man and wife; there's no good talking about it till then.' That was what he said.

"The next evening the princess was rather put out. She could see with half an eye,' she said, 'that he couldn't care very much for his sweetheart, when he wouldn't tell her what she asked him. So it would be with all the rest of his love-making, when he wouldn't meet her wishes in such a little thing.'

"Now the lad was quite cut to the heart, and that they might be friends again he told her the whole story from beginning to end. She was not slow in telling it to the king and queen, and so they laid their heads together how they might get the ring from the lad, and when they had done that they thought it would be no such hard thing to be rid of him.

"At night the princess came with some sleeping-drops, and said, now she would pour out a little philtre for her own true love, for she was sure he did not care enough for her; that was what she said. Yes! he thought no harm could come of it, and so he drained off the drink like a man, and in a trice he fell so sound asleep, they might have pulled the house down over his head without waking him. So the princess took the ring off his finger and put it on her own, and wished the lad might lie on the dungheap outside in the street, just as tattered and beggarly as he was when he came in, and in his place she wished for the handsomest prince in the world. In the twinkling of an eye it all happened. As the night wore on the lad woke up on the dunghill, and at first he thought it was only a dream, but when he found the ring was gone he knew how it had all happened, and then he got so bewildered that he set off and was just going to jump into the lake and drown himself.

"But just then he met the cat which his master had bought for him.

"'Whither away?' asked the cat.

"'To the lake to drown myself,' said the lad.

"'Don't think of it,' said the cat; 'you shall get your ring back again, never fear.'

"'Oh, shall I, shall I?' said the lad.

"By this time the cat was already off, and as she started she met a rat.

"'Now I'll take and gobble you up,' said the cat.

"'Oh! pray don't,' said the rat, 'and I'll get you the ring again.'

"'If so, be quick about it,' said the cat, 'or ——'

"So after they had taken up their abode in the palace, the rat ran about poking his nose into everything, trying to get into the prince and princess's bedroom. At last he found a little hole and crept through it. Then he heard how they lay awake talking, and the rat could tell that the prince had the ring on his finger, for the princess said, 'Mind you take great care of my ring, dear.' That was what she said; but what the prince said was,—

"'Pooh, no one will come in hither after the ring through stone and mortar; but, for all that, if you think it isn't safe on my finger, I can just as well put it into my mouth.'

In a little while the prince turned over on his back, and tried to go to sleep, and as he did so the ring was just slipping down into his throat, and then he coughed it up, so that it shot out of his mouth and rolled away over the floor—Pop!—up the rat snapped it and crept off with it to the cat who sat outside watching at the rat-hole.

"All this while the king had laid hands on the lad and put him into a strong tower and doomed him to lose his life, for that he had made jeers and gibes at him and his daughter, and there he was to stay till the day of his death. Now, as the cat was hard at work prowling about trying to steal into the tower with the ring to the lad, a great eagle came flying and pounced down on her and caught her up in his claws and flew away with her over the sea. But just in the nick of time came a falcon and struck at the eagle, so that he let the cat fall into the sea; but when the cat felt the cold water, she got so frightened she dropped the ring and swam to shore. She had not shaken the water off her, and smoothed her coat, before she met the dog which his master had bought for the lad.

"'Nay! nay!' said the cat, and purred and was in a sad way, 'what's to be done now? the ring is gone and they will take the lad's life.'

"'I'm sure I don't know,' said the dog, 'all I know is that something is riving and rending my inside. It couldn't be worse, if I were going to turn inside out.'

"'Now you see what comes of over-eating yourself,' said the cat.

"'I never eat more than I can carry,' said the dog; 'and this time I have eaten nothing but a dead fish which lay floating up and down on the ebb.'

"'May be that fish had swallowed the ring,' said the cat. 'And now I dare say you are going to pay for it too, for you know you can't digest gold.'

"'It may well be,' said the dog. 'It's much the same whether one loses life first or last. Perhaps, the lad's life might then be saved.'

"'Oh!' said the rat, for he was there too, "don't say that. I don't want much of a hole to creep into, and if the ring is there may I never tell the truth, if I don't poke it out.'

"Well! the rat crept down the dog's throat, and it was not long before he came out again with the ring. Then the cat set off to the tower and clambered up about it, till she found a hole into which she could put her paw, and so she gave back his ring to the lad.

"The lad no sooner got it on his finger than he wished the tower might rend asunder, and at the same moment he stood in the doorway and scolded both the king and queen and the princess as a pack of rogues. The king was not slow in calling out his warriors, and bade them throw a ring round the tower and seize the lad and settle him whether they took him dead or alive. But the lad only wished that all the soldiers might stand up to the armpits in the big moss up in the fjeld, and then they had more than enough to get out again, all that were not left sticking there. After that he began again where he left off with the king and his folk, and when he had got his mouth to say all the bad of them that he knew and willed, he wished they might be shut up all their days in the tower into which they had thrown him. And when they were safe shut up there, he took the land and realm as his own. Then the dog became a prince and the cat a princess again, her he took and married, and the last I heard of them, was, that they kept it up at the bridal both well and long.

OUR PARISH CLERK.

"ONCE on a time there was a clerk in our parish, who was very sharp set after all that was nice and good. All the parish said his brains were in his belly, for though he was very fond of pretty girls and buxom wives, still he liked good meat and drink even better.

"'Aye, aye,' said our clerk; 'one can't live long on love and the south wind.' That was his motto, and that was why he kept company most with well-to-do-house-wives, with those who were new wedded, or with pretty lasses who were sure to marry rich husbands, for there you were sure to find titbits both of beauty and food. That was what our clerk thought. It wasn't every one, indeed, who thought it so fine to have such a cupboard lover, but yet there were some who looked on it as fine enough for them, for, after all, a parish clerk stands a little higher than a farmer.

"Now it fell out there was a rich young lass who had married our clerk's next-door neighbour. There he crept in and out, and soon got good friends with the husband, and better friends still with his wife. When the husband was at home all went well between them, but as soon as he was away at the mill, or in the wood, or at floating timber, or at a meeting, the goody sent word to the clerk, and then they two spent the day in revelling and mirth. There was no one who found this out, before the plough-boy got wind of it, and he thought he would just speak of it to his master; but, somehow or other, he couldn't find a fitting time till one day when they were together in the outfield gathering leaves for litter. There they chatted this and that about lasses and wives, and the master thought he had made a lucky hit in marrying such a rich and pretty wife, and he said as much outright.

"'Thank God, she is both good and clever.'

"'Aye, aye,' said the lad; 'every man is welcome to believe what he likes, but if you knew her as well as I do, you wouldn't say such words at random. Pretty women are like wind in warm summer weather.

> 'And love is such that, willy, nilly,
> It takes up with a clerk as well as a lily.'

"'What's that you say?' said the man.

"'I have long thought I would tell you that there's a black bull that walks hoof to hoof and horn to horn with that milk-white cow in your mead, master—that's what I wanted to say.'

"'One can say much in a summer day,' said the man; 'but I can't understand what this points to.'

"'Is it so?' said the lad. 'Well, I have long thought of telling you that our clerk is often and ever in our house with the mistress, and how they lived as though there was a bridal every day, while we scarce get so much as the leavings of their good cheer.'

"'He who will ever taste and try,
Will burn his fingers in the pie,'

said his master. 'I don't believe a word of what you say.'

"'It's a strange ear that will never hear," said the lad; "but seeing is believing, and if you will listen to me, I'm ready to wager ten dollars that you shall soon have the proof in your own hands.'

"'Done,' said the master; 'he would bet ten dollars; nay, for that matter, he would bet horse and farm, and a hundred dollars into the bargain.'

"Well, that wager was to stand. 'But an old fox is hard to hunt,' said the lad, and so his master must say and do all that his ploughboy wished. When they got home he was to say they must set off for the river and land timber, and his wife must put up some food for them in hot haste; it was best to look out while the weather was fine, it might turn to storm in a trice. Yes! That was what the husband said, and the food was ready to the minute. The lad put the horses to the timber drags, and off they went, but no farther than half a mile; there they put the horses up at a farm, and turned in themselves. As the night came on they went back, and when they got home, the door was locked fast.

"'Now we have him,' said the lad; 'it's hard to keep off the field to which one is wont.'

"So they went by the back way from the garden, and so

through a trapdoor in the cellar into the kitchen. Then they struck a light and went into the parlour, and saw what they saw. Well! our clerk had eaten so well that he lay snoring with his mouth open and his nose in the air; as for the goody, she was not awake either.

"'Now you see I was right; seeing is believing, master,' said the lad.

"'May I never speak the truth again,' said the man, 'if I would have believed ten men telling it.'

"'Hush, be still,' said the lad, and took him out again.

"'Man's law is not land's law,' said the lad; 'but even a bear can be tamed if you know how to deal with him. Have you any lead, master?

"Yes! He had, he was sure, more than seventy bullets in his pouch. Then it was all right. They took a saucepan, and melted the lead on the spot, and ran it down our clerk's throat.

"'Every man has his own taste,' said the lad, "and that's why all meat is eaten,' as he heard the molten lead bubbling and frizzling in our clerk's throat.

"Then they went out by the way they got in, and began to knock and thunder at the front door. The wife woke up and asked who was there.

"'It is I, open the door, I say,' said the husband.

"Then she gave our clerk a nudge in the ribs. 'It is the master; the master is back,' she said. But no! he did not mind her, and never so much as stirred. Then she put her knees to his side, and tumbled him on to the floor, and jumped up and took him by the legs, and dragged him to the heap of wood behind the stove, and there she hid him. Till she had done that she had no time to open the door to her husband.

"'Were you gone after christening water, that you were gone so long?' asked the man.

"'Oh!' she answered; 'I dozed off again to sleep, and I did not think it could ever be you either.'

"Well!' said her husband; 'now you must bring out some food, for me and the boy, we are a'most starved.'

"'I've got no food ready,' said the goody 'How can you think of such a thing? I never thought you would be back either to-day or to-morrow. Why you know you were to go to the river to land timber.'

"'One can't hang a hungry man up on the wall like a clock,' said the lad; 'and self-help is the best help; shall I bring in the food we packed up, master.'

"Yes; they did that, and they sat down to eat out of the knapsack; but when they got up to put a log or two on the fire, there lay our clerk among the pile of wood.

"'Why who in the world is this?' asked the man.

"'Oh! oh! It's only a beggar man who came here so late and begged for houseroom; he was quite content if he might only lie among the firewood,' said the goody.

"'A pretty beggar,' said the man; 'why he has got silver buckles to his shoes, and silver buttons at his knees.'

"'All are not beggars who are tattered and torn,' said the lad; 'but I'm blessed if this isn't our parish clerk.'

"'What was he doing here, mistress,' asked her husband, who all the while kept on pulling and kicking at him.

But our clerk never so much as stirred or lifted a finger. There stood the goody fumbling and stammering, and not knowing what to say. All she could do was to bite her thumb.

"'I see it in your face, what you have done, mistress,' said her husband. "But life is hard to lose, and, after all, he was our parish clerk. If I did what was right, I should send off at once for the sheriff.'

"'Heaven help us," said his wife; "only get our clerk out of the way.'

"'This is your matter, and not mine,' said the man. 'I never asked him hither, nor sent for him; but if you can get any one to help you to get rid of him, I won't stand in your way.'

"Then she took the lad on one side, and said,—

"'I've laid up some woollen stuff for my husband, but I'll give it to you for clothes, if you'll only get our clerk buried, so that he shall never be seen or heard of again.'

"'There's no saying what one can do till one tries. If we drive in the frost, we shall find it slippery, to our cost. Have you ropes and cord, master? if so, I'll see if I can't cure this.'

"Well! he got our clerk fast in a slipknot, threw him on his back, caught up his hat as well, and away he went. But he hadn't gone far along the path in the meadow when he met some horses; so he caught one of these, and tied and bound our clerk fast on his back. He put his hat, too, on his head, and his hand down on his thigh, and there he sat upright, and jogged up and down just as a man on horseback.

"'One may kill trolls at any time of night,' said the lad, when he got home; 'who can say when a man is 'fey.' But he will never rise up who is safe buried under ground, and the cock that is slain crows never again.',

"Now, whether all this were true or no, there was a way from the meadow across the fields to a barn, and along it they had carted hay, and dropped it as they went along; so the horse went that way, picking up the hay as he went, and out in that barn were two men watching for thieves who used to steal the hay, for it had been a bad year for fodder.

"'Here comes the thief,' they said, when they heard the horse's hoofs; 'now we shall catch him.'

"'Who's there,' they called out, so that it rang against the hill-side. No! there was no answer, the horse paid little heed, and our clerk less.

"'If you don't answer I'll send a bullet through your brains, you horse-thief,' they both called out, and then off went the gun, at which the horse gave such a sudden jump, that our clerk gave a bob, and fell bump on the ground.

"'I think,' said one of the watchers, as he jumped up to look, 'I think you've shot him dead as mutton;' and then, when he saw who it was, 'Oh Lord!' he said, 'if it ain't our parish clerk. You ought to have aimed at his legs, and not killed him outright.'

"'What's done is done, and can't be helped," said the

other. 'Least said soonest mended. We must keep our ears close, and bury him for a little while among the hay in the barn.'

"Yes! They did that, and when it was over, they lay them down to rest. In a little while came some one puffing and stamping, that the field shook again. The two who lay among the hay nudged one another, for they thought it was thieves again. Close to the barn was a stepping-stone, and there the new-comer sat down with his load, and began to talk to himself. He had been killing pigs at a farm a few days before, and thought he had been paid too little for his work, too little pay and too little board, and so he had set off and stolen the biggest porker. 'He that swaps with a bear always comes worst off,' he said; 'and so it's best to help one's self to what is right, and a little share is better than a long law-suit. But, bitter death! If I haven't forgotten my gloves; if they find them at the farm, they'll soon find out who has inherited their porker.' And, as he said this, he bolted back after his gloves.

"The two who were in the barn lay and listened to all this.

"'He who lays traps for others, comes into the trap himself,' said one.

"'There's no sin in stealing from a thief,' said the other; 'and no one is hanged, save those who can't steal right. It would be fine fun to get rid of our clerk in an easy way, and get a fat pig instead. I think, old chap, we had better make a swap.'

"The other burst out laughing at this, and so they tumbled the pig out of the sack and tossed in our clerk, head foremost, hat and all, and tied up the mouth of the sack as tight as they could.

"Just as they had done, back came the thief flying with his gloves, snatched up the sack, and strode off home. There he cast the sack down on the floor at his goody's feet.

"'Here's what I call a porker, old lass,' he said.

"'How grand!' said the goody. 'Nothing is all very fine to the eye, but not to the mouth. One can't get on without meat, for meat is man's strength. Thank Heaven we have now a bit of meat in the house, and shall be able to live well awhile.'

"'I took the biggest I could,' said the man, who sat down in his armchair, and puffed and wiped the sweat off his brow. 'He had both breeches and drawers, he was well covered, that he was.' By which he meant the pig was well fed and fat. Then he went on, 'Have you any meat in the house, old lass?'

"'No,' she said; 'meat! where should I get meat?'

"'Make up the fire then,' said the man; 'and sharpen your knife, and cut off a wee bit, and fry it with salt, and let's have a pork chop.'

"She did as he bade, and tore open the mouth of the sack, and was just going to cut off a steak.

"'What's all this?' she cried. 'He has got his trotters on,' when she saw his shoes; 'and he's as black as a coal.'

"'Don't you know,' said her husband; "all cats are grey in the dark, and all pigs black.'

"'I dare say,' she said; 'but black or white is always bright, and a fog is not like a bilberry. This pig has got breeches on.'

"'Plague take him!' said the man. 'I know well enough he is covered with fat all down his legs. Haven't I carried him till the sweat ran down my face?'

"'Nay, nay!' said the goody. 'He has silver buckles in his shoes, and silver buttons at his knees. My! if it isn't our Parish Clerk!' she screamed out.

"'I tell you it was a fat pig I took,' said the man, as he jumped up to see how things stood. 'Well! Well! Seeing is believing.' It was our clerk, both with shoes and buckles; but, for all, he stuck to it, it was the fattest pig he had put into the sack.

"'But what's done can't be undone,' he said; 'the best servant is one's own self; but, for all that, help is good, even if it comes out of the porridge-pot; wake up our Mary, old girl.'

"Now you must know Mary was their daughter, a ready and trusty lass; she had the strength of a man too, and always had her wits about her. So she was to take our clerk and bury him in an out-of-the-way dale, so that nothing should ever be heard of him. If she did this, she was to have a new suit of working clothes, which were meant for her mother.

"Well! The lassie took our clerk round the body, tossed him on her back, and strode off from the farm, not forgetting to take his hat. But when she had gone a bit of the way, she heard a fiddle going, for there was a dance at a farm near the road, and so she crept in and set our clerk down upright behind the back-stairs. There he sat with his hat between his hands, just as though he were begging an alms, and leaning against the wall and a post.

"After a while came a girl in a flurry.

"'I wonder whoever this can be,' she said. 'The master of the house is as grey as a goose, but this fellow is black as a raven. Halloa, you sir, why are you sitting there, blocking up the way? One can scarce get by.'

"But our clerk said never a word.

"'Are you poor? Do you beg for a penny for Heaven's sake? Ah! poor fellow! Here's two pence for you,' and as she said this she tossed them into his hat. Still our clerk said never a word. She waited a little, for she thought he would say 'Thank you,' but our clerk did not so much as nod his head.

"'No, I never,' said the girl, when she went back into the ball-room. 'I never did see the like of a beggar who sits out yonder by the staircase. He isn't at all like a starling on a fence,' she went on; 'for he won't answer, and he won't say "Thank you," and won't so much as lift a finger, though I did give him two pence.'

"'The least a beggar can do is to say "Thank you,"' cried a young sheriff's clerk who was of the party. 'He must be a pretty fellow whom I cannot get to speak, for I've made thieves and stiff-necked folk open their mouths wide before this.'

"As he said this he ran out to the stairs, and bawled out in our clerk's ear, for he thought he was hard of hearing.

"'What do you sit here for, you sir?' And then again, 'Are you poor? Do you beg?'

"No, our clerk said never a word. So he took out half-a-dollar, and threw it into his hat, saying, 'There's something for you.' But our clerk was still silent, and made no sign. So when he could get no thanks out of him, the sheriff's officer gave him a blow under the ear, as hard as he could, and down fell our clerk head over heels across the staircase. And you may be sure the girl Mary was not slow in running to the spot.

"'Are you in a swoon, or are you dead, father,' she screeched out, and then she went on screaming and bewailing herself.

"'It's quite true,' she said; 'there's no peace for the poor after all, but I never yet heard of any one laying themselves out to strike beggars dead.'

"'Hush! Hold your tongue,' said the sheriff's officer. 'Don't make a fuss. Here you have ten dollars, keep your peace and take him away. I only gave him a blow that made him swoon.'

"Well! She was glad enough. 'Money brings money,' she thought; 'with fair words and money, one can go far in a day, and one need never care for food with a purse full of pence.' So she took our clerk on her back again, and strode off to the nearest farm, and there she put him athwart the brink of the well. When our Mary got home she said she had borne him off to the wood, and buried him far far away in a side dale.

"'Thank Heaven,' said the goody. 'Now we are well quit of him, you shall have all I promised, and more besides. Be sure of that.'

"So there lay our clerk, as though he were peering down into the well, till at dawn of day the ploughboy came running up to draw water.

"'Why are you lying there, and what are you gazing at? Out of the way. I want some water,' said the lad.

"No! He neither stirred hand or foot. Then the lad let drive at him, so that it went *plump*, and there lay our clerk in the well. Then he must have help to get him out, but there was no help for it till the hind came with a boat-hook and dragged him out.

"'Why! it's our Parish Clerk!' they all bawled out, and they all thought he had eaten and drank so much at some feast, that he had fallen asleep by the well-side.

"But when the master of the house came and saw our clerk, and heard how it had all happened, he said,—

"'Harm watches while men sleep; but man's scathe is the worst scathe. When one pot strikes against another, both break. Take the saddle and lay it on Blackie, and ride to fetch the sheriff, my lad, and then we shall be out of harm's way, for our clerk's sake. Mishaps never come single, but it's hard to drown on dry land.' That was what the master said.

"Yes! The lad rode off to the sheriff, and after a while the sheriff came. But, as the saying is, more haste, worse speed, and work done in haste will never last. So it took time before they got the doctor and witnesses to come. Now you all know we owe a death to God; but then it was made as plain as day that our clerk had been killed three times before he tumbled into the well. First the ladle of lead had taken away his breath, next he had a bullet through his forehead, and third and last his neck was broken. Surely he was 'fey' when he set out to see the goody. It is hard to tell how all this was found out at last; but tongues will clack behind a man's back, and hard things are said of a man when he's dead."

SILLY MEN AND CUNNING WIVES.

"ONCE on a time there were two Goodies, who quarrelled, as women often will; and when they had nothing else to quarrel about, they fell to fighting about their husbands, as to which was the silliest of them. The longer they strove the worse they got, and at last they had almost come to pulling caps about it, for, as every one knows, it is easier to begin than to end, and it is a bad look out when wit is wanting. At last, one of them said there was nothing she could not get her husband to believe, if she only said it, for he was as easy as a Troll. Then the other said there was nothing so silly that she could not get her husband to do, if she only said it must be done, for he was such a fool, he could not tell B from a bull's foot.

"'Well! let us put it to the proof, which of us can fool them best, and then we'll see which is the silliest.' That was what they said once, and so it was settled.

"Now when the first husband, Master Northgrange came home from the wood, his goody said—

"'Heaven help us both! what is the matter! you are surely ill, if you are not at death's door?'

" 'Nothing ails me but want of meat and drink,' said the man.

" 'Now, Heaven be my witness!' screamed out the wife, 'it gets worse and worse. You look just like a corpse in face; you must go to bed! Dear! dear! this never can last long! And so she went on till she got her husband to believe he was hard at death's door, and she put him to bed; and then she made him fold his hands on his breast, and shut his eyes; and so she stretched his limbs, and laid him out, and put him into a coffin; but that he might not be smothered while he lay there, she had some holes made in the sides, so that he could breathe and peep out.

"The other goody, she took a pair of carding combs, and began to card wool; but she had no wool on them. In came the man, and saw this tomfoolery.

" 'There's no use,' he said, 'in a wheel without wool; but carding combs, without wool, is work for a fool.'

" 'Without wool!' said the goody; 'I have wool, only you can't see it; it's of the fine sort.' So, when she had carded it all, she took her wheel, and fell a-spinning.

" 'Nay! nay! this is all labour lost!" said the man. 'There you sit, wearing out your wheel, as it spins and hums, and all the while you've nothing on it.'

" 'Nothing on it!' said the goody; 'the thread is so fine, it takes better eyes than yours to see it, that's all.'

"So, when her spinning was over, she set up her loom, and put the woof in, and threw the shuttle, and wove cloth. Then she took it out of the loom and pressed it and cut it out, and sewed a new suit of clothes for her husband out of it, and when it was ready, she hung the suit up in the linen closet. As for the man, he could see neither cloth nor clothes; but as he had once for all got it into his head that it was too fine for him to see, he went on saying, 'Aye, aye, I understand it all, it is so fine because it is so fine.'

"Well! in a day or two his goody said to him,

"'To-day you must go to a funeral. Farmer North-grange is dead, and they bury him to-day, and so you had better put on your new clothes.'

"'Yes, very true, he must go to the funeral;' and she helped him on with his new suit, for it was so fine, he might tear it asunder if he put it on alone.

"So when he came up to the farm, where the funeral was to be, they had all drank hard and long, and you may fancy their grief was not greater when they saw him come in in his new suit. But when the train set off for the churchyard, and the dead man peeped through the breathing holes, he burst out into a loud fit of laughter.

"'Nay! nay!' he said, 'I can't help laughing, though it is my funeral, for if there isn't Olof Southgrange walking to my funeral stark naked!'

"When the bearers heard that, they were not slow in taking the lid off the coffin, and the other husband, he in the new suit, asked how it was that he, over whom they had just drank his funeral ale, lay there in his coffin and chatted and laughed, when it would be more seemly if he wept.

"'Ah!' said the other; 'you know tears never yet dug up any one out of his grave—that's why I laughed myself to life again.'

"But the end of all their talk was that it came out that their goodies had played them those tricks. So the husbands went home, and did the wisest thing either of them had done for a long time; and if any one wishes to know what it was, he had better go and ask the birch cudgel."

"ONCE on a time there was a King, who had a daughter, and she was so lovely, that her good looks were well known far and near; but she was so sad and serious, she could never be got to laugh; and, besides, she was so high and mighty, that she said 'No' to all who wooed her to wife, and she would have none of them, were they ever so grand—lords and princes, it was all the same. The king had long ago got tired of this, for he thought she might just as well marry, she, too, like the rest of the world. There was no good waiting; she was quite old enough, nor would she be any richer, for she was to have half the kingdom, that came to her as her mother's heir.

"So he had it given out at the church door both quick and soon, that any one who could get his daughter to laugh should have her and half the kingdom. But if there were any one who tried and could not, he was to have three red stripes cut out of his back, and salt rubbed in; and sure it was that there were many sore backs in that kingdom, for lovers and wooers came from north and south, and east and west, thinking it nothing at all to make a king's daughter laugh; and brave fellows they were, some of them, too; but for all their tricks and capers, there sat the princess, just as sad and serious as she had been before.

"Now, hard by the Palace lived a man who had three sons, and they too had heard how the king had given it out that the man who could make the princess laugh was to have her to wife and half the kingdom.

"The eldest, he was for setting off first; so he strode off; and when he came to the king's grange, he told the king he would be glad to try to make the princess laugh.

"'All very well, my man,' said the king; 'but it's sure to be no good, for so many have been here and tried. My daughter is so sorrowful, it's no use trying, and I don't at all wish that any one should come to grief.'

"But he thought there was use. It couldn't be such a very hard thing for him to get a princess to laugh, for so many had laughed at him, both gentle and simple, when he listed for a soldier, and learnt his drill under Corporal Jack. So he went off to the courtyard, under the princess's window, and began to go through his drill as Corporal Jack had taught him. But it was no good, the princess was just as sad and serious, and did not so much as smile at him once. So they took him, and cut three broad red stripes out of his back, and sent him home again.

"Well! he had hardly got home before his second brother wanted to set off. He was a schoolmaster, and a wonderful figure of fun besides; he was lop-sided, for he had one leg shorter than the other, and one moment he was as little as a boy, and in another, when he stood on his long leg, he was as tall and long as a Troll. Besides this, he was a powerful preacher.

"So when he came to the king's grange, and said he wished to make the princess laugh, the king thought it might not be so unlikely after all. 'But Heaven help you!' he said, 'if you don't make her laugh. We are for cutting the stripes broader and broader for every one that tries.'

"Then the schoolmaster strode off to the courtyard, and put himself before the princess's window, and read and preached like seven parsons, and sang and chanted like seven clerks, as loud as all the parsons and clerks in the country round. The king laughed loud at him, and was forced to hold the posts in the gallery, and the princess was just going to put a smile on her lips, but all at once she got as sad and serious as ever; and so it fared no better with Paul the schoolmaster than with Peter the soldier—for you must know one was called Peter and the other Paul. So they took him and cut three red stripes out of his back, and rubbed the salt well in, and then they sent him home again.

"Then the youngest was all for setting out, and his name was Taper Tom; but his brothers laughed and jeered at him, and showed him their sore backs, and his father would not give him leave, for he said, how could it be of any use to him, when he had no sense, for, wasn't it true that he neither knew anything or could do anything? There he sat in the ingle by the chimney corner, like a cat, and grubbed in the ashes and split fir tapers. That was why they called him 'Taper Tom.' But Taper Tom wouldn't give in, for he growled and grizzled so long, that they got tired of his growling, and so, at last, he too got leave to go to the king's grange, and try his luck.

"When he got to the king's grange he did not say he wished to try to make the princess laugh, but asked if he could get a place there. 'No,' they had no place for him; but for all that Taper Tom wouldn't take an answer; they must want some one, he said, to carry wood and water for the kitchenmaid, in such a big grange as that— that was what he said; and the king thought it might very well be, for he, too, got tired of his worry, and the end was, Taper Tom got leave to stay there and carry wood and water for the kitchenmaid.

" So, one day, when he was going to fetch water from the beck, he set eyes on a big fish, which lay under an old fir stump, where the water had eaten into the bank, and he put his bucket so softly under the fish, and caught it. But as he was going home to the grange he met an old woman who led a golden goose by a string.

"'Good day, godmother,' said Taper Tom; 'that's a pretty bird you have got; and what fine feathers!—they dazzle one a long way off. If one only had such feathers one might leave off splitting fir tapers.'

" The goody was just as pleased with the fish Tom had in his bucket, and said, if he would give her the fish, he might have the golden goose; and it was such a goose, that when any one touched it, he stuck fast to it, if Tom only said, 'Hang on, if you care to come with us.'

"Yes! that swap Taper Tom was willing enough to make.

"'A bird is as good as a fish, any day,' he said to himself; and if it's such a bird as you say, I can use it as a fish-hook.' That was what he said to the goody, and was so pleased with the goose. Now, he hadn't gone far before he met another old woman, and as soon as she saw the lovely gold goose she was all for running up to it and patting it; and she spoke so prettily, and coaxed him so, and begged him give her leave to stroke his lovely golden goose.

"'With all my heart,' said Taper Tom; 'but, mind you don't pluck out any of its feathers.'

"Just as she stroked the goose, he said,

"'Hang on, if you care to come with us!'

"The goody pulled and tore, but she was forced to hang on, whether she would or no, and Taper Tom went before, as though he alone were with the golden goose. So when he had gone a bit further, he met a man who had a thorn in his side against the goody for a trick she had played him. So, when he saw how hard she struggled and strove to get free, and how fast she stuck, he thought he would be quite safe in giving her one for her nob, to pay off the old grudge, and so he just gave her a kick with his foot.

"'Hang on, if you care to come with us!' called out Tom, and then the man had to limp along on one leg, whether he would or no, and when he jibbed and jibed, and tried to break loose, it was still worse for him, for he was all but falling flat on his back every step he took.

"So they went on a good bit till they had about come to the king's grange. There they met the king's smith, who was going to the smithy, and had a great pair of tongs in his hand. Now you must know this smith was a merry fellow, who was as full of tricks and pranks as an egg is full of meat, and when he saw this string come hobbling and limping along, he laughed so that he was almost bent in two, and then he bawled out, ' Surely this is a new flock of geese the princess is going to have; who can tell which is goose and which gander! Ah! I see, this must be the gander that toddles in front. Goosey! goosey! goosey!' he called out; and with that he coaxed them to him, and threw his hands about as though he were scattering corn for the geese.

"But the flock never stopped—on it went, and all that the goody and the man did was to look daggers at the smith for making game of them. Then the smith went on,

" ' It would be fine fun to see if I could hold the whole flock, so many as they are;' for he was a stout strong fellow, and so he took hold, with his big tongs, by the old man's coat tail, and the man all the while bellowed and wriggled; but Taper Tom only said,

" ' Hang on, if you care to come with us.'

"So the smith had to go along too. He bent his back and stuck his heels into the hill, and tried to get loose;

but it was all no good, he stuck fast, as though he had been screwed tight with his own anvil, and, whether he would or no, he had to dance along with the rest.

"So, when they came near to the king's grange, the mastiff ran out and began to bay and bark as though they were wolves or beggars; and when the princess looked out of the window to see what was the matter, and set eyes on this strange pack, she laughed inwardly. But Taper Tom was not content with that.

"'Bide a bit,' he said, 'she'll soon have to open the door of her mouth wider;' and as he said that he turned off with his band to the back of the grange.

"So, when they passed by the kitchen, the door stood open, and the cook was just beating the porridge; but when she saw Taper Tom and his pack she came running out at the door, with her brush in one hand, and a wooden ladle full of smoking porridge in the other, and she laughed as though her sides would split; and when she saw the smith there too, she slapped her thigh and went off again in a loud peal. But when she had laughed her laugh out, she too thought the golden goose so lovely she must just stroke it.

"'Taper Tom! Taper Tom!' she bawled out, and came running out with the ladle of porridge in her fist, 'may I have leave to stroke that pretty bird of yours?'

"'Better let her stroke me,' said the smith.

"'I daresay,' said Taper Tom.

"But when the cook heard that she got angry.

" ' What is that you say !' she cried, and let fly at the smith with the ladle.

" ' Hang on, if you care to come with us,' said Taper Tom. So she stuck fast, she, too; and for all her kicks and plunges, and all her scolding and screaming, and all her riving and striving, and all her rage, she too had to limp along with them.

" But when they came outside the window of the princess, there she stood, waiting for them; and when she saw they had taken the cook too, with her ladle and brush, she opened her mouth wide, and laughed loud, so that the king had to hold her upright. So Taper Tom got the princess and half the kingdom; and they had such a merry wedding, it was heard and talked of far and wide."

"UP at a place in Vaage, in Gudbrandsdale, there lived once on a time in the days of old a poor couple. They had many children, and two of the sons who were about half grown up had to be always roaming about the country begging. So it was that they were well known with all the highways and by-ways, and they also knew the short cut into Hedale.

"It happened once that they wanted to get thither, but at the same time they heard that some falconers had built themselves a hut at Mæla, and so they wished to kill two birds with one stone, and see the birds, and how they are taken, and so they took the cut across Longmoss. But you must know it was far on towards autumn, and so the milkmaids had all gone home from the shielings, and they could neither get shelter nor food. Then they had to keep straight on for Hedale, but the path was a mere track, and when night fell they lost it; and, worse still, they could not find the falconers' hut either, and before they knew where they were, they found themselves in the very depths of the forest. As soon as they saw they could not get on, they began to break boughs, lit a fire, and built themselves a bower of branches, for they had a hand-axe with them; and, after that, they plucked heather and moss and made themselves a bed. So a little while after they had lain down, they heard something which sniffed and snuffed so with its nose; then the boys pricked up their ears and listened sharp to hear whether it were wild beasts or wood trolls, and just then something snuffed up the air louder than ever, and said—

"'There's a smell of Christian blood here!'

"At the same time they heard such a heavy foot-fall that the earth shook under it, and then they knew well enough the trolls must be about.

"'Heaven help us! what shall we do?' said the younger boy to his brother.

"'Oh! you must stand as you are under the fir, and be ready to take our bags and run away when you see them coming; as for me, I will take the hand-axe,' said the other.

"All at once they saw the trolls coming at them like mad, and they were so tall and stout, their heads were just as high as the fir-tops; but it was a good thing they had only one eye between them all three, and that they used turn and turn about. They had a hole in their foreheads into which they put it, and turned and twisted it with their hands. The one that went first, he must have it to see his way, and the others went behind and took hold of the first.

"'Take up the traps,' said the elder of the boys, 'but don't run away too far, but see how things go; as they carry their eye so high aloft they'll find it hard to see me when I get behind them.'

"Yes ! the brother ran before and the trolls after him, meanwhile the elder got behind them and chopped the hindmost troll with his axe on the ankle, so that the troll gave an awful shriek, and the foremost troll got so afraid he was all of a shake and dropped the eye. But the boy was not slow to snap it up. It was bigger than two quart pots put together, and so clear and bright, that though it was pitch dark, everything was as clear as day as soon as he looked through it.

"When the trolls saw he had taken their eye and done one of them harm, they began to threaten him with all the evil in the world if he didn't give back the eye at once.

"'I don't care a farthing for trolls and threats,' said the boy, 'now I've got three eyes to myself and you three have got none, and besides two of you have to carry the third.'

"'If we don't get our eye back this minute, you shall be both turned to stocks and stones,' screeched the trolls.

"But the boy thought things needn't go so fast; he was not afraid for witchcraft or hard words. If they didn't leave him in peace he'd chop them all three, so that they would have to creep and crawl along the earth like cripples and crabs.

"When the trolls heard that, they got still more afraid and began to use soft words. They begged so prettily that he would give them their eye back, and then he should have both gold and silver and all that he wished to ask. Yes! that seemed all very fine to the lad, but he must have the gold and silver first, and so he said, if one of them would go home and fetch as much gold and silver as would fill his and his brother's bags, and give them two good cross-bows beside, they might have their eye, but he should keep it until they did what he said.

"The trolls were very put out, and said none of them could go when he hadn't his eye to see with, but all at once one of them began to bawl out for their goody, for you must know they had a goody between them all three as well as an eye. After a while an answer came from a knoll a long way off to the north. So the trolls said she must come with two steel cross-bows and two buckets full of gold and silver, and then it was not long, you may fancy, before she was there. And when she heard what had happened, she too began to threaten them with witchcraft. But the trolls got so afraid, and begged her beware of the little wasp, for she couldn't be sure he would not take away her eye too. So she threw them the cross-bows and the buckets and the gold and the silver, and strode off to the knoll with the trolls; and since that time no one has ever heard that the trolls have walked in Hedale wood snuffing after Christian blood."

THE SKIPPER AND OLD NICK.

"ONCE on a time there was a skipper who was so wonderfully lucky in everything he undertook; there was no one who got such freights, and no one who earned so much money, for it rolled in upon him on all sides, and, in a word, there was no one who was good to make such voyages as he, for whithersoever he sailed he took the wind with him;—nay! men did say he had only to turn his hat and the wind turned the way he wished it to blow.

"So he sailed for many years, both in the timber trade and to China, and he had gathered money together like grass. But it so happened that once he was coming home across the North sea with every sail set, as though he had stolen both ship and lading; but he who wanted to lay hold on him went faster still. It was Old Nick, for with him he had made a bargain, as one may well fancy, and that very day the time was up, and he might look any moment that Old Nick would come and fetch him.

"Well! the skipper came up on deck out of the cabin and looked at the weather; then he called for the carpenter and some others of the crew, and said they must go down into the hold and hew two holes in the ship's bottom, and when they had done that they were to lift the pumps out of their beds and drive them down tight into the holes they had made, so that the sea might rise high up into the pumps.

"The crew wondered at all this, and thought it a funny bit of work, but they did as the skipper ordered; they hewed holes in the ship's bottom and drove the pumps in so tight that never a drop of water could come to the cargo, but up in the pump itself the North sea stood seven feet high.

"They had only just thrown the chips overboard after their piece of work when Old Nick came on board in a gust of wind and caught the skipper by the throat.

"'Stop, father!' said the skipper, 'there's no need to be in such a hurry,' and as he said that he began to defend himself and to loose the claws which Old Nick had stuck into him by the help of a marling-spike.

"'Haven't you made a bargain that you would always keep the ship dry and tight?' asked the skipper. 'Yes! you're a pretty fellow; look down the pumps, there's the water standing seven feet high in the pipe. Pump, devil, pump! and pump the ship dry, and then you may take me and have me as soon and as long as you choose.'

"Old Nick was not so clever that he was not taken in; he pumped and strove, and the sweat ran down his back like a brook, so that you might have turned a mill at the end of his backbone, but he only pumped out of the North sea and into the North sea again. At last he got tired of that work, and when he could not pump a stroke more, he set off in a sad temper home to his grandmother to take a rest. As for the skipper, he let him stay a skipper as long as he chose, and if he isn't dead, he is still perhaps sailing on his voyages whithersoever he will, and twisting the wind as he chooses only by turning his hat."

"ONCE on a time there was a man who had a goody who was so cross-grained that there was no living with her. As for her husband he could not get on with her at all, for whatever he wished she set her face right against it.

"So it fell one Sunday in summer that the man and his wife went out into the field to see how the crop looked; and when they came to a field of rye on the other side of the river, the man said—

"'Ay! now it is ripe. To-morrow we must set to work and reap it.'

"'Yes,' said his wife, 'to-morrow we can set to work and shear it.'

"'What do you say,' said the man; 'shall we shear it? Mayn't we just as well reap it?'

"'No,' said the goody, 'It shall be shorn.'

"'There is nothing so bad as a little knowledge,' said the man, 'but you must have lost the little wit you had. When did you ever hear of shearing a field?'

"'I know little, and I care to know little, I dare say,'

said the goody, 'but I know very well that this field shall be shorn and not reaped.'

" That was what she said, and there was no help for it; it must and should be shorn.

" So they walked about and quarrelled and strove till they came to the bridge across the river, just above a deep hole.

" ' 'Tis an old saying,' said the man, 'that good tools make good work, but I fancy it will be a fine swathe that is shorn with a pair of shears. Mayn't we just as well reap the field after all ?' he asked.

" ' No ! no ! shear, shear,' bawled out the goody, who jumped about and clipped like a pair of scissors under her husband's nose. In her shrewishness she took such little heed that she tripped over a beam on the bridge, and down she went *plump* into the stream.

" ' 'Tis hard to wean any one from bad ways,' said the man, ' but it were strange if I were not sometimes in the right, I too.'

" Then he swam out into the hole and caught his wife by the hair of her head, and so got her head above water.

" ' Shall we reap the field now ?' were the first words he said.

" ' Shear ! shear ! shear !' screeched the goody.

" ' I'll teach you to shear,' said the man, as he ducked her under the water; but it was no good, they must shear it, she said, as soon as ever she came up again.

" ' I can't think anything else than that the goody is mad,' said the man to himself. 'Many are mad and never know it; many have wit and never show it; but all the same, I'll try her once more.'

"But as soon as ever he ducked her under the water again, she held her hands up out of the water and began to clip with her fingers like a pair of shears. Then the man fell into a great rage and ducked her down both well and long; but while he was about it, the goody's head fell down below the water, and she got so heavy all at once, that he had to let her go.

"'No! no!' he said, 'you wish to drag me down with you into the hole, but you may lie there by yourself.'

"So the goody was left in the river.

"But after a while the man thought it was ill she should lie there and not get Christian burial, and so he went down the course of the stream and hunted and searched for her, but for all his pains he could not find her. Then he came with all his men and brought his neighbours with him, and they all in a body began to drag the stream and to search for her all along it. But for all their searching they found no goody.

"'Oh!' said the man, 'I have it. All this is no good, we search in the wrong place. This goody was a sort by herself; there was not such another in the world while she was alive. She was so cross and contrary, and I'll be bound it is just the same now she is dead. We had better just go and hunt for her up stream, and drag for her above the force,* maybe she has floated up thither.'

* Waterfall.

"And so it was. They went up stream and sought for her above the force, and there lay the goody, sure enough! Yes! She was well called GOODY GAINST-THE-STREAM."

HOW TO WIN A PRINCE.

"ONCE on a time there was a king's son who made love to a lass, but after they had become great friends and were as good as betrothed, the prince began to think little of her, and he got it into his head that she wasn't clever enough for him, and so he wouldn't have her.

" So he thought how he might be rid of her ; and at last he said he would take her to wife all the same, if she could come to him—

> ' Not driving,
> And not riding ;
> Not walking,
> And not carried ;
> Not fasting,
> And not full-fed ;
> Not naked,
> And not clad ;
> Not in the daylight,
> And not by night.'

" For all that he fancied she could never do.

" So she took three barleycorns and swallowed them.

and then she was not fasting, and yet not full-fed ; and
next she threw a net over her, and so she was

> ‘ Not naked,
> And yet not clad.’

Next she got a ram and sat on him, so that her feet
touched the ground ; and so she waddled along, and
was

> ‘ Not driving,
> And not riding ;
> Not walking,
> And not carried.’

And all this happened in the twilight, betwixt night
and day.

“ So when she came to the guard at the palace, she
begged that she might have leave to speak with the
prince; but they wouldn’t open the gate, she looked such
a figure of fun.

“ But for all that the noise woke up the prince, and he
went to the window to see what it was.

“ So she waddled up to the window, and twisted off one
of the ram’s horns, and took it and rapped with it against
the window.

“ And so they had to let her in, and have her for their
princess.”

BOOTS AND THE BEASTS.

"ONCE on a time there was a man who had an only son, but he lived in need and wretchedness, and when he lay on his death-bed, he told his son he had nothing in the world but a sword, a bit of coarse linen, and a few crusts of bread—that was all he had to leave him. Well! when the man was dead, the lad made up his mind to go out into the world to try his luck; so he girded the sword about him, and took the crusts and laid them in the bit of linen for his travelling fare; for you must know they lived far away up on a hillside in the wood, far from folk. Now the way he went took him over a fell, and when he had got up so high that he could look over the country, he set his eyes on a lion, a falcon, and an ant, who stood there quarrelling over a dead horse. The lad was sore afraid when he saw the lion, but he called out to him and said he must come and settle the strife between them and share the horse, so that each should get what he ought to have.

"So the lad took his sword and shared the horse, as well as he could. To the lion he gave the carcass and the greater portion; the falcon got some of the entrails and other titbits; and the ant got the head. When he had done, he said,—

"'Now I think it is fairly shared. The lion shall have most, because he is biggest and strongest; the falcon shall have the best, because he is nice and dainty; and the ant shall have the skull, because he loves to creep about in holes and crannies.'

"Yes! they were all well pleased with his sharing; and so they asked him what he would like to have for sharing the horse so well.

"'Oh,' he said, 'if I have done you a service, and you are pleased with it, I am also pleased; but I won't be paid.'

"'Yes; but he must have something,' they said.

"'If you won't have anything else,' said the lion, 'you shall have three wishes.'

"But the lad knew not what to wish for; and so the lion asked him if he wouldn't wish that he might be able to turn himself into a lion; and the two others asked him if he wouldn't wish to be able to turn himself into a falcon and an ant. Yes! all that seemed to him good and right; and so he wished these three wishes.

"Then he threw aside his sword and wallet, turned himself into a falcon, and began to fly. So he flew on and on, till he came over a great lake; but when he had almost flown across it he got so tired and sore on the wing he couldn't fly any longer; and as he saw a steep rock that rose out of the water, he perched on it and rested himself. He thought it a wondrous strong rock, and walked about it for a while ; but when he had taken a good rest, he turned himself again into a little falcon, and flew away till he came to the king's grange. There he perched on a tree, just before the princess's windows. When she saw the falcon she set her heart on catching it. So she lured it to her ; and as soon as the falcon came under the casement she was ready, and pop! she shut to the window, and caught the bird and put him into a cage.

"In the night the lad turned himself into an ant and crept out of the cage; and then he turned himself into his own shape, and went up and sat down by the princess's bed. Then she got so afraid that she fell to screeching out and awoke the king, who came into her room and asked whatever was the matter.

"'Oh !' said the princess, 'there is some one here.'

"But in a trice the lad became an ant, crept into the cage, and turned himself into a falcon. The king could see nothing for her to be afraid of; so he said to the princess it must have been the nightmare riding her. But he was hardly out of the door before it was all the same story over again. The lad crept out of the cage as an ant, and then became his own self, and sat down by the bedside of the princess.

"Then she screamed loud, and the king came again to see what was the matter.

"'There is some one here,' screamed the princess.

But the lad crept into the cage again, and sat perched up there like a falcon. The king looked and hunted high and low; and when he could see nothing he got cross that his rest was broken, and said it was all a trick of the princess.

"'If you scream like that again,' he said, 'you shall soon know that your father is the king.'

"But for all that, the king's back was scarcely turned before the lad was by the princess's side again. This time she did not scream, although she was so afraid she did not know which way to turn.

"So the lad asked why she was so afraid.

"Didn't he know? She was promised to a hill-ogre, and the very first time she came under bare sky he was to come and take her; and so when the lad came she thought it was the hill-ogre. And, besides, every Thursday morning came a messenger from the hill-ogre, and that was a dragon, to whom the king had to give nine fat pigs every time he came; and that was why he had given it out that the man who could free him from the dragon should have the princess and half the kingdom.

"The lad said he would soon do that; and as soon as it was daybreak the princess went to the king and said there was a man in there who would free him from the dragon and the tax of pigs. As soon as the king heard that, he was very glad, for the dragon had eaten up so many pigs, there would soon have been no more left in the whole kingdom. It happened that day was just a

Thursday morning, and so the lad strode off to the spot where the dragon used to come to eat the pigs, and the shoeblack in the king's grange showed him the way.

"Yes! the dragon came; and he had nine heads, and he was so wild and wroth that fire and flame flared out of his nostrils when he did not see his feast of pigs; and he flew upon the lad as though he would gobble him up alive. But, pop! he turned himself into a lion and fought with the dragon, and tore one head off him after another. The dragon was strong, that he was; and he spat fire and venom. But as the fight went on he hadn't more than one head left, though that was the toughest. At last the lad got that torn off, too; and then it was all over with the dragon.

"So he went to the king, and there was great joy all over the palace; and the lad was to have the princess. But once on a time, as they were walking in the garden, the hill-ogre came flying at them himself, and caught up the princess and bore her off through the air.

"As for the lad, he was for going after her at once; but the king said he mustn't do that, for he had no one else to lean on now he had lost his daughter. But for all that, neither prayers nor preaching were any good: the lad turned himself into a falcon and flew off. But when he could not see them anywhere, he called to mind that wonderful rock in the lake, where he had rested the first time he ever flew. So he settled there, and after he had done that he turned himself into an ant, and crept down through a crack in the rock. So when he had crept about awhile, he came to a door which was locked. But he knew a way how to get in, for he crept through the key-hole, and what do you think he saw there? Why, a strange princess, combing a hill-ogre's hair that had three heads.

"'I have come all right,' said the lad to himself; for he had heard how the king had lost two daughters before, whom the trolls had taken.

"'Maybe, I shall find the second also,' he said to himself, as he crept through the keyhole of a second door. There sat a strange princess combing a hill-ogre's hair who had six heads. So he crept through a third keyhole still, and there sat the youngest princess, combing a hill-ogre's hair with nine heads. Then he crept up her leg and stung her, and so she knew it was the lad who wished to talk to her; and then she begged leave of the hill-ogre to go out.

"When she came out the lad was himself again, and so he told her she must ask the hill-ogre whether she would never get away and go home to her father. Then he turned himself into an ant and sat on her foot, and so the princess went into the house again, and fell to combing the hill-ogre's hair.

"So when she had done this awhile, she fell a-thinking.

"'You're forgetting to comb me,' said the hill-ogre. 'What is it you're thinking of?'

"'Oh, I am doubting whether I shall ever get away

from this place, and home to my father's grange,' said the princess.

"'Nay! nay! that you'll never do!' said the hill-ogre; 'not unless you can find the grain of sand which lies under the ninth tongue of the ninth head of the dragon to which your father paid tax; but that no one will ever find, for if that grain of sand came over the rock all the hill-ogres would burst, and the rock itself would become a gilded palace, and the lake green meadows.'

"As soon as the lad heard that he crept out through the keyholes, and through the crack in the rock, till he got outside. Then he turned himself into a falcon, and flew whither the dragon lay. Then he hunted till he found the grain of sand under the ninth tongue of the ninth head, and flew off with it; but when he came to the lake he got so tired, so tired, that he had to sink down and perch on a stone by the strand. And just as he sat there he dozed and nodded for the twinkling of an eye; and, meantime, the grain of sand fell out of his bill down among the sand on the shore. So he searched for it three days before he found it again. But as soon as he had found it he flew straight off to the steep rock with it, and dropped it down the crack. Then all the hill-ogres burst, and the rock was rent, and there stood a gilded castle, which was the grandest castle in all the world; and the lake became the loveliest fields and the greenest meads any one ever saw.

"So they travelled back to the king's grange, and there arose, as you may fancy, joy and gladness. The lad and the youngest princess were to have one another ; and they kept up the bridal feast over the whole kingdom for seven full weeks. And if they did not fare well, I only hope you may fare better still."

THE SWEETHEART IN THE WOOD.

"ONCE on a time there was a man who had a daughter,
and she was so pretty her name was spread over
many kingdoms, and lovers came to her as thick as autumn
leaves. One of these made out that he was richer than
all the rest; and grand and handsome he was too; so he
was to have her, and after that he came over and over
again to see her.

"As time went on, he said he should like her to come
to his house and see how he lived; he was sorry he could
not fetch her and go with her, but the day she came he
would strew peas all along the path right up to his house
door; but somehow or other it fell out that he strewed the
peas a day too early.

"She set out and walked a long way, through wood and
waste, and at last she came to a big grand house, which
stood in a green field in the midst of the wood; but her
lover was not at home, nor was there a soul in the house
either. First, she went into the kitchen, and there she
saw nothing but a strange bird which hung in a cage from
the roof. Next she went into the parlour, and there

everything was so fine it was beyond belief. But as she went into it, the bird called after her,—

"'Pretty maiden, be bold, but not too bold.'

"When she passed on into an inner room, the bird called out the same words. There she saw ever so many chests of drawers, and when she pulled open the drawers, they were filled with gold and silver, and everything that was rich and rare. When she went on into a second room the bird called out again,—

"'Pretty maiden! be bold, but not too bold.'

"In that room the walls were all hung round with women's dresses, till the room was crammed full. She went on into a third room, and then the bird screamed out,—

"'Pretty maiden! Pretty maiden, be bold, but not too bold.'

"And what do you think she saw there? Why! ever so many pails full of blood.

"So she passed on to a fourth room, and then the bird screamed and screeched after her,—

"'Pretty maiden! Pretty maiden, be bold, but not too bold.'

"'That room was full of heaps of dead bodies, and skeletons of slain women, and the girl got so afraid that she was going to run away out of the house, but she had only got as far as the next room, where the pails of blood stood, when the bird called out to her,—

"'Pretty maiden! Pretty maiden! Jump under the bed, jump under the bed, for now he's coming.'

"She was not slow to give heed to the bird, and to hide under the bed. She crept as far back close to the wall as she could, for she was so afraid she would have crept into the wall itself, had she been able !

"So in came her lover with another girl; and she begged so prettily and so hard he would only spare her life, and then she would never say a word against him, but it was all no good. He tore off all her clothes and jewels, down to a ring which she had on her finger. That he pulled and tore at, but when he couldn't get it off he hacked off her finger, and it rolled away under the bed to the girl who lay there, and she took it up and kept it. Her sweetheart told a little boy who was with him, to creep under the bed and bring out the finger. Yes ! he bent down and crept under, and saw the girl lying there ; but she squeezed his hand hard, and then he saw what she meant.

"'It lies so far under, I can't reach it,' he cried. 'Let it bide there till to-morrow, and then I'll fetch it out.'

"Early next morning the robber went out, and the boy was left behind to mind the house, and he then went to meet the girl to whom his master was betrothed, and who had come, as you know, by mistake the day before. But before he went, the robber told him to be sure not to let her go into the two farthermost bed-rooms.

"So when he was well off in the wood, the boy went and said she might come out now.

"'You were lucky, that you were,' he said, 'in coming so soon, else he would have killed you like all the others.'

"She did not stay there long, you may fancy, but hurried back home as quick as ever she could, and when her father asked her why she had come so soon, she told him what sort of a man her sweetheart was, and all that she had heard and seen.

"A short time after her lover came passing by that way, and he looked so grand that his raiment shone again, and he came to ask, he said, why she had never paid him that visit as she had promised.

"'Oh!' said her father; 'there came a man in the way with a sledge and scattered the peas, and she couldn't find her way; but now you must just put up with our poor house, and stay the night, for you must know we have guests coming, and it will be just a betrothal feast.'

"So when they had all eaten and drunk, and still sat round the table, the daughter of the house said she had dreamt such a strange dream a few nights before. If they cared to hear it she would tell it them, but they must all promise to sit quite still till she came to the end.

"Yes! They were all ready to hear, and they all promised to sit still, and her sweetheart as well.

"'I dreamt I was walking along a broad path, and it was strewn with peas.'

"'Yes! Yes!' said her sweetheart; 'just as it will be when you go to my house, my love.'

"'Then the path got narrower and narrower, and it went far far away through wood and waste.'

"'Just like the way to my house, my love,' said her sweetheart.

"'And so I came to a green field, in which stood a big grand house.'

"'Just like my house, my love,' said her sweetheart.

"'So I went into the kitchen, but I saw no living soul, and from the roof hung a strange bird in a cage, and as I passed on into the parlour, it called after me, "Pretty maiden, be bold, but not too bold."'

"'Just like my house that too, my love!' said her sweetheart.

"'So I passed on into a bed-room, and the bird bawled after me the same words, and in there were so many chests of drawers, and when I pulled the drawers out and looked into them, they were filled with gold and silver stuffs, and everything that was grand.'

"'That is just like it is at my house, my love,' said her sweetheart. 'I, too, have many drawers full of gold and silver, and costly things.'

"'So I went on into another bed-room, and the bird screeched out to me the very same words; and that room was all hung round on the walls with fine dresses of women.'

"'Yes, that too, is just as it is in my house,' he said; 'there are dresses and finery there both of silk and satin.'

"'Well! when I passed on to the next bed-room, the bird began to screech and scream—pretty maiden, pretty maiden! be bold, but not too bold; and in this room were casks and pails all round the walls, and they were full of blood.'

"'Fie,' said her sweetheart, 'how nasty. It isn't at all like that in my house, my love,' for now he began to grow uneasy and wished to be off.

"'Why!' said the daughter, 'it's only a dream, you know, that I am telling. Sit still. The least you can do is to hear my dream out.' Then she went on,

"When I went on into the next bed-room the bird began to scream out as loudly as before, the same words—pretty maiden, pretty maiden! be bold, but not too bold. And there lay many dead bodies and skeletons of slain folk.'

"'No! no,' said her sweetheart, 'there's nothing like that in my house,' and again he tried to run out.

"'Sit still, I say,' she said, 'it is nothing else than a dream, and you may very well hear it out. I, too, thought it dreadful, and ran back again, but I had not got farther than the next room where all those pails of blood stood, when the bird screeched out that I must jump under the bed and hide, for now *He* was coming; and so he came, and with him he had a girl who was so lovely I thought I had never seen her like before. She prayed and begged so prettily that he would spare her life. But he did not care a pin for all her tears and prayers; he tore off her clothes, and took all she had, and he neither spared her life nor aught else; but on her left hand she had a ring, which he could not tear off, so he hacked off her finger, and it rolled away under the bed to me.'

"'Indeed! my love,' said her sweetheart, 'there's nothing like that in my house.'

" ' Yes, it was in your house,' she said, ' and here is the finger and the ring, and you are the man who hacked it off.'

" So they laid hands on him, and put him to death, and burnt both his body and his house in the wood."

HOW THEY GOT HAIRLOCK HOME.

"ONCE on a time there was a goody who had three sons. The first was called Peter, the second Paul, and the third Osborn Boots. One single nanny-goat she had who was called Hairlock and she never would come home in time for tea.

"Peter and Paul both went out to get her home, but they found no nanny-goat, so Boots had to set off, and when he had walked a while he saw Hairlock high high upon a crag.

"'Dear Hairlock, pretty Hairlock,' he cried, 'you can't stand any longer on yon crag, for you must come home in good time for tea, to-day.'

"'No, no, that I shan't,' said Hairlock, 'I won't wet my socks for any one, and if you want me you must carry me.'

"But Osborn Boots would not do that, so he went and told his mother.

"'Well!' said his mother, 'go to the fox and beg him to bite Hairlock.'

"So the lad went to the fox.

" ' My dear fox, bite Hairlock, for Hairlock won't come home in good time for tea to-day.'

" ' No,' said the fox, ' I won't blunt my snout on pig's bristles and goat's beards.'

" So the lad went and told his mother.

" ' Well, then ! ' she said, ' go to Graylegs, the wolf.'

" So the lad said to Graylegs,—

" ' Dear Graylegs ! do, Graylegs, tear the fox, for the fox won't bite Hairlock, and Hairlock won't come home in good time for tea to-day.'

" ' No,' said Graylegs, ' I won't wear out my paws and teeth on a dry fox's carcass.'

" So the lad went and told his mother.

" ' Well then, go to the bear,' said his mother, ' and beg him to slay Graylegs.'

" So the lad said to the bear,—

" ' My dear bear, do, bear, slay Graylegs, for Graylegs won't tear the fox, and the fox won't bite Hairlock, and Hairlock won't come home in good time for tea to-day.'

" ' No, I won't,' said the bear, ' I won't blunt my claws in that work, that I won't.'

" So the lad told his mother.

" ' Well then,' she said, ' go to the Finn and beg him shoot the bear.'

" So the lad said to the Finn,—

" ' Dear Finn ! do, Finn, shoot the bear, the bear won't slay Graylegs, Graylegs won't tear the fox, the fox won't bite Hairlock, and Hairlock won't come home in good time for tea to-day.'

"'No! that I won't,' said the Finn, 'I'm not going to shoot away my bullets for that.'

"So the lad told his mother.

"'Well then,' she said, 'go to the fir, and beg him fall on the Finn.'

"So the lad said to the fir,—

"'My dear fir! fir, do fall on the Finn, the Finn won't shoot the bear, the bear won't slay the wolf, the wolf won't tear the fox, the fox won't bite Hairlock, and Hairlock won't come home in good time to tea to-day.'

"'No! that I won't,' said the fir, 'I'm not going to break off my boughs for that.'

"So the lad told his mother.

"'Well then,' said she, 'go to the fire and beg it to burn the fir.'

"So the lad said to the fire, 'My dear fire! do, fire, burn the fir, the fir won't fall on the Finn, the Finn won't shoot the bear, the bear won't slay the wolf, the wolf won't tear the fox, the fox won't bite Hairlock, and Hairlock won't come home in good time to tea to-day.'

"'No! that I won't,' said the fire, 'I'm not going to burn myself out for that, that I won't.'

"So the lad told his mother.

"'Well then,' she said, 'go to the water and beg it to quench the fire.'

"So the lad said to the water,—

"'My dear water! do, water, quench the fire, the fire won't burn the fir, the fir won't fall on the Finn, the Finn won't shoot the bear, the bear won't slay the wolf, the wolf won't tear the fox, the fox won't bite Hairlock, and Hairlock won't come home in good time to tea to-day.'

"'No, I won't,' said the water, 'I'm not going to run to waste for that, be sure.'

"So the lad told his mother.

"'Well then,' she said, 'go to the ox, and beg him to drink up the water.'

"So the lad said to the ox,—

"'My dear ox! do, ox, drink up the water, for the water won't quench the fire, the fire won't burn the fir, the fir won't fall on the Finn, the Finn won't shoot the bear, the bear won't slay the wolf, the wolf won't tear the fox, the fox won't bite Hairlock, and Hairlock won't come home in good time to tea to-day.'

"'No! I won't,' said the ox, 'I'm not going to burst asunder in doing that, I trow.'

"So the lad told his mother.

"'Well then,' said she, 'you must go to the yoke, and beg him to pinch the ox.'

"So the lad said to the yoke,—

"'My dear yoke! yoke, do pinch the ox, for the ox won't drink up the water, the water won't quench the fire, the fire won't burn the fir, the fir won't fall on the Finn, the Finn won't shoot the bear, the bear won't slay the wolf, the wolf won't tear the fox, the fox won't bite

Hairlock, and Hairlock won't come home in good time to tea to-day.'

" ' No, that I won't,' said the yoke, ' I'm not going to break myself in two in doing that.'

" So the lad told his mother.

" ' Well then,' she said, ' you must go to the axe, and beg him to chop the yoke.'

" So the lad said to the axe,—

" ' My dear axe, do, axe, chop the yoke, for the yoke won't pinch the ox, the ox won't drink up the water, the water won't quench the fire, the fire won't burn the fir, the fir won't fall on the Finn, the Finn won't shoot the bear, the bear won't slay the wolf, the wolf won't tear the fox, the fox won't bite Hairlock, and Hairlock won't come home in good time to tea to-day.'

" ' No, that I won't,' said the axe, ' I'm not going to spoil my edge for that, that I won't.'

" So the lad told his mother.

" ' Well then,' she said, ' go to the smith, and beg him to hammer the axe.'

" So the lad said to the smith,—

" ' My dear smith ! do, smith, hammer the axe, for the axe won't chop the yoke, the yoke won't pinch the ox, the ox won't drink up the water, the water won't quench the fire, the fire won't burn the fir, the fir won't fall on the Finn, the Finn won't shoot the bear, the bear won't slay the wolf, the wolf won't tear the fox, the fox won't bite Hairlock, and Hairlock won't come home in good time to tea to-day.'

"'No, I won't,' said the smith, 'I'm not going to burn up my coal, and wear out my sledge hammer for that,' he said.

"So the lad told his mother.

"'Well then,' she said, 'you must go to the rope, and beg it to hang the smith.'

"So the lad said to the rope,—

"'My dear rope! do, rope, hang the smith, for the smith won't hammer the axe, the axe won't chop the yoke, the yoke won't pinch the ox, the ox won't drink up the water, the water won't quench the fire, the fire won't burn the fir, the fir won't fall on the Finn, the Finn won't shoot the bear, the bear won't slay the wolf, the wolf won't tear the fox, the fox won't bite Hairlock, and Hairlock won't come home in good time to tea to-day.'

"'No!' said the rope, 'that I won't, I'm not going to fray myself out for that.'

"So the lad told his mother.

"'Well then!' she said, 'you must go to the mouse, and beg him to gnaw the rope.'

"So the lad said to the mouse,—

"'My dear mouse! do, mouse, gnaw the rope, for the rope won't hang the smith, the smith won't hammer the axe, the axe won't chop the yoke, the yoke won't pinch the ox, the ox won't drink up the water, the water won't quench the fire, the fire won't burn the fir, the fir won't fall on the Finn, the Finn won't shoot the bear, the bear won't slay the wolf, the wolf won't tear the fox, the fox won't bite Hairlock, and Hairlock won't come home in good time to tea to-day.'

" ' No ! I won't,' said the mouse, ' I'm not going to wear down my teeth for that.'

" So the lad told his mother.

" ' Well then,' she said, ' you must go to the cat, and beg her to catch the mouse.'

" So the lad said to the cat,—

" ' My dear cat ! do, cat, catch the mouse, for the mouse won't gnaw the rope, the rope won't hang the smith, the smith won't hammer the axe, the axe won't chop the yoke, the yoke won't pinch the ox, the ox won't drink up the water, the water won't quench the fire, the fire won't burn the fir, the fir won't fall on the Finn, the Finn won't shoot the bear, the bear won't slay the wolf, the wolf won't tear the fox, the fox won't bite Hairlock, and Hairlock won't come home in good time to tea to-day.'

" ' Well !' said the cat, ' just give me a drop of milk for my kittens and then ——' that's what the cat said, and the lad said, ' yes, she should have it.'

" So the cat bit mouse, and mouse gnawed rope, and rope hanged smith, and smith hammered axe, and axe chopped yoke, and yoke pinched ox, and ox drank water, and water quenched fire, and fire burnt fir, and fir felled Finn, and Finn shot bear, and bear slew graylegs, and graylegs tore fox, and fox bit Hairlock, so that she sprang home and knocked off one of her hind legs against the barn wall.

"So there lay the nanny-goat, and if she's not dead she limps about on three legs.

"But as for Osborn Boots, he said it served her just right, because she would not come home in good time for tea that very day."

OSBORN BOOTS AND MR. GLIBTONGUE.

"ONCE on a time there was a king who had many hundred sheep, and many hundred goats and kine; and many hundred horses he had too, and silver and gold in great heaps. But for all that he was so given to grief, that he seldom or ever saw folk, and much less say a word to them. Such he had been ever since his youngest daughter was lost, and if he had never lost her it would still have been bad enough, for there was a troll who was for ever making such waste and worry there that folk could hardly pass to the king's grange in peace. Now the troll let all the horses loose, and they trampled down mead and corn-field, and ate up the crops; now he tore the heads off the king's ducks and geese; sometimes he killed the king's kine in the byre, sometimes he drove the king's sheep and goats down the rocks and broke their necks, and every time they went to fish in the mill-dam he had hunted all the fish to land and left them lying there dead.

"Well! there was a couple of old folk who had three sons, the first was called Peter, the second Paul, and the third

Osborn Boots, for he always lay and grubbed about in the ashes.

"They were hopeful youths, but Peter, who was the eldest, was said to be the hopefullest, and so he asked his father if he might have leave to go out into the world and try his luck.

"'Yes! you shall have it,' said the old fellow. 'Better late than never, my boy.'

"So he got brandy in a flask, and food in his wallet, and then he threw his fare on his back and toddled down the hill. And when he had walked a while, he fell upon an old wife who lay by the road side.

"'Ah! my dear boy, give me a morsel of food to-day,' said the old wife.

"But Peter hardly so much as looked on one side, and then he held his head straight and went on his way.

"'Ay, ay,' said the old wife, 'go along, and you shall see what you shall see.'

"So Peter went far and farther than far, till he came at last to the king's grange. There stood the king in the gallery, feeding the cocks and hens.

"'Good evening and God bless your majesty," said Peter.

"'Chick-a-biddy! chick-a-biddy!' said the king, and scattered corn both east and west, and took no heed of Peter.

"'Well!' said Peter to himself, 'you may just stand there and scatter corn and cackle chicken-tongue till you turn into a bear,' and so he went into the kitchen and sat down on the bench as though he were a great man.

"'What sort of a stripling are you,' said the cook, for Peter had not yet got his beard. That he thought jibes and mocking, and so he fell to beating and banging the kitchen-maid. But while he was hard at it, in came the king, and made them cut three red stripes out of his back, and then they rubbed salt into the wound, and sent him home again the same way he came.

"Now as soon as Peter was well home, Paul must set off in his turn. Well! well! he too got brandy in his flask and food in his wallet, and he threw his fare over his back and toddled down the hill. When he had got on his way he, too, met the old wife, who begged for food, but he strode past her and made no answer; and at the king's grange he did not fare a pin better than Peter. The king called 'chick-a-biddy,' and the kitchen-maid called him a clumsy boy, and when he was going to bang and beat her for that, in came the king with a butcher's knife, and cut three red stripes out of him, and rubbed hot embers in, and sent him home again with a sore back.

"Then Boots crept out the cinders, and fell to shaking himself. The first day he shook all the ashes off him, the second he washed and combed himself, and the third he dressed himself in his Sunday best.

"'Nay! nay! just look at him,' said Peter. 'Now we have got a new sun shining here. I'll be bound you are off to the king's grange to win his daughter and half the kingdom.   Far better bide in the dusthole and lie in the ashes, that you had.'

"But Boots was deaf in that ear, and he went in to his father and asked leave to go out a little into the world.

"'What are you to do out in the world?' said the greybeard.   'It did not fare so well either with Peter or Paul, and what do you think will become of you?'

"But Boots would not give way, and so at last he had leave to go.

"His brothers were not for letting him have a morsel of food with him, but his mother gave him a cheese rind and a bone with very little meat on it, and with them he toddled away from the cottage.   As he went he took his time.   'You'll be there soon enough,' he said to himself.   'You have all the day before you, and afterwards the moon will rise, if you have any luck.'   So he put his best foot foremost, and puffed up the hills, and all the while looked about him on the road.

"After a long, long way he met the old wife, who lay by the road side.

"'The poor old cripple,' said Boots, 'I'll be bound you are starving.'

"'Yes! she was,' said the old wife.

"'Are you? then I'll go shares with you,' said Osborn Boots, and as he said that he gave her the rind of cheese.

"You're freezing too,' he said, as he saw how her teeth chattered.   'You must take this old jacket of mine. It's not good in the arms, and thin in the back, but once on a time, when it was new, it was a good wrap.'

" ' Bide a bit,' said the old wife, as she fumbled down in her big pocket, ' Here you have an old key, I have nothing better or worse to give you, but when you look through the ring at the top, you can see whatever you choose to see.'

"So when he got to the king's grange the cook was hard at work drawing water, and that was great toil to her.

" ' It's too heavy for you,' said Boots, ' but it's just what I am fit to do.'

" The one that was glad then, you may fancy, was the kitchen-maid, and from that day she always let Boots scrape the porridge-pot; but it was not long before he got so many enemies by that, that they told lies of him to the king, and said he had told them he was man enough to do this and that.

" So one day the king came and asked Boots if it were true that he was man enough to keep the fish in the mill-dam, so that the troll could not harm them, ' for that's what they tell me you have said,' spoke the king.

" ' I have not said so,' said Boots, ' but if I had said it I would have been as good as my word.'

" Well, however it was, whether he had said it or not, he must try, if he wished to keep a whole skin on his back; that was what the king said.

" ' Well, if he must he must,' said Boots, for he said he had no need to go about with red stripes under his jacket.

"In the evening Boots peeped through his key ring, and then he saw that the troll was afraid of thyme. So he fell to plucking all the thyme he could find, and some of it he strewed in the water, and some on land, and the rest he spread over the brink of the dam.

"So the troll had to leave the fish in peace, but now the sheep had to pay for it, for the troll was chasing them over all the cliffs and crags the whole night.

"Then one of the other servants came and said again that Boots knew a cure for the stock as well, if he only chose, for that he had said he was man enough to do it, was the very truth.

"Well! the king went out to him and spoke to him as he had spoken the first time, and threatened that he would cut three broad stripes out of his back if he did not do what he had said.

"So there was no help for it. Boots thought, I dare say it would be very fine to go about in the king's livery and a red jacket, but he thought he would rather be without it, if he himself had to find the cloth for it out of the skin of his back. That was what he thought and said.

"So he betook himself to his thyme again, but there was no end to his work, for as soon as he bound thyme on the sheep they ate it off one another's backs, and as he went on binding they went on eating, and they ate faster than he could bind. But at last he made an ointment of thyme and tar, and rubbed it well into them, and then they left off eating it. Then the kine and the horses got the same ointment, and so they had peace from the troll.

"But one day when the king was out hunting he trod upon wild grass and got bewildered, and lost his way in the wood; so he rode round and round for many days, and had nothing either to eat or drink, and his clothing fared so ill in the thorns and thickets that at last he had scarce a rag to his back. So the troll came to him and said if he might have the first thing the king set eyes on when he got on his own land, he would let him go home to his grange. Yes! he should have that, for the king thought it would be sure to be his little dog, which always came frisking and fawning to meet him. But just as he got near his grange, that they could see him, out came his eldest daughter at the head of all the court, to meet the king, and to welcome him back safe and sound.

"So when he saw that she was the first to meet him, he was so cut to the heart he fell to the ground on the spot, and since that time had been almost half-witted.

"One evening the troll was to come and fetch the princess, and she was dressed out in her best, and sat in a field out by the tarn, and wept and bewailed. There was a man called Glibtongue, who was to go with her, but he was so afraid he clomb up into a tall spruce fir, and there he stuck. Just then up came Boots, and sat down on the ground by the side of the princess. And she was so glad, as you may fancy, when she saw there were still Christian folk who dared to stay by her after all.

"'Lay your head on my lap,' she said, 'and I'll comb your hair;' so Osborn Boots did as she bade him, and while she combed his hair he fell asleep, and. she took a gold ring off her finger and knitted it into his hair. Just then up came the troll puffing and blowing. He was so heavy footed that all the wood groaned and cracked a whole mile round.

"And when the troll saw Glibtongue sitting up in the tree-top, like a little black cock, he spat at him.

"'Pish,' he said, that was all, and down toppled Glibtongue and the spruce fir to the ground, and there he lay sprawling like a fish out of water.

"Hu! hu!' said the troll, 'are you sitting here combing Christian folk's hair? Now I'll gobble you up.'

"'Stuff,' said Boots, as soon as he woke up, and then he fell to peering at the troll through the ring on his key.

"'Hu! hu!' said the troll, 'what are you staring at? Hu! hu!'

"And as he said that he hurled his iron club at him, so that it stood fifteen ells deep in the rock ; but Boots was so quick and ready on his feet that he got on one side of the club, just as the troll hurled it.

"'Stuff! for such old wives' tricks,' said Boots, 'out with your toothpick, and you shall see something like a throw.'

"Yes! the troll plucked out the club at one pull, and it was as big as three weaver's beams. Meanwhile Boots stared up at the sky, both south and north.

" ' Hu! hu!' said the troll, 'what are you gazing at now ?'

" ' I'm looking out for a star at which to throw,' said Boots. 'Do you see that tiny little one due north, that's the one I choose.'

" ' Nay ! nay !' said the troll, ' let it bide as it is. You mustn't throw away my iron club.'

" ' Well! well!' said Boots, ' you may have it again then, but perhaps you wouldn't mind if I tossed you up to the moon just for once.'

" No! the troll would have nothing to say to that either.

" ' Oh ! but blindman's buff,' said Boots, ' haven't you a mind to play blindman's buff ?'

" Yes, that would be fine fun, the troll thought ; ' but you shall be blindfold first,' said the troll to Boots.

" ' Oh, yes, with all my heart,' said the lad, ' but the fairest way is that we draw lots, and then we shan't have anything to quarrel about.'

" Yes! yes! that was best, and then you may fancy Boots took care the troll should be the first to have the hand-kerchief over his eyes, and was the first ' buff.'

" But that just was a game. My! how they went in and out of the wood, and how the troll ran and stumbled over the stumps, so that the dust flew and the wood rang.

" ' Haw ! haw !' bawled the troll at last, ' the deil take me if I'll be buff any longer,' for he was in a great rage.

" ' Bide a bit,' said Boots, ' and I'll stand still and call till you come and catch me.'

" Meanwhile he took a hemp-comb and ran round to the other side of the tarn, which was so deep it had no bottom.

" ' Now come, here I stand,' bawled out Boots.

" ' I dare say there are logs and stumps in the way,' said the troll.

" ' Your ears can tell you there is no wood here,' said Boots, and then he swore to him there were no stumps or stocks.

" ' Now come along.'

" So the troll set off again, but ' squash ' it said, and there lay the troll in the tarn, and Boots hacked at his eyes with the hemp-comb every time he got his head above water.

" Now the troll begged so prettily for his life, that Boots thought it was a shame to take it, but first he had to give up the princess, and to bring back the other whom he had stolen before.   And besides he had to promise that folk and flock should have peace, and then he let the troll out, and he took himself off home to his hill.

" But now Glibtongue became a man again, and came down out of the tree-top, and carried off the princess to the grange, as though he had set her free.   And then he stole down and gave his arm to the other also, when Boots had brought her as far as the garden.   And now there was such joy in the king's grange, that it was heard and talked of over land and realm, and Glibtongue was to be married to the youngest daughter.

" Well, it was all good and right, but after all it was

not so well, for just as they were to have the feast, if that old troll had not gone down under earth and stopped all the springs of water.

"'If I can't do them any other harm,' he said, 'they sha'n't have water to boil their bridal brose.'

"So there was no help for it but to send for Boots again. Then he got him an iron bar, which was to be fifteen.ells long, and six smiths were to make it red hot. Then he peeped through his key ring, and saw where the troll was, just as well underground as above it, and then he drove the bar down through the ground, and into the troll's back-bone, and all I can say was, there was a smell of burnt horn fifteen miles round.

"'Haw! haw!' bellowed out the troll, 'let me out,' and in a trice he came tearing up through the hole, and all his back was burnt and singed up to the nape of his neck.

"But Boots was not slow, for he caught the troll and laid him on a stake that had thyme twisted round it, and there he had to be till he told him where he had got eyes from after those had been hacked out with the hemp-comb.

"'If you must know,' said the troll, 'I stole a turnip, and rubbed it well over with ointment, and then I cut it to the sizes I needed, and nailed them in tight with ten-penny nails, and better eyes I hope no Christian man will ever have.'

"Then the king came with the two princesses, and wanted to see the troll, and Glibtongue walked so bent and bowed, his coat tails were higher than his neck. But then the king caught sight of something glistening in the hair of Boots.

" ' What have you got there ? ' he said.

" ' Oh ! ' said Boots, ' nothing but the ring your daughter gave me when I freed her from the troll.'

" And now it came out how it had all happened. Glibtongue begged and prayed for himself, but for all his trying and all his crying there was no help for it, down he had to go into a pit full of snakes, and there he lay till he burst.

" Then they put an end to the troll, and then they began to be noisy and merry, and to drink and dance at the bridal of Boots, for now he was king of that company, and he got the youngest princess and half the kingdom.

> " And here I lay my tale upon a sledge,
> And send it thee whose tongue hath sharper edge,
> But if thy tongue in wit is not so fine,
> Then shame on thee that throwest blame on mine."

THIS IS THE LAD WHO SOLD THE PIG.

"ONCE on a time there was a widow who had a son and he had set his heart on being nothing else than a tradesman. But you must know they were so poor that they had nothing that he could begin his trading with. The only thing his mother owned in the world was a sow pig, and he begged and prayed so long and so prettily for that, at last she was forced to let him have it.

"When he had got it he was to set off to sell it, that he might have some money to begin his trading. So he offered it to this man and that, good and bad alike; but there was no one who just then cared to buy a pig. At last he came to a rich old hunks; but you know much will always have more, and that man was one of the sort that never can have enough.

"'Will you buy a pig to-day?' said the lad; 'a good pig, and a long pig, and a fine fat pig.' That was what he said.

"The old hunks asked what he would have for it. It was at least worth six dollars, even between brothers, said the lad; but the times were so hard, and money so scarce, he didn't mind selling it for four dollars. And that was as good as giving it away.

"No, that the old hunks would not do—he wouldn't give so much as a dollar even ; he had more pigs already than he wanted, and was well off for pigs of that sort. But as the lad was so eager to sell, he would be willing to do him a turn, and deal with him ; but the most he could give for the whole pig, every inch of it, was fourpence. If he would take that down, he might turn his pig into the sty with the rest. That was what the old hunks said.

"The lad thought it shameful that he should not get more for his pig; but then he thought that something was better than nothing, and so he took the fourpence and turned in the pig. And then he fingered the money and went about his business. But when he got out into the road, he could not get it out of his head that he had been cheated out of his pig, and that he was not much better off with fourpence than with nothing. The longer he went and thought of this the angrier he got, and at last he thought to himself,—

"'If I could only play him a pretty trick, I wouldn't care either for the pig or the pence.'

"So he went away and got him a pair of stout thongs and a cat-o'-nine-tails, and then he threw over him a big cloak, and put on a billygoat's beard ; and so he went back to the skinflint and said he was from outlandish parts, where he had learnt to be a master builder—for you must know he had heard the old hunks was going to build a house.

"Yes, he would gladly take him as master builder, he said; for thereabouts there were none but home-taught carpenters. So off they went to look at the timber, and it was the finest heart of pine that any one would wish to have in the wall of his house: and even the lad said it was brave timber—he couldn't say otherwise; but in out-landish parts they had got a new fashion, which was far better than the old. They did not take long beams and fit them into the wall, but they cut the beams up into nice small logs, and then they baked them in the sun and fastened them together again; and so they were both stronger and prettier than an old-fashioned timber building.

"'That's how they build all the houses now-a-days in outlandish parts,' said the lad.

"'If it must be so, it must,' said the hunks. With that he set all the carpenters and woodmen who were to be found round about to chop and hew all his beams up into small logs.

"'But,' said the lad, 'we still want some big trees— some of the real mast-firs—for our sill-beams; maybe, there are no such big trees in your wood?'

"'Well!' said the man; 'if they're not to be found in my wood, it will be hard to find them anywhere else.'

"And so they strode off to the wood, both of them; and a little way up the hill they came to a big tree.

"'I should think that's big enough,' said the man.

"'No, it isn't big enough,' said the lad. 'If you haven't

bigger trees, we sha'n't make much way with our building after the new fashion.'

" 'Yes! I have bigger ones,' said the man. 'You sha soon see ; but we must go further on.'

"So they went a long way over the hill, and at last they came to a big tree, one of the finest trees for a mast in all the wood.

" 'Do you think this is big enough ?' said the man.

" 'I almost think it is,' said the lad. 'We will fathom it, and then we shall soon see. You go on the other side of the fir, and I will stand here. If we are not good enough to make our hands meet, it will be big enough ; but mind you stretch out well. Stretch out well, do you hear ?' said the lad, as he took out his thongs. As for the man, he did all the lad told him.

" 'Yes !' said the lad, 'we shall meet nicely, I can see. But stop a bit, and I'll stretch your hands better,' he said, as he slipped a running knot over his wrists and drew it tight and bound him fast to the tree ; then out came the cat-o'-nine-tails, and he fell to flogging the old hunks as fast as he could, and all the while he cried out,—

" 'This is the lad who sold the pig, and this is the lad who sold the pig.'

"Nor did he leave off till he thought the old hunks had enough, and that he had got his rights for the pig ; and then he loosed him, and left him lying under the tree.

"Now when the man did not come home they made

a hue and cry for him over the neighbourhood, and searched the country round; and at last they found him under the fir-tree, more dead than alive.

"So when they had got him home the lad came, and had dressed himself up as a doctor, and said he had come from foreign parts, and knew a cure for all kinds of hurt. And when the man heard that, he was all for having him to doctor him, and the lad said he would not be long in curing him; but he must have him all alone in a room by himself, and no one must be by.

"'If you hear him screech and cry out,' he said, 'you must not mind it; for the more he screeches, the sooner he will be well again.'

"So when they were alone, he said,—

"'First of all I must bleed you.' And so he threw the man roughly down on a bench and bound him fast with the thongs; and then out came the cat-o'-nine-tails, and he fell to flogging him as fast as he could. The man screeched and screamed, for his back was sore, and every lash went into the bare flesh; and the lad flogged and flogged as though there were no end to it, and all the while he bawled out,—

"'This is the lad who sold the pig. This is the lad who sold the pig.'

"The old hunks bellowed as though a knife were being stuck into him; but there was not a soul that cared about it, for the more he screeched the sooner he would be well, they thought.

"So when the lad had done his doctoring, he set off

from the farm as fast as he could; but they followed fast on his heels, and overtook him and threw him into prison, and the end was he was doomed to be hanged.

" And the old hunks was so angry with him, even then, that he would not have him hanged till he was quite well, so that he might hang him with his own hands.

" So while the lad sat there in prison waiting to be hanged, one of the serving-men came out by night and stole kail in the garden of the old hunks, and the lad saw him.

" ' So, so ! ' said he to himself; ' master thief, it will be odd if I don't play off a trick or two with you before I am hanged.'

" And so when time went on, and the man was so well he thought he had strength enough to hang him, he made them set up a gallows down by the way to the mill, so that he might see the body hanging every time he went to the mill. So they set out to hang the lad, and when they had gone a bit of the way, the lad said,—

" ' You will not refuse to let me talk alone with your servant who grinds down yonder at the mill ? I did him a bad turn once, and I wish now to confess it, and beg him for forgiveness before I die.'

" Yes ! he might have leave to do that.

" ' Heaven help you ! ' he said to the miller's man. ' Now your master is coming to hang you because you stole kail in his garden.'

" As soon as the miller's man heard that, he was so taken aback he did not know which way to turn ; and so he asked the lad what he should do.

"'Take and change clothes with me and hide yourself behind the door,' said the lad; 'and then he will not know that 'it isn't me. And if he lays hands on any one, then it will not be you, but me.'

"It was some time before they had changed clothes and dressed again, and the old hunks began to be afraid lest the lad should have run away. So he posted down to the mill door.

"'Where is he?' he said to the lad, who stood there as white as a miller.

"'Oh, he was here just now,' said the lad. 'I think he went and hid himself behind the door.'

"'I'll teach you to hide behind the door, you rogue,' said the old hunks, as he seized the man in a great rage, and hurried him off to the gallows and hanged him in a breath; and all the while he never knew it was not the lad that he hanged.

"After that was done, he wanted to go into the mill to talk to his man, who was busy grinding. Meantime the lad had wedged up the upper millstone, and was feeling under it with his hands.

"'Come here, come here,' he called out as soon as he saw the old hunks; 'and you shall feel what a wonderful millstone this is.'

"So the man went and felt the millstone with one hand.

"'Nay, nay,' said the lad; 'you'll never feel it unless you take hold of it with both hands.'

"Well, he did so; and just then the lad snatched out

the wedge and let the upper millstone down on him, so that he was caught fast by the hands between the stones. Then out came the cat-o'-nine-tails again, and he fell to flogging him as fast as he could.

"'This is the lad who sold the pig,' he cried out, till he was hoarse.

"And when he had flogged him as much as he could he went home to his mother; and as time went on, and he thought the man had come to himself again, he said to her,—

"'Yes! now I daresay that man will be coming to whom I sold the pig; and now I know no other trick to screen me any longer from him, unless I dig a hole here south of the house, and there I will lie all day; and you must mind and say to him just what I tell you.'

"So the lad told his mother all she was to say and do.

"Then he dug such a hole as he had said, and took with him a long butcher's knife, and lay down in it; and his mother covered him over with boughs, and leaves, and moss, so that he was quite hidden! There he lay by day; and after a while the man came travelling along and asked for the lad.

"'Ay, ay,' said his mother. 'He was a man, that he was; though he never got from me more than one sow pig. For he became both a doctor and a master builder, and he was hanged after that, and rose again from the dead; and yet I never heard anything but ill of him. Here he came flying home the other day, and then he gave me the greatest joy I ever had of him, for he laid him down and died. As for me, I did not care enough for him to spend money on a priest and Christian earth; but I just buried him yonder, south of the house, and raked over him boughs and leaves.'

" 'See now,' said the old hunks; 'if he hasn't cheated me after all, and slipped through my fingers. But though I have not been avenged on him living, I will do him a dishonour in his grave.'

" As he said this he strode away south to the grave, and stooped down to spit into it ; but at that very moment the lad stuck the knife into him up to the handle, and bawled out,—

" 'This is the lad who sold the pig ! This is the lad who sold the pig !'

"Away flew the man with the knife sticking in him, and he was so scared and afraid, that nothing has ever been heard or seen of him since."

THE SHEEP AND THE PIG WHO SET UP HOUSE.

" ONCE on a time there was a sheep who stood in the pen to be fattened; so he lived well, and was stuffed and crammed with everything that was good. So it went on, till, one day, the dairymaid came and gave him still more food, and then she said,

" 'Eat away, sheep; you won't be much longer here; we are going to kill you to-morrow.'

"It is an old saying, that women's counsel is always worth having, and that there is a cure and physic for everything but death. 'But, after all,' said the sheep to himself, 'there may be a cure even for death this time.'

"So he ate till he was ready to burst; and when he was crammed full, he butted out the door of the pen, and took his way to the neighbouring farm. There he went to the pigsty to a pig whom he had known out on the common, and ever since had been the best friends with.

" 'Good day!' said the sheep, 'and thanks for our last merry meeting.'

" 'Good day!' answered the pig, 'and the same to you.'

" 'Do you know,' said the sheep, 'why it is you are so

well off, and why it is they fatten you and take such pains
with you ? '

" ' No, I don't,' said the pig.

" ' Many a flask empties the cask ; I suppose you know
that,' said the sheep. ' They are going to kill and eat
you.'

" ' Are they ? ' said the pig ; ' well, I hope they'll say
grace after meat.'

" ' If you will do as I do,' said the sheep, ' we'll go off
to the wood, build us a house, and set up for ourselves.
A home is a home be it ever so homely.'

" Yes ! the pig was willing enough. ' Good company is
such a comfort,' he said, and so the two set off.

" So, when they had gone a bit they met a goose.

" ' Good day, good sirs, and thanks for our last merry
meeting,' said the goose ; ' whither away so fast to-day ? '

" ' Good day, and the same to you,' said the sheep ; ' you
must know we were too well off at home, and so we are
going to set up for ourselves in the wood, for you know
every man's house is his castle.'

" ' Well ! ' said the goose, ' it's much the same with me
where I am. Can't I go with you too, for it's child's play
when three share the day.'

" ' With gossip and gabble is built neither house nor
stable,' said the pig, ' let us know what you can do.'

" ' By cunning and skill a cripple can do what he will,'
said the goose. ' I can pluck moss and stuff it into the
seams of the planks, and your house will be tight and
warm.'

"Yes! they would give him leave, for, above all things piggy wished to be warm and comfortable.

"So, when they had gone a bit farther—the goose had hard work to walk so fast—they met a hare, who came frisking out of the wood.

"'Good day, good sirs, and thanks for our last merry meeting,' she said, 'how far are you trotting to-day?'

"'Good day, and the same to you,' said the sheep; 'we were far too well off at home, and so we're going to the wood, to build us a house, and set up for ourselves, for you know, try all the world round, there's nothing like home.'

"'As for that,' said the hare, 'I have a house in every bush—yes, a house in every bush; but, yet, I have often said, in winter, 'if I only live till summer, I'll build me a house;' and so I have half a mind to go with you and build one up, after all.'

"'Yes!' said the pig, 'if we ever get into a scrape, we might use you to scare away the dogs, for you don't fancy you could help us in house building.'

"'He who lives long enough always finds work enough to do,' said the hare. 'I have teeth to gnaw pegs, and paws to drive them into the wall, so I can very well set up to be a carpenter, for "good tools make good work," as the man said, when he flayed the mare with a gimlet.'

"Yes! he too got leave to go with them and build their house, there was nothing more to be said about it.

"When they had gone a bit farther they met a cock.

"'Good day, good sirs,' said the cock, 'and thanks for our last merry meeting; whither are ye going to-day, gentlemen?'

"'Good day, and the same to you,' said the sheep. 'At home we were too well off, and so we are going off to the wood to build us a house, and set up for ourselves; for he who out of doors shall bake, loses at last both coal and cake.'

"'Well!' said the cock, 'that's just my case; but it's better to sit on one's own perch, for then one can never be left in the lurch, and, besides, all cocks crow loudest at home. Now, if I might have leave to join such a gallant company, I also would like to go to the wood and build a house.'

"'Ay! ay!' said the pig, 'flapping and crowing sets tongues a-going; but a jaw on a stick never yet laid a brick. How can you ever help us to build a house?'

"'Oh!' said the cock, 'that house will never have a clock, where there is neither dog nor cock. I am up early, and I wake every one.'

"'Very true,' said the pig, 'the morning hour has a golden dower; let him come with us;' for, you must know, piggy was always the soundest sleeper. 'Sleep is the biggest thief,' he said; 'he thinks nothing of stealing half one's life.'

"So they all set off to the wood, as a band and brotherhood, and built the house. The pig hewed the timber, and the sheep drew it home; the hare was carpenter, and gnawed pegs and bolts, and hammered them into the walls and roof; the goose plucked moss and stuffed it into the seams; the cock crew, and looked out that they did not oversleep themselves in the morning; and when the house was ready, and the roof lined with birch bark, and thatched with turf; there they lived by themselves, and were merry and well. ' 'Tis good to travel east and west,' said the sheep, ' but after all a home is best.'

"But you must know that a bit farther on in the wood was a wolf's den, and there lived two graylegs. So when they saw that a new house had risen up hard by, they wanted to know what sort of folk their neighbours were, for they thought to themselves that a good neighbour was better than a brother in a foreign land, and that it was better to live in a good neighbourhood than to know many people miles and miles off.

"So one of them made up an errand, and went into the new house and asked for a light for his pipe. But as soon as ever he got inside the door, the sheep gave him such a butt that he fell head foremost into the stove. Then the pig began to gore and bite him, the goose to nip and peck him, the cock upon the roost to crow and chatter; and as for the hare he was so frightened out of his wits, that he ran about aloft and on the floor, and scratched and scrambled in every corner of the house.

" So after a long time the wolf came out.

" 'Well!' said the one who waited for him outside, ' neighbourhood makes brotherhood. You must have come into a perfect paradise on bare earth, since you stayed so long. But what became of the light, for you have neither pipe nor smoke.'

" 'Yes, yes !' said the other ; 'it was just a nice light and a pleasant company. Such manners I never saw in all my life. But then you know we can't pick and choose in this wicked world, and an unbidden guest gets bad treatment. As soon as I got inside the door, the shoe-maker let fly at me with his last, so that I fell head foremost into the stithy fire; and there sat two smiths who blew the bellows and made the sparks fly, and beat and punched me with red hot tongs and pincers, so that they tore whole pieces out of my body. As for the hunter he went scrambling about looking for his gun, and it was good luck he did not find it. And all the while there was another who sat up under the roof, and slapped his arms and sang out,

" 'Put a hook into him, and drag him hither, drag him hither.' That was what he screamed, and if he had only got hold of me, I should never have come out alive."

THE GOLDEN PALACE THAT HUNG
IN THE AIR.

"ONCE on a time there was a poor man who had three sons. When he died the two eldest were to go out into the world to try their luck; but as for the youngest they would not have him at any price.

"'As for you,' they said, 'you are fit for nothing but to sit and hold fir tapers, and grub in the ashes and blow up the embers. That's what you are fit for.'

"'Well, well,' said Boots, 'then I must e'en go alone by myself: at any rate I shan't fall out with my company.'

"So the two went their way, and when they had travelled some days they came to a great wood. There they sat down to rest, and were just going to take out a meal from their knapsack, for they were both tired and hungry. So as they sat there up came an old hag out of a hillock, and begged for a morsel of meat. She was so old and feeble that her nose and mouth met, and she nodded with her head, and could only walk with a stick. As for meat she had not had, she said, a morsel in her mouth these hundred years. But the lads only laughed at her, and ate on and told her as she had lived so long on nothing, she might very well hold out the rest of her life, even though she did not eat up their scanty fare, for they had little to eat and nothing to spare.

" So when they had eaten their fill and could eat no more, and were quite rested, they went on their way again, and, sooner or later, they came to the King's Grange, and there they each of them got a place.

" A while after they had started from home, Boots gathered together the crumbs which his brothers had thrown on one side, and put them into his little scrip, and he took with him the old gun which had no lock, for he thought it might be some good on the way; and so he set off. So when he had wandered some days, he too came into the big wood, through which his brothers had passed, and as he got tired and hungry, he sat down under a tree that he might rest and eat; but he had his eyes about him for all that, and as he opened his scrip he saw a picture hanging on a tree, and on it was painted the likeness of a young girl or princess, whom he thought so lovely he couldn't keep his eyes off her. So he forgot both food and scrip, and took down the painting and lay and stared at it. Just then came up the old hag out of the hillock, who hobbled along with her stick, whose nose and mouth met, and whose head nodded. Then she begged for a little food, for she hadn't had a morsel of bread in her mouth for a hundred years. That was what she said.

" ' Then it's high time you had a little to live on, granny,' said the lad; and with that he gave here some

of the crumbs he had. The old hag said **no one** had
ever called her 'granny' these hundred years, and she
would be as a mother **to him in** her turn. Then she
gave him a grey ball of wool, which he had only **to roll**
on before him and he would come to whatever **place he**
wished; but as for the **painting** she said he **mustn't**
bother himself about that, he would only fall into ill luck
if he did. As for Boots, he thought it was very kind of
her **to say that,** but he could not bear to be without the
painting, so he took it under his arm and rolled the ball
of wool before him, **and it was** not long before he came
to the King's Grange, where his brothers **served.** There
he too begged for a place, but all the answer he got was
they had nothing to put him to, for they had just got
two new serving men. But as he begged so prettily, at
last he got leave to be with the coachman, and learn
how to groom and handle horses. That he was right glad
to do, for he was fond of horses, and he was both quick
and ready, so that he soon learnt how to bed and rub
them down, and it was not long before every one in the
King's Grange was fond of him; but every hour he had
to himself he was up in the loft looking at the picture,
for he had hung it up in a corner of the hay-loft.

"As for his brothers, they were dull and lazy, and so
they often got scolding and stripes, and when they saw
that Boots fared better than they, they got jealous of
him, and told the coachman he was a worshipper of false
gods, for he prayed to a picture and not to Our Lord.
Now, even though the coachman thought well of the lad,

still he wasn't long before he told the king what he had heard. But the king only swore and snapped at him, for he had grown very sad and sorrowful since his daughters had been carried off by trolls. But they so dinned it into the king's ears, that at last he must and would know what it was that the lad did. But when he went up into the hay-loft and set his eyes on the picture, he saw it was his youngest daughter who was painted on it. But when the brothers of Boots heard that, they were ready with an answer, and said to the coachman,

"'If our brother only would, he has said he was good to get the king's daughter back.'

"You may fancy it was not long before the coachman went to the king with this story, and when the king heard it, he called for Boots, and said,

"'Your brothers say you can bring back my daughter again, and now you must do it.'

"Boots answered, he had never known it was the king's daughter till the king said so himself, and if he could free her and fetch her he would be sure to do his best; but two days he must have to think over it and fit himself out. Yes, he might have two days.

"So Boots took the grey ball of wool and threw it down on the road, and it rolled and rolled before him, and he followed it till he came to the old hag, from whom he had got it. Her he asked what he must do, and she said he must take with him that old gun of his and three hundred chests of nails and horseshoe brads, and three hundred barrels of barley, and three hundred barrels of grits, and three hundred carcases of pigs, and three hundred beeves, and then he was to roll the ball of wool before him till he met a raven and a baby troll, and then he would be all right, for they were both of her stock.   Yes, the lad did as she bade him; he went right on to the King's Grange, and took his old gun with him, and he asked the king for the nails and the brads, and meat and flesh, and grain, and for horses and men, and carts to carry them in.   The king thought it was a good deal to ask, but if he could only get his daughter back, he might have whatever he chose, even to the half of his kingdom.

" So when the lad had fitted himself out, he rolled the ball of wool before him again, and he hadn't gone many days before he came to a high hill, and there sat a raven, up in a fir tree.   So Boots went on till he came close under the tree, and then he began to aim and point at the raven with his gun.

" ' No, no,' cried the raven, ' don't shoot me, don't shoot me, and I'll help you.'

" ' Well,' said Boots, ' I never heard of anyone who boasted he had eaten roast raven, and since you are so eager to save your life, I may just as well spare it.'

" So he threw down his gun, and the raven came flying down to him, and said,

" ' Here, up on this fell there is a baby troll walking up and down, for he has lost his way and can't get down again.   I will help you up, and then you can lead him home, and ask a boon which will stand you in good stead.   When you get to the troll's house he will offer you all the grandest things he has, but you should not heed them a pin.   Mind you take nothing else but the little grey ass which stands behind the stable door.'

"Then the raven took Boots on his back and flew up on the hill with him, and put him off there.   When he had gone about on it a bit, he heard the baby troll howling and whining, because it couldn't get down again.   So the lad talked kindly to it, and they got the best friends in the world, and he said he would help it down and guide it to the old troll's house, that it mightn't lose itself on the way back.   Then they went to the raven, and he took them both on his back, and carried them off the hill troll's house.

"And when the old troll saw his baby, he was so glad he was beside himself, and told Boots he might come in-doors and take whatever he chose, because he had freed his child.   Then they offered him both gold and silver, and all that was rare and costly; but the lad said he would rather have a horse than anything else.   Yes, he should have a horse, the troll said, and off they went to the stable.   It was full of the grandest horses, whose coats shone like the sun and moon; but Boots thought they were all too big for him.   So he peeped behind the stable door, and when he set eyes on the little grey ass that stood there, he said,

" ' I'll take this one.   It will suit me to a T, and if I fall off I shall be no farther from the ground than that —— high.'

" The old troll did not at all like to part with his ass, but as he had given his word he had to stand by it. So Boots got the ass, and saddle, and bridle, and all that belonged to it, and then he set off. They travelled through wood and field, and over fells and wide wastes. So when they had gone farther than far, the ass asked Boots if he saw anything.

" 'No, I see naught else than a hill, which looks blue in the distance,' said Boots.

" 'Oh,' said the ass, 'that hill we have to pass through.'

" 'All very fine, I daresay,' said Boots, for he didn't believe a word of it.

" So when they got close to the hill, an unicorn came tearing along at them, just as if he were going to eat them up all alive.

" ' I almost think now I'm afraid,' said Boots.

" ' Oh,' said the ass, 'don't say so ; just throw it a score or so of beeves, and beg it to bore a hole, and break a way for us through the hill.'

" So Boots did as he was told, and when the unicorn had eaten his fill, they said they would give him a score or two of pigs' carcasses, if he would go before them and bore a hole in the hill, so that they might get through it. So when he heard that he set to work and bored the hole, and broke a way so fast that they had hard work to keep up with him, and when he had done his work they threw him two score of pigs.

" So when they had got well out of that they travelled

far away, until they passed again through woods and fields, and across fells and wide wastes.

"'Do you see anything now?' asked the ass.

"'Now I see naught but the bare sky and wild fells,' said Boots.

"So they travelled on far and farther than far, and the higher up they came the fell got smoother and flatter, so that they could see farther about them.

"'Do you see anything now?' said the ass.

"'Yes, I see something far, far away,' said Boots, 'and it gleams and twinkles like a little star.'

"'It's not so very little for all that,' said the ass.

"So when they had gone on farther and farther than far again, the ass asked again,

"'Do you see anything now?'

"'Yes,' said Boots, 'I see something a long way off, that shines like a moon.'

"'It is no moon,' said the ass, 'but the silver castle we are bound for. Now, when we get there you will see three dragons lying on the watch before the gate. They have not been awakened for hundreds of years, and so the moss has grown over their eyes.'

"'I almost think I shall be afraid of them,' said Boots.

"'Oh, don't say that,' said the ass, 'you've only got to wake up the youngest, and throw it a score or so of beeves and swine, and then it will talk to the others, and so you'll come into the castle.'

"So on they travelled far and farther than far again before they came up to the castle, but when they reached it

it was both grand and great, and everything they saw was
cast in silver, and outside the gate lay the dragons, and
blocked up the way so that no one could get in; but
they had a nice easy time of it, and had not been much
troubled in their watch; for they were so overgrown
with moss that no one could tell what they were made of,
and at their sides underwood was springing up between
the tufts of moss. So Boots woke up the youngest of
them, and it began to rub its eyes and clear the moss
out of them. But when the dragon saw there was foik
there, he came at them with his maw wide agape; but
then the lad stood ready, and tossed into it the carcasses
of beeves, and swung after them salted swine, till the
dragon had got his fill, and grew a little more sensible
to talk to. Then the lad begged he would wake up his
fellows, and ask them to be so good as to get out of the
way, so that he might get into the castle; but the dragon
neither would nor dared to do that at first, for he said,
as they had not been awake or tasted anything for hundreds
of years, he was afraid lest they should get raving mad,
and swallow up everything alive or dead.

"But Boots thought there was no need to fear that, for
they could leave behind them a hundred carcasses of
beeves, and a hundred salt swine, and go a little way off
and then the dragons would have time to eat their fill,
and to come to themselves before the others came back
to the castle.

"Yes, the dragon was ready to do that, and so they
did it; but before the dragons were well awake, and got

the moss rubbed off their eyes, they went about roaring and raving, and riving and rending at everything alive or dead, so that the youngest dragon had enough to do to shield himself from them till they had snuffed up the smell of flesh. Then they swallowed down whole oxen and swine, and ate and ate till they were full. And after that they were just as tame and buxom as the youngest, and let Boots pass between them into the castle.

"When he got inside it was all so grand he never could have thought anything could be so good anywhere; but there was not a soul in it, for he went from room to room, and opened all the doors, but he could see no one. Well, at last he peeped through a door that led to a bed-room, which he had not seen before, and in there sat a princess, spinning, and she was so glad and happy when she saw him.

" ' No, no,' she cried, ' can it be that Christian folk dare to come hither ? but it will be best for you to be off again, else the troll might kill you, for you must know a troll lives with three heads.'

" But Boots said he would not fly even if he had seven heads. When the princess heard that, she said she wished him to try if he could brandish the great rusty sword that hung behind the door. No, he could not brandish it, he could not so much as even lift it.

" ' Ah,' said the princess, ' if you can't do that you must take a drink of that flask yonder, that hangs by the side of the sword, for that's what the troll does when he goes out to use it.'

" So Boots took two or three drinks, and then he could brandish the sword as though it were a rolling pin.

" Just then came the troll, so that the wind sung after him.

" ' Hu!' he screeched out, ' what a smell of Christian blood there is in here.'

" ' I know there is,' said Boots, ' but you needn't blow and snort so at it; you shan't suffer long from that smell,' and in a trice he cut off all his heads.

" The princess was so glad, just as if she had got something so good; but in a little while she got heavy-hearted, for she pined for her sister, who had been stolen by a troll with six heads, and lived in a golden castle three hundred miles on this side of the world's end.   Boots thought that was not so very bad, for he could go and fetch both the princess and the castle; and so he took the sword and the flask, and got on the ass, and bade the dragons follow him, and carry the meat, and grain, and nails which he had.

" So when they had been a while on the way, and had travelled far, far away over land and strand, the ass said one day,

" ' Do you see anything ? '

" ' I see naught,' said Boots, ' but land and water and bare sky and high crags.'

" So they went on far and farther than far, and then the ass said again,

" ' Do you see anything now ? '

" ' Yes,' when he had looked well before him, he saw

something a long, long way off, that shone like a little star.

"'It will be big enough by-and-by,' said the ass.

"When they had gone a good bit still, the ass asked,

"'Do you see anything now?'

"'Now I see it shining like a moon,' said the lad.

"'Ay, ay,' said the ass, and on they went.

"So when they had gone far, and farther than far away, over land and strand, and hill and heath, the ass asked,

"'Do you see anything now?'

"'Now, methinks,' said Boots, 'it shines most like the sun.'

"'Ay,' said the ass, 'that's the golden castle for which we are bound; but outside it lives a worm, which stops the way and keeps watch and ward.'

"'I think I shall be afraid of it,' said Boots.

"'Oh, don't say so,' said the ass, 'we must spread over it heaps of boughs, and lay between them layers of horse-shoe brads and nails, and set fire to them all, and so we shall be rid of it.'

"So after a long, long time they came up to where the castle hung in the air, but the worm lay underneath it and stopped the way. So the lad gave the dragons a good meal of beeves and salted swine, that they might help him, and they spread over the worm heaps of boughs and wood, and laid between them layers of nails and brads, till they had used up the three hundred chests, and when it was all done they set fire to the pile and burned up the worm alive, in a fire at white heat.

" So when they had done with him one dragon flew under the castle and lifted it up, and the two others went up high, high into the air, and unloosed the links and hooks by which it hung, and so they lowered it down and set it on the ground. When that was done Boots went inside, and there it was grander far than in the silvern castle, but he could see no folk till he came to the innermost room, and there lay a princess on a bed of gold. She slept so sound, as though she were dead, but she was not, though he was not able to wake her up, for her face was as red and white as milk and blood. And just as Boots stood there gazing at her, back came the troll tearing along. As soon as he put his first head through the door he screamed out,

" ' Hu ! what a smell of Christian blood there is in here.'

" ' Maybe,' said Boots, ' but you've no need to smell and snort about that ; you shan't suffer long from it.'

" And with that he cut off all his heads, as though they stood on a kail stalk.

" So the dragons took the golden castle on their backs and went home with it—I fancy they were not long on the way—and set it down side by side with the silvern castle, so that it shone both far and wide.

" Now when the princess of the silvern castle came to her window in the morning, and caught sight of it, she was so glad that she sprang over to the golden castle at once ; but when she saw her sister lying there and sleeping as though she were dead, she said to Boots that they would never get life into her before they found the water of life and death, and that stood in two wells on either side of a golden castle which hung in the air, nine hundred miles beyond the world's end, and where the third sister dwelt.

" Well, Boots thought there was no help for it; he must go and fetch it, and it was not long before he was on his way. So he travelled far and farther than far, through many realms, across wood and field, over fell and firth, along hill and heath, and at last he got to the world's end, and after that he travelled far, far over crags and wastes and high rocks.

" ' Do you see anything ?' asked the ass one day.

" ' I see naught but heaven and earth,' said the lad.

" ' Do you see anything now ?' asked the ass again, when some days were past.

" ' Yes,' said Boots, ' now I see something that glimmers very high up, far, far away, like a little star.'

" ' It's not so little for all that,' said the ass.

" So when they had travelled on a while, the ass asked,

" ' Do you see anything now ?'

" ' Yes,' said Boots, ' now it shines like the sun.'

" ' That's whither we are bound,' said the ass; ' it's the golden castle that hangs in the air, and there lives a princess who has been stolen by a troll with nine heads; but all the wild beasts there are in the world lie on watch, and stop the way thither.'

" ' Uf,' said Boots, ' I almost think I'm afraid of them.'

" ' Don't say so,' said the ass; and then he told him there was no danger, if he would only make up his mind not to linger there, but to set off on his way back as soon as ever he had filled his flasks with the water, for there was no going thither but during one hour in the day, and that began at high noon; but if he were not man enough to be ready in time and to get away, the beasts would tear him into a thousand pieces.

" Well, Boots said he would be sure to do that, he would not think of staying too long.

" At the stroke of twelve they reached the castle, and there lay all the wild and savage beasts that ever were, as it were a fence before the gate, and on either side of the way. But they all slumbered like stocks and stones, and there wasn't one of them that so much as lifted a paw. So Boots passed between them, and took good heed not to tread on their toes or the tips of their tails, and he filled his flasks with the waters of life and death, and while he did that he looked up at the castle, which was as though it were cast in pure gold. It was the grandest he had ever seen, and he thought it would be grander still inside than out.

" ' Stuff,' thought Boots, ' I have time enough, I can always look about me in half an hour,' and so he opened the door and went in. Well, inside it was grander than grand itself, and as he went out of one gorgeous room into another, it was as if it was all made of gold and pearls, and everything that was costliest in the world. Folk there were none; but at last he came into a bedroom where there lay another princess on a bed of gold, just as though she were dead too, but she was as grand as the grandest queen, and as red and white as blood on snow, and so lovely he had never seen anything so lovely but her picture ; for she it was that was painted on it.

" Then Boots forgot both the water he was to fetch, and the wild beasts, and the castle and everything, and could only gaze at the princess ; and he thought he could never have his fill of looking at her ; but all the while she slept as though she were dead, and he was not able to wake her up.

" So when it drew towards evening, the troll came tearing along so that the wind sung after him, and he rattled and slammed the gates and doors till the whole castle rang again.

" ' Huf,' he cried ; ' what a strong smell of Christian blood there is in here ; ' and then he stuck his first head inside the door and snuffed up the air.

" ' I daresay there is,' said Boots, ' but you've no need to puff and blow as though you were about to burst, for it shan't vex you long ; ' and as he said that he cut off all his nine heads. But when he had done that he got so weary he couldn't keep his eyes open. So he laid him down on the bed by the side of the princess, and all the while she slept both night and day, as though she would never wake again ; only at midnight she just woke up for the twinkling of an eye, and then she told him that he had set her free, but she must bide there three years still, and if she didn't come home to him then he must just come and fetch her.

" When the clock began to go towards one next day,

Boots woke for the first time, and the first thing he heard was the ass braying and screaming and making a stir, and so he thought he would get up and set off home, but before he went he cut a breadth out of the princess's skirt, and took it away with him.   And however it was, he had loitered so long there that the beasts began to wake and stir, and by the time he had mounted his ass they stood in a ring round him, so that he thought it had rather a ghastly look.   But the ass said he must sprinkle on them a few drops of the water of death, and he did so, and in a trice they all fell headlong on the spot, and never stirred a limb more.

"As they were on their way home, the ass said to Boots,—

"'Now when you come to honour and glory, see if you don't forget me and all I have done for you, so that I shall be broken-kneed for hunger.'

"'Nay, nay! that should never be,' said the lad.

"So when he got home to the princess with the water of life, she sprinkled a few drops over her sister, and woke her up, and then there was such great joy and they were so happy.   Then they travelled home to the king, and he too was glad and joyful, because he had got those two back; but still he went about longing and longing that the three years might pass away, and his youngest daughter come home.

"As for Boots, who had brought them back, the king made him a mighty man, so that he was the first in the land after the king himself. But there were many who were jealous that he should have grown to be such a man of mark, and one of them was Ritter Red, who they did say wished to have the eldest princess, and he got her to sprinkle over Boots a little of the water of death, so that he swooned off and lay as dead.

" So when the three years were over, and a bit of the fourth was gone, there came sailing up a strange ship of war, 'and on board was the third sister, and with her she had a boy three years old. She sent word up to the King's Grange, and said she would not set her foot on land till they had sent him who had been in the golden castle and set her free. So they sent down to her one of the highest men about the court, the master of the ceremonies himself; and when he came on board the princess' ship, he took off his hat and bowed and scraped, and bent himself before her.

" ' Can that be your father ? my son,' said the princess to her boy, who was playing with a golden apple.

" ' No,' said the child, ' my father doesn't crawl about like a cheesemite.'

" So they sent another of the same stamp, and this time it was Ritter Red. But it fared no better with him than with the first one, and the princess sent word by him, if they didn't make haste and send the right one, it should go ill with them. When they heard that they were forced to wake up Boots with the water of life ; and so he went down to the ship to the princess, but he didn't make too low a bow, I should think ; he only nodded his head and brought out the breadth he had cut out of the skirt of the princess in the golden castle.

" ' That's my father! that's my father!' bawled out the boy, and gave him the golden apple he was playing with.

" Then there was great joy and mirth all over the realm, and the old king was the gladdest of all of them, because he had got his darling back again. But when what Ritter Red and the eldest princess had done to Boots came out, the king asked to have them both rolled down a hill, each in a cask full of spikes and nails; but Boots and the youngest princess begged hard for them, and so they got off with life.

" Now it happened one day, as they were about to begin the bridal feast, that they stood looking out of window,—it was towards spring, just when they were turning out the horses and cows after the winter—and the last that came out of the stable was the ass; but it was so starved that it came out of the stable-door on its knees.

" Then Boots was cut to the heart because he had forgotten it, and he went down and did not know how to make it up to the poor beast. But the ass said the best thing he could do was to cut his head off. That he was very loath to do, but the ass begged so prettily that he had to yield, and did it at last; and as soon as ever his head fell in the yard, it was all over with the shape which had been thrown over him by witchcraft, and there stood the handsomest prince any one cared to see. He got the second princess to wife, and they fell to keeping the bridal feast, so that it was heard and talked of over seven kingdoms.

> ' Then they built themselves houses,
>   And stitched themselves shoon,
>   And had so many bairns
>   They reached up to the moon.' "

LITTLE FREDDY WITH HIS FIDDLE.

"ONCE on a time there was a cottager who had an only son, and this lad was weakly, and hadn't much health to speak of; so he couldn't go out to work in the field.

"His name was Freddy, and undersized he was, too; and so they called him Little Freddy. At home there was little either to bite or sup, and so his father went about the country trying to bind him over as a cowherd or an errand-boy; but there was no one who would take his son till he came to the sheriff, and he was ready to take him, for he had just packed off his errand-boy, and there was no one who would fill his place, for the story went that he was a skinflint.

"But the cottager thought it was better there than nowhere: he would get his food, for all the pay he was to get was his board—there was nothing said about wages or clothes. So when the lad had served three years he wanted to leave, and then the sheriff gave him all his wages at one time. He was to have a penny a year. 'It couldn't well be less,' said the sheriff. And so he got threepence in all.

"As for little Freddy, he thought it was a great sum, for he had never owned so much; but for all that he asked if he wasn't to have something more.

"'You have already had more than you ought to have,' said the sheriff.

"'Sha'n't I have anything, then, for clothes?' asked little Freddy; 'for those I had on when I came here are worn to rags, and I have had no new ones.'

"And, to tell the truth, he was so ragged that the tatters hung and flapped about him.

"'When you have got what we agreed on,' said the sheriff, 'and three whole pennies beside, I have nothing more to do with you. Be off!'

"But for all that he got leave just to go into the kitchen and get a little food to put in his scrip; and after that he set off on the road to buy himself more clothes. He was both merry and glad, for he had never seen a penny before; and every now and then he felt in his pockets as he went along to see if he had them all three. So when he had gone far, and farther than far, he got into a narrow dale, with high fells on all sides, so that he couldn't tell if there were any way to pass out; and he began to wonder what there could be on the other side of those fells, and how he ever should get over them.

"But up and up he had to go, and on he strode; he was not strong on his legs, and had to rest every now and then—and then he counted and counted how many pennies he had got. So when he had got quite up to the very top, there was nothing but a great plain overgrown with moss. There he sat him down, and began to see if his money were all right; and before he was aware of him a beggarman came up to him—and he was so tall and big that the lad began to scream and screech when he got a good look of him, and saw his height and length.

"'Don't you be afraid,' said the beggarman, 'I'll do you no harm; I only beg for a penny, in God's name.'

"'Heaven help me!' said the lad. 'I have only three pennies, and with them I was going to the town to buy clothes.'

"'It is worse for me than for you,' said the beggarman. 'I have got no penny, and I am still more ragged than you.'

"'Well! then you shall have it,' said the lad.

"So when he had walked on awhile he got weary, and sat down to rest again. But when he looked up there he saw another beggarman, and he was still taller and uglier than the first; and so when the lad saw how very tall and ugly and long he was he fell a-screeching.

"'Now, don't you be afraid of me,' said the beggar; 'I'll not do you any harm. I only beg for a penny, in God's name.'

"'Now, may heaven help me!' said the lad. 'I've only got two pence, and with them I was going to the town to buy clothes. If I had only met you sooner, then——'

"'It's worse for me than for you,' said the beggarman. I have no penny, and a bigger body and less clothing.'

"'Well, you may have it,' said the lad.

"So he went awhile farther, till he got weary, and then he sat down to rest; but he had scarce sat down than a third beggarman came to him. He was so tall and ugly and long, that the lad had to look up and up, right up to the sky. And when he took him all in with his eyes, and saw how very, very tall and ugly and ragged he was he fell a-screeching and screaming again.

"'Now, don't you be afraid of me, my lad,' said the beggarman. 'I'll do you no harm; for I am only a beggarman, who begs for a penny in God's name.'

"'May heaven help me!' said the lad. 'I have only one penny left, and with it I was going to the town to buy clothes. If I had only met you sooner, then——'

"'As for that,' said the beggarman, 'I have no penny at all—that I haven't, and a bigger body and less clothes, so it is worse for me than for you.'

"'Yes!' said little Freddy, he must have the penny then—there was no help for it; for so each would have what belonged to him, and he would have nothing.

"'Well!' said the beggarman, 'since you have such a good heart that you gave away all that you had in the world, I will give you a wish for each penny.' For you must know it was the same beggarman who had got them all three; he had only changed his shape each time, that the lad might not know him again.

"'I have always had such a longing to hear a fiddle go,

and see folk so glad and merry that they couldn't help dancing,' said the lad; and so, if I may wish what I choose, I will wish myself such a fiddle, that everything that has life must dance to its tune.'

" 'That he might have,' said the beggarman; but it was a sorry wish. 'You must wish something better for the other two pennies.'

" ' I have always had such a love for hunting and shooting,' said little Freddy; 'so if I may wish what I choose, I will wish myself such a gun that I shall hit everything I aim at, were it ever so far off.'

" ' That he might have,' said the beggarman; 'but it was a sorry wish. You must wish better for the last penny.'

" ' I have always had a longing to be in company with folk who were kind and good,' said little Freddy; and so, if I could get what I wish, I would wish it to be so that no one can say ' Nay ' to the first thing I ask.'

" 'That wish was not so sorry,' said the beggarman; and off he strode between the hills, and he saw him no more. And so the lad laid down to sleep, and the next day he came down from the fell with his fiddle and his gun.

" First he went to the storekeeper and asked for clothes, and at one farm he asked for a horse, and at another for a sledge; and at this place he asked for a fur-coat, and no one said him ' Nay,'—even the stingiest folk, they were all forced to give him what he asked for. At last he went through the country as a fine gentleman, and had his horse and his sledge; and so when he had gone a bit he met the sheriff with whom he had served.

"'Good-day, master,' said Little Freddy, as he pulled up and took off his hat.

"'Good-day,' said the sheriff. And then he went on, 'When was I ever your master?'

"'Oh, yes!' said little Freddy. 'Don't you remember how I served you three years for three pence?'

"'Heaven help us!' said the sheriff. 'How you have got on all of a hurry! And pray how was it that you got to be such a fine gentleman?'

"'Oh, that's tellings!' said little Freddy.

"'And are you full of fun, that you carry a fiddle about with you?' asked the sheriff.

"'Yes! yes!' said Freddy. 'I have always had such a longing to get folk to dance; but the funniest thing of all is this gun, for it brings down almost anything that I aim at, however far it may be off. Do you see that magpie yonder, sitting in the spruce fir? What'll you bet I don't bag it, as we stand here?'

"On that the sheriff was ready to stake horse and groom, and a hundred dollars beside, that he couldn't do it; but, as it was, he would bet all the money he had about him; and he would go to fetch it when it fell—for he never thought it possible for any gun to carry so far.

"But as the gun went off down fell the magpie, and into a great bramble thicket; and away went the sheriff up into the brambles after it, and he picked it up and showed it to the lad. But in a trice Little Freddy began to scrape his fiddle, and the sheriff began to dance, and the thorns to tear him; but still the lad **played** on, and the sheriff danced, and cried, and begged till **his clothes** flew to tatters, and he scarce had a thread to his back.

"' Yes!''said Little Freddy; 'now I think you're about as ragged as I was when I left your service. So now **you** may get off with **what** you have got.'

"But, first of all, the sheriff had **to pay him** what he had wagered that **he** could not hit **the** magpie.

"So when the lad came to the town he turned aside into an inn, **and** he began to play, and all who **came** danced, and he lived merrily and well. He **had no care,** for **no** one could say him 'Nay' to anything he asked.

"But just as they were all in the midst of their fun **up** came the watchmen to drag the lad off to the town-hall : for the sheriff had laid a charge against him, and said he had **waylaid** him **and robbed him,** and nearly taken his life. And now he was to be hanged—they would not hear of anything else. But Little Freddy had a cure for **all trouble, and that was his fiddle. He** began to play on it, and the watchmen fell a-dancing, till **they** lay down and gasped for breath.

"So they sent soldiers and the guard on their way; but it was no better with them than with the watchmen. As **soon** as ever Little Freddy scraped his fiddle, they were **all bound** to dance, so long as he could lift a finger to play a tune; but **they** were half dead long before he was tired. At last **they stole a** march on him, and took him while he lay asleep by night; and when they had caught him he was doomed to be hanged on the spot, and away they hurried him to the gallows-tree.

"There a great crowd of people flocked together to see this wonder, and the sheriff, he, too, was there; and he was so glad at last at getting amends for the money and the skin he had lost, and that he might see him hanged with his own eyes. But they did not get him to the gallows very fast, for little Freddy was always weak on his legs, and now he made himself weaker still. His fiddle and his gun he had with him also—it was hard to part him from them; and so, when he came to the gallows, and had to mount the steps, he halted on each step; and when he got to the top he sat down, and asked if they could deny him a wish, and if he might have leave to do one thing? He had such a longing, he said to scrape a tune and play a bar on his fiddle before they hanged him.

"'No! no!' they said. 'It were sin and shame to deny him that.' For, you know, no one could gainsay what he asked.

"But the sheriff he begged them, for God's sake, not to let him have leave to touch a string, else it was all over with them altogether; and if the lad got leave, he begged them to bind him to the birch that stood there.

"So little Freddy was not slow in getting his fiddle to speak, and all that were there fell a-dancing at once—those who went on two legs, and those who went on four; both the dean and the parson, and the lawyer, and the bailiff, and the sheriff; masters and men, dogs and swine, they all danced and laughed and screeched at one another. Some danced till they lay for dead; some danced till they fell into a swoon. It went badly with all of them, but worst of all with the sheriff, for there he stood bound to the birch, and he danced and scraped great bits off his back against the trunk. There was not one of them who thought of doing anything to little Freddy, and away he went with his fiddle and his gun, just as he chose; and he lived merrily and happily all his days, for there was no one who could say him 'Nay' to the first thing he asked for." .

"ONCE on a time there was a goody who had a son, and he was so lazy and slow he would never turn his hand to anything that was useful; but singing and dancing he was very fond of, and so he danced and sang as long as it was day, and sometimes even some way on in the night. The longer this lasted the harder it was for the goody, the boy grew, and meat he must have without stint, and more and more was spent in clothing as he grew bigger and bigger, and it was soon worn out, I should think; for he danced and sprang about both in wood and field.

" At last the goody thought it too bad ; so she told the lad that now he must begin to turn his hand to work, and live steadily, or else there was nothing before both of them but starving to death. But that the lad had no mind to do; he said he would far rather woo Mother Roundabout's daughter, for if he could only get her he would be able to live well and good all his days, and sing and dance and never do one stroke of work.

" When his mother heard that, she too thought it would be a very fine thing, and so she fitted out the lad as well as she could that he might look tidy when he got to Mother Roundabout's house, and so he set off on his way.

"Now when he got out of doors the sun shone warm and bright; but it had rained the night before, so that the ways were soft and miry, and all the bog-holes stood full of water. The lad took a short cut to Mother Roundabout, and he sang and jumped, as was ever his wont, but just as he sprang and leapt he got to a bog-hole, and over it lay a little bridge, and from the bridge he had to make a spring across a hole on to a tuft of grass, that he might not dirty his shoes. But '*plump*,' it said all at once, and just as he put his foot on the tuft it gave way under him, and there was no stopping till he found himself in a nasty deep dark hole. At first he could see nothing, but when he had been there a while he had a glimpse of a rat which came wiggle-waggle up to him with a bunch of keys at the tip of her tail.

"'What, you here, my boy?" said the rat. 'Thank you kindly for coming to me. I have waited long for you· You come, of course, to woo me, and you are eager at it, I can very well see; but you must have patience yet awhile, for I shall have a great dower, and I am not ready for my wedding just yet, but I'll do my best that it shall be as soon as ever I can.'

"When she had said that she brought out ever so many eggshells with all sorts of bits and scraps, such as rats are wont to eat, and set them before him, and said,

"'Now, you must sit down and eat; I am sure you must be both tired and hungry.'

" But the lad thought he had no liking for such food.

" ' If I were only well away from this, above ground again,' he thought to himself, but he said nothing out loud.

" ' Now, I daresay, you'ld be glad to go home again,' said the rat. ' I know your heart is set on this wedding, and I'll make all the haste I can, and you must take with you this linen thread, and when you get up above you must not look round, but go straight home, and on the way you must mind and say nothing but

> ' Short before, and long back,
> Short before, and long back ;'

and as she said this she put the linen thread into his hand.

" ' Heaven be praised !' said the lad, when he got above ground.   ' Thither I'll never come again, if I can help it.'

" But he still had the thread in his hand, and he sprang and sang as he was wont ; but even though he thought no more of the rat-hole, he had got his tongue into the tune, and so he sang,

> ' Short before, and long back,
> Short before, and long back ;'

" So when he got back home into the porch he turned round, and there lay many many hundred ells of the whitest linen, so fine that the handiest weaving girl could not have woven it finer.

" ' Mother ! mother ! come out,' he cried and roared.

Out came the goody in a bustle, and asked what ever was the matter; but when she saw the linen woof, which stretched as far back as she could see and a bit beside, she couldn't believe her eyes, till the lad told her how it had all happened. And when she had heard it and tried the woof between her fingers, she got so glad that she too began to dance and sing.

"So she took the linen and cut it out, and sewed shirts out of it both for herself and her son, and the rest she took into the town and sold, and got money for it. And now they both lived well and happily a while; but when the money was all gone the goody had no more food in the house, and so she told her son he really must now begin to go to work, and live like the rest of the world, else there was nothing for it but starving for them both.

" But the lad had more mind to go to Mother Round-about and woo her daughter. Well, the goody thought that a very fine thing, for now he had good clothes on his back, and he was not such a bad looking fellow either. So she made him smart and fitted him out as well as she could, and he took out his new shoes and brushed them till they were as bright as glass, and when he had done that off he went.

" But all happened just as it did before. When he got out of doors the sun shone warm and bright, but it had rained over night, so that it was soft and miry, and all the bog-holes were full of water. The lad took the short cut to Mother Roundabout, and he sang and sprang as he was ever wont. Now he took another way than the one he went before, but just as he leaped and jumped he got upon the bridge over the moor again, and from it he had to jump over a bog-hole on to a tuft that he might not dirty his shoes. But *plump* it went, and down it went under him, and there was no stopping till he found himself in a nasty deep dark hole. At first he could see nothing, but when he had been there a while he got a glimpse of a rat with a bunch of keys at the tip of her tail, who came wiggle-waggle up to him.

"'What, you here, my boy?' said the rat. 'That was nice of you to wish to see me so soon again. You are very eager, that I can see; but you really must wait a while, for there is still something wanting to my dower, but the next time you come it shall be all right.'

"When she had said this she set before him all kinds of scraps and bits in eggshells, such as rats eat and like; but the lad thought it all looked like meat that had been already eaten once, and he wasn't hungry, he said; and all the time he thought, 'If I could only once get above ground, well out of this hole.' But he said nothing out loud.

"So after a while the rat said,

"I dare say now you would be glad to get home again; but I'll hasten on the wedding as fast as ever I can. And now you must take with you this thread of wool, and when you come above ground you must not look round, but go straight home, and all the way you must mind and say nothing than

  'Short before, and long back,
   Short before, and long back;'

and as she said that she gave him a thread of wool into his hand.

"'Heaven be praised!' said the lad, 'that I got away. Thither I'll never go again if I can help it;' and so he sang and jumped as he was wont. As for the rat-hole he thought no more about it, but as he had got his tongue into tune and he sang,

> 'Short before, and long back,
> Short before, and long back;'

so he kept on the whole way home.

"So when he had got into the yard at home again he turned and looked behind him, and there lay the finest cloth more than many hundred ells; ay! almost above half a mile long, and so fine that no town dandy could have had finer cloth to his coat.

"'Mother! mother! come out,' bawled the lad.

"So the goody came out of doors, and clapped her hands, and was almost ready to swoon for joy when she saw all that lovely cloth, and then he had to tell her how he had got it, and how it had all happened from first to last. Then they had a fine time of it, you may fancy. The lad got new clothes of the finest sort, and the goody went off to the town and sold the cloth by little and little, and made heaps of money. Then she decked out her cottage and got so smart in her old days as though she had been a born lady. So they lived well and happily, but at last that money came to an end too, and so the day came when the goody had no more food in the house, and then she told her son, he really must turn his hand to work, and live like the rest of the world, else there was nothing but starving staring both of them in the face.

"But the lad thought it far better to go to Mother Round-about and woo her daughter. This time the goody thought so too, and said not a word against it, for now he had new clothes of the finest kind, and he looked so well she thought it quite out of the question that any one could say, 'No!' to so smart a lad. So she smartened him up, and made him as tidy as she could, and he himself brought out his new shoes and rubbed them till they shone so he could see his face in them, and when he had done that off he went.

"This time he did not take the short cut, but made a great bend, for down to the rats he would not go if he could help it, he was so tired of all that wiggle-waggle and that everlasting bridal gossip. As for the weather and the ways they were just as they had been twice before. The sun shone, so that it was dazzling on the pools and bog-holes, and the lad sang and sprang as he was wont; but just as he sang and jumped, before he knew where he was, he was on the very same bridge across the bog again. So he was to jump from the bridge over a bog-hole on to a tuft, that he might not dirty his bright shoes. '*Plump*,' it said, and it gave way with him, and there was no stopping till he was down in the same nasty deep dark hole again. At first he was glad, for he could see nothing, but when he had been there a while he had a glimpse of the ugly rat, and he was so loath to see her with the bunch of keys at the end of her tail.

" ' Good day, my boy!' said the rat. 'You shall be heartily welcome again, for I see you can't bear to be any longer without me. Thank you, thank you kindly; but now everything is ready for the wedding, and we shall set off to church at once.'

" ' Something dreadful is going to happen,' thought the lad, but he said nothing out loud.

" Then the rat whistled, and there came swarming out such a lot of small rats and mice out of all the holes and crannies, and six big rats came harnessed to a frying-pan; two mice got up behind as footmen, and two got up before and drove; some, too, got into the pan, and the rat with the bunch of keys at her tail took her seat among them. Then she said to the lad,

" ' The road is a little narrow here, so you must be good enough to walk by the side of the carriage, my darling boy, till it gets broader, and then you shall have leave to sit up in the carriage alongside of me.'

" ' Very fine that will be, I dare say,' thought the lad. ' If I were only well above ground, I'd run away from the whole pack of you.' That was what he thought, but he said nothing out loud!

" So he followed them as well as he could; sometimes he had to creep on all fours, and sometimes he had to stoop and bend his back well, for the road was low and narrow in places; but when it got broader he went on in front, and looked about him how he might best give them the slip and run away. But as he went forward he heard a clear, sweet voice behind him, which said,

"'Now the road is good. Come, my dear, and get up into the carriage.'

"The lad turned round in a trice, and had near lost both nose and ears. There stood the grandest carriage with six white horses to it, and in the carriage sat a maiden, as bright and lovely as the sun, and round her sat others who were as pretty and soft as stars. They were a princess and her playfellows, who had been bewitched all together. But now they were free because he had come down to them, and never said a word against them.

"'Come now,' said the princess. So the lad stepped up into the carriage, and they drove to church, and when they drove from church again the princess said, 'Now, we will drive first to my house, and then we'll send to fetch your mother.'

"'That is all very well!' thought the lad, for he still said nothing, even now; but, for all that, he thought it would be better to go home to his mother than down into that nasty rat-hole. But just as he thought that, they came to a grand castle; into it they turned, and there they were to dwell. And so a grand carriage with six horses was sent to fetch the goody, and when it came back they set to work at the wedding feast. It lasted fourteen days, and maybe they are still at it. So let us all make haste; perhaps, we too may come in time to drink the bridegroom's health and dance with the bride."

THE GREEN KNIGHT.

"ONCE on a time there was a king who was a widower,
and he had an only daughter. But it is an old
saying, that widower's grief is like knocking your funny-
bone, it hurts, but it soon passes away ; and so the king
married a queen who had two daughters. Now, this queen
—well ! she was no better than step-mothers are wont to
be, snappish and spiteful she always was to her step-
daughter.

" Well ! a long time after, when they were grown up,
these three girls, war broke out, and the king had to go
forth to fight for his country and his kingdom. But before
he went the three daughters had leave to say what the
king should buy and bring home for each of them, if he won
the day against the foe.

" So the step-daughters were to speak first, as you may
fancy, and say what they wished.

" Well ! the first wished for a golden spinning-wheel, so
small that it could stand on a sixpenny-piece ; and the
second, she begged for a golden winder, so small that it
could stand on a sixpenny-piece ; that was what they
wanted to have, and till they had them there was no

spinning or winding to be got out of them. But his own daughter, she would ask for no other thing than that he would greet the Green Knight in her name.

"So the king went out to war, and whithersoever he went he won, and however things turned out he brought the things he had promised his step-daughters; but he had clean forgotten what his own daughter had begged him to do, till at last he made a feast because he had won the day.

"Then it was that he set eyes on a Green Knight, and all at once his daughter's words came into his head, and he greeted him in her name. The Green Knight thanked him for the greeting, and gave him a book which looked like a hymn-book with parchment clasps. That the king was to take home and give her; but he was not to unclasp it, or the princess either, till she was all alone.

"So, when the king had done fighting and feasting he went home again, and he had scarce got inside the door before his step-daughters clung round him to get what he had promised to buy them. 'Yes,' he said, he had brought them what they wished; but his own daughter, she held back and asked for nothing, and the king forgot all about it too, till one day, when he was going out, and he put on the coat he had worn at the feast, and just as he thrust his hand into his pocket for his handkerchief, he felt the book and knew what it was.

"So he gave it to his daughter, and said he was to greet her with it from the Green Knight, and she mustn't unclasp it till she was all alone.

" Well ! that evening when she was by herself in her bed-room she unclasped the book, and as soon as she did so she heard a strain of music, so sweet she had never heard the like of it, and then, what do you think ! Why, the Green Knight came to her and told her the book was such a book that whenever she unclasped it he must come to her, and it would be all the same wherever she might be, and when she clasped it again he would be off and away again.

" Well ! she unclasped the book often and often in the evenings when she was alone and at rest, and the knight always came to her and was almost always there. But her step-mother, who was always thrusting her nose into everything, she found out there was some one with her in her room, and she was not long in telling it to the king. But he wouldn't believe it. 'No !' he said, they must watch first and see if it was so before they trumped up such stories, and took her to task for them.

" So one evening they stood outside the door and listened, and it seemed as though they heard some one talking inside ; but when they went in there was no one.

" ' Who was it you were talking with ?' asked the step-mother, both sharp and cross.

" ' It was no one, indeed,' said the princess.

" ' Nay ! said she ; ' I heard it as plain as day.'

" ' Oh !' said the princess, ' I only lay and read aloud out of a prayer-book.'

" ' Show it me,' said the queen.

" ' Well ! then it was only a prayer-book after all, and she must have leave to read that,' the king said.

"But the step-mother thought just the same as before, and so she bored a hole through the wall and stood prying about there. So one evening, when she heard that the knight was in the room she tore open the door and came flying into her step-daughter's room like a blast of wind; but she was not slow in clasping the book either, and he was off and away in a trice; but however quick she had been, for all that her step-mother caught a glimpse of him, so that she was sure some one had been there.

"It happened just then that the king was setting out on a long, long journey, and while he was away the quéen had a deep pit dug down into the ground, and there she built up a dungeon, and in the stone and mortar she laid ratsbane and other strong poisons, so that not so much as a mouse could get through the wall. As for the master-mason he was well paid, and gave his word to fly the land, but he didn't, for he stayed where he was. Then the princess was thrown into that dungeon with her maid, and when they were inside the queen walled up the door and left only a little hole open at the top to let down food to them. So there she sat and sorrowed, and the time seemed long, and longer than long; but at last she remembered she had her book with her, and took it out and unclasped it. First of all she heard the same sweet strain she had heard before, and then arose a grievous sound of wailing, and just then the Green Knight came.

"'I am at death's door,' he said, and then he told her that her step-mother had laid poison in the mortar, and he did not know if he should ever come out alive. So when she clasped the book up as fast as she could she heard the same wailing sound.

"But you must know the maid who was shut up with her had a sweetheart, and she sent word to him to go to the master-mason, and beg him to make the hole at top big enough for them to creep out at it. If he would do that the princess would pay him so well he could live in plenty all his days. Yes! he did so, and they set out and travelled far, far away in strange lands, she and her maid, and wherever they came they asked after the Green Knight.

"So after a long, long time they came to a castle, which was all hung with black, and just as they were passing by it a shower of rain fell, and so the princess stepped into the church porch to wait till the rain was over. As she stood there, a young man and an old man came by, who also wished to take shelter; but the princess drew away further into a corner, so that they did not see her.

" ' Why is it,' said the young man, 'that the king's castle is hung with black ? '

" ' Don't you know,' said the greybeard, 'the prince here is sick to death, he whom they call the Green Knight ;' And so he went on telling him how it had all happened. So when the young man had listened to the story, he asked if there was anyone who could make him well again.

" ' Nay, nay ! ' said the other. 'There is but one cure, and that is if the maiden who was shut up in the dungeon were to come and pluck healing plants in the fields, and boil them in sweet milk, and wash him with them thrice.'

"Then he went on reckoning up the plants that were needful before he could get well again.

"All this the princess heard, and she kept it in her head, and when the rain was over the two men went away, nor did she bide there long either.

"So when they got home to the house in which they lived, out they went at once to get all kinds of plants and grasses in the field and wood, she and the maid, and they plucked and gathered early and late till she had got all that she was to boil. Then she bought her a doctor's hat and a doctor's gown, and went to the king's castle, and offered to make the prince well again.

"'No, no; it is no good,' said the king. So many had been there and tried, but he always got worse instead of better. But she would not yield, and gave her word he should be well, and that soon and happily. Well, then, she might have leave to try, and so she went into the Green Knight's bedroom and washed him the first time. And when she came the next day he was so well he could sit up in bed; the day after he was man enough to walk about the room, and the third he was as well and lively as a fish in the water.

"'Now he may go out hunting,' said the doctor.

"Then the king was so overjoyed with the doctor as a bird in broad day. But the doctor said he must go home.

"Then she threw off her hat and gown, and dressed herself smart, and made a feast, and then she unclasped the book. Then arose the same joyful strain as of old, and in

a trice the Green Knight was there, and he wondered much
to know how she had got thither.

" So she told him all about it, and how it had happened,
and when they had eaten and drunk he took her straight
up to the castle, and told the king the whole story from
beginning to end. Then there was such a bridal and such
a feast, and when it was over they set off to the bride's
home, and there was great joy in her father's heart, but
they took the stepmother and rolled her down hill in a
cask full of spikes."

BOOTS AND HIS CREW.

" ONCE on a time there was a king, and that king had heard talk of a ship that went as fast by land as it did by water; so he set his heart on having such a ship, and he gave his word that the man who could build it should have the princess and half the kingdom. And this promise he had given out in every parish church in the realm, and at every parish meeting. There were many that tried their hands you may fancy, for it was a nice thing to have half the kingdom, and it was brave to get the princess into the bargain, but it went ill with most of them.

" So there were three brothers away in the wood; the eldest was called Peter, the second Paul, and the youngest Osborn Boots, because he was for ever sitting and grubbing in the ashes. But it so happened that on the Sunday, when the king's promise was given out, he was at church too. So when he got home and told the story, his eldest brother, Peter, begged his mother for some food, for he was bent on setting off, and trying his luck, if he couldn't build the ship and win the princess and half the realm.

So when he had got his wallet full he strode off from the farm, and on the way he met an old, old man, who was so bent and wretched.

" ' Whither away ? ' asked the old man.

" ' Oh ! ' said Peter, ' I'm off to the wood to make a platter for my father, for he doesn't like to eat out of the same dish with us.'

" ' A platter it shall be,' said the man ; ' but what have you in your knapsack ? '

" ' Muck,' said Peter.

" ' Muck it shall be,' said the man, and they parted.

" So Peter strode on till he came to a grove of oaks, and then he fell to chopping and carpentering, but for all his hewing and all his carpentering he could turn out nothing but platter after platter. So when it got towards mid-day, he was going to take a snack, and opened his wallet. But there was not a morsel of food in it, and as he had nothing to eat, and did not get on any better with the carpentering, he got weary of the work, and took his axe and wallet on his back and strode off home to his mother again.

" Next Paul was for setting off to try if he had any luck in shipbuilding, and could win the king's daughter and half the kingdom. He, too, begged his mother for food, and when he had got it he threw his wallet over his shoulder and set off from their farm. On the way he met an old man who was so bent and wretched.

" ' Whither away ? ' said the man.

"'Oh! I'm just going to the wood to make a pig trough for our little pig,' said Paul.

"'A pig trough it shall be,' said the man.

"'What have you got in your wallet?' asked the man.

"'Muck,' said Paul.

"'Muck it shall be,' said the man.

"'So Paul trudged off to the wood, and fell to hewing and carpentering as hard as he could; but however he hewed and however he carpentered, he could turn out nothing but pig troughs and pig tubs. Still he wouldn't give in, but worked till far on in the afternoon before he thought of taking a little snack; then he got so hungry all at once that he must take out his knapsack, but when he opened it there was not a morsel of food in it. Then Paul got so cross that he rolled up the knapsack and dashed it against a stump, and then he shouldered his axe and trudged away home from the wood as fast as he could.

"So when Paul had come home, Boots was all for setting out in his turn, and begged his mother for food.

"'May be I might be man enough to get the ship built and win the princess and half the kingdom.' That was what he said.

"'Yes! yes! a likely thing,' said his mother. 'You look like winning the princess and the kingdom, that you do, by my troth; you, who have done naught else than grub and poke about in the ashes! No! no! you don't get any food,' said the goody.

"'But Boots would not give in; he begged so long

that at last he got leave. As for food he got none, was it likely ? But he got by stealth two oat cakes and a drop of stale beer, and with them he trudged off from the farm.

"Well ! when he had walked a while he met the same old man, who was so bent and vile and wretched.

" ' Whither away ? ' asked the man.

"Oh ! I'm going into the wood to build me a ship which will go as well on land as on sea ; for you must know that the king has given out that the man who can build such a ship shall have the princess and half the realm.'

" ' What have you got in your wallet ? ' asked the man.

" ' Not much to brag of,' said Boots, ' though it's called travelling fare.'

" ' If you'll give me some of your food, I'll help you,' said the man.

" ' With all my heart,' said Boots ; ' but there's nothing but two oat cakes and a drop of stale beer.'

" ' It was all the same to him what it was,' said the man, so that he got something ; and he would be sure to help him.

" So when they got up to the old oak in the wood, the man said to the lad,—

" ' Now you must chop out one chip, and you must put it back where it came from, and when you have done that you may lie down and sleep.

" Yes ! Boots did as he said, he lay him down to sleep, and in his slumber he thought he heard some one hewing and hammering, and carpentering and sawing, and planing, but he could not wake up till the man called him, and then there stood the ship all ready alongside the oak.

" ' Now you must go aboard her, and every one you meet you must take as one of your crew,' he said.

" Yes! Boots thanked him for the ship, and sailed off saying he'd be sure to do what he said.

" So when he had sailed a while, he came upon a great, long, thin fellow, who lay away by the hillside and ate granite.

" ' What kind of chap are you ?' said Boots, 'that you lie here eating granite ?'

" Well! he was so sharp set for meat he could never have his fill, and that was why he was forced to eat granite. That was what he said; and then he begged if he might have leave to be one of the ship's company.

" ' Oh, yes,' said Boots, ' if you care to come, step on board.'

" Yes, he was willing enough, and he took with him a few big granite boulders as his sea stores.

" So when they had sailed a bit farther they met a man who lay on a sunny brae and sucked at a tap.

" ' What sort of a chap are you ?' asked Boots, and what good is it that you lie there sucking at that tap ?'

" ' Oh !' said he, when one hasn't got the cask, one must be thankful for the tap. I am always so thirsty for ale, that I can never drink enough ale or wine;' and then he asked if he might have leave to be one of the ship's company.

" ' If you care to come, step on board,' said Boots.

" Yes, he was willing enough, and he stepped on board and took the tap with him lest he should be a-thirst.

" So when they had sailed a bit farther they met one who lay with one ear on the ground, listening.

" ' What sort of a chap are you?' asked Boots ' and what good is it that you lie there on the ground, listening?'

" ' I am listening to the grass growing,' he said, ' for I am so quick of hearing that I can hear it grow;' and so he begged that he might be one of the ship's company. Well, he too did not get ' Nay.'

" ' If you care to come, step on board,' said Boots.

" Yes, he was willing enough, and so up he too stepped into the ship.

" So when they had sailed a bit farther, they came to a man who stood aiming and aiming.

" ' What sort of a chap are you?' said Boots, ' and why is it that you stand there aiming and aiming?'

" ' I am so sharp-sighted,' he said, ' that I'm a dead shot up to the world's end;' and so he too asked if he might have leave to be one of the ship's company.

" ' If you care to come, step in,' said Boots.

" Yes, he was willing enough, and so he stepped up into the ship and joined Boots and his comrades.

" So when they had sailed a bit farther, they came on

a man who went about hopping on one leg, and on the other he had seven hundred weight.

" What sort of a chap are you ?' asked Boots ; 'and what's the good of your limping and hopping on one leg, with seven hundred weight on the other ?'

" ' Oh ?' said he, ' I'm as light as a feather, and if I went on both legs I should be at the world's end in less than five minutes ;' and so he too begged if he might have leave to be one of the ship's company.

" ' If you care to come, step in,' said Boots.

" Yes, he was willing enough, and he stepped on board to Boots and his comrades.

" So when they had sailed a bit farther, they met a man who stood holding his throat.

" ' What sort of a chap are you ?' asked Boots, ' and why in the world do you stand here holding your throat ?'

" ' Oh !' said he, ' you must know I have got seven summers and fifteen winters inside me, so I've good need to hold my gullet, for if they all slipped out at once they'd freeze the whole world in a trice.' That was what he said, and so he begged leave to be with them.

" ' If you care to come, step in,' said Boots. Yes, he was willing enough, and so he too stepped on board the ship to the rest.

" So when they had sailed a good bit farther, they came to the king's grange. Then Boots strode straight into the king, and said, that the ship was ready out in the court-yard, and now he was come to claim the princess, as the king had given his word.

"But the king wouldn't hear of it, for Boots did not look very nice; he was grimy and sooty, and the king was loath to give his daughter to such a fellow. So he said he must wait a little, he couldn't have the princess until they cleared a barn which the king had with three hundred casks of salt meat in it.

"'All the same,' said the king, 'if you can do it by this time to-morrow you shall have her.'

"'I can but try,' said Boots; 'I may have leave, perhaps, to take one of my crew with me?'

"'Yes, he might have leave to do that, even if he took them all six,' said the king, for he thought it quite beyond his power though he had six hundred to help him.

"But Boots only took with him the man who ate granite, and was always so sharp set; and so when they came next morning and unlocked the barn, if he hadn't eaten all the casks, so that there was nothing left but half a dozen spare-ribs, and that was only one for each of his other comrades. So Boots strode into the king, and said, now the barn was empty, and now he might have the princess.

"Then the king went out to the barn, and empty it was, that was plain enough; but still Boots was so sooty and smutty, that the king thought it a shame that such a fellow should have his daughter. So he said he had a cellar full of ale and old wine, three hundred casks of each kind, which he must have drunk out first, and said the king,—

" ' All the same, if you are man enough to drink them out by this time to-morrow, you shall have her.'

" ' I can but try,' said Boots ; ' but I may have leave, perhaps, to take one of my comrades with me.

" With all my heart,' said the king, who thought he had so much ale and wine that the whole seven of them would soon get more than their skins could hold.

" But Boots only took with him the man who sucked the tap, and who had such a swallow for ale, and then the king locked them both up in the cellar.

" So he drank cask after cask as long as there were any left, but at last he spared a drop or two, about as much as a quart or two, for each of his comrades. Next morning they unlocked the cellar, and Boots strode off at once to the king, and said he was done with the ale and wine, and now he must have his daughter as he had given his word.

" ' Ay, ay, but I must first go down into the cellar and see,' said the king, for he didn't believe it. But when he got to the cellar, there was nothing in it but empty casks. But Boots was still black and smutty, and the king thought he never could bear to have such a fellow for his son-in-law. So he said, ' No,' but all the same if he could fetch him water from the world's end, in ten minutes, for the princess's tea, he should have both her and half the realm, for he thought that quite out of his power.

" ' I can but try,' said Boots ; so he laid hand on him who limped on one leg, with seven hundred weight on the other, and said he must unbuckle the weights and use both his legs as fast as ever he could, for he must have water from the world's end for the princess's tea in ten minutes.

"So he took off the weights, and got a pail, and set off and was out of sight in a trice. But time went on and on, for seven lengths and seven breadths, and yet he did not come back. At last there were no more than three minutes left till the time was up, and the king was as pleased as though some one had given him a horse. But just then Boots bawled out to him who heard the grass grow, and bade him listen and hear what had become of him.

"'He has fallen asleep at the well,' he said. 'I can hear him snoring, and the trolls are combing his hair.'

"So Boots called him, who could shoot to the world's end, and bade him put a bullet into the troll. Yes! he did that, and shot him right in the eye, and the troll set up such a howl that he woke up at once, he that was to fetch the water for tea; and when he got back to the king's grange, there was still one minute left of the ten.

"Then Boots strode into the king, and said there was the water, and now he must have the princess, there must be no more words about it. But the king thought him just as sooty and smutty as before, and did not at all like to have him for a son-in-law. So the king said he had three hundred fathoms of wood, with which he was about to dry corn in the malt-house, and 'all the same, if you are man enough to get inside it while I burn up all that fuel, you shall have her, and I will make no more bones about it.'

" ' I can but try,' said Boots; 'but I must have leave to take one of my crew with me.'

" ' Yes, yes !' said the king, 'all six of them if you like ;' for he thought it would be warm enough in there for all of them.

" But Boots took with him the man who had fifteen winters and seven summers inside him, and they trudged off to the malt-house at night. But the king had laid the fuel on thick, and there was such a pile burning, it almost melted the stove. Out again they could not come, for they had scarce set foot inside than the king shot the bolt behind them, and hung two padlocks on the door besides. Then Boots said,—

" ' You'd better slip out six or seven winters at once, so that it may be a nice summer heat.'

" Then the heat fell, and they could bear it, but on in the night it began to grow chilly ; so Boots said he must make it milder, with two summers, and then they slept till far on next day.

" But when they heard the king rattling at the door outside, Boots said,—

" ' Now you must let slip two more winters, but lay them so that the last may go full on his face.'

" Yes, he did so, and when the king unlocked the malt-house door, and thought to find them lying there burnt to cinders, there they sat shivering and shaking till their teeth chattered, and the man with the fifteen winters let

slip the last right into the king's face, so that it swelled up
at once into a big frost-bite.

"'MAY I HAVE YOUR DAUGHTER NOW?'
said Boots.

"'Yes, yes! Pray take her and keep her, and half the
realm besides,' said the king, for he couldn't say 'No' any
longer.

"So they held the bridal feast, and kept it up and
rejoiced and fired off witch shots, and meanwhile they
went looking about for charges, and then they took me
and gave me porridge in a flask, and milk in a basket,
and then they shot me off here to you, that I might tell
you all how the wedding went off."

THE TOWN-MOUSE AND THE FELL-MOUSE.

"ONCE on a time there was a fell-mouse and a town-mouse, and they met on a hill brae, where the fell-mouse sat in a hazel thicket and plucked nuts.

"'God help you, sister,' said the town-mouse. 'Do I meet my kinsfolk here so far out in the country?'

"'Yes! so it is;' said the fell-mouse.

"'You gather these nuts and carry them to your house?' said the town mouse.

"'Yes; I must do it,' said the fell-mouse, 'if we are to have anything to live on.'

"'The husks are long and the kernels full this year,' said the town-mouse; 'so I dare say they will help to fill out a starveling body.'

"'You are quite right,' said the fell-mouse, and then she told her how well and happily she lived. But the town-mouse thought she was better off, and the fell-mouse would not give in, but said there was no place so good as wood and fell, and as for herself, she had far the best of it.

"Still the town-mouse said she was sure she had the best of it, and they could not agree at all. So, at last, they promised to pay one another a visit at Yule, that they might taste and see which lived best. The town-mouse was the one that had to pay the first visit, and she went through woods and deep dales, for though the fell-mouse had come down to the lowlands for the winter, the road was both long and heavy. It was up-hill work, and the snow was both deep and soft, so that she was both weary and hungry by the time she got to her journey's end.

" 'Now I shall be glad to get some food,' she said, when she got there. As for the fell-mouse, she had scraped together all sorts of good things. There were kernels of nuts, and liquorish-root and other roots, and much else that grows in wood and field. All this she had in a hole deep under ground where it would not freeze, and close by was a spring which was open all the winter, so that she could drink as much water as she chose. There was plenty of what was to be had, and they fed both well and good; but the town-mouse thought it was not more than sorry fare.

" 'One can keep life together with this,' she said; 'but it isn't choice, not at all. But now you must be so kind as come to me, and taste what we have in town.'

" Well, the fell-mouse was willing, and it was not long before she came. Then the town-mouse had gathered together something of all the Christmas fare which the mistress of the house had dropped as she went about, when she had taken a drop too much at Yule. There were bits of cheese, and odds and ends of butter and tallow, and cheesecakes and tipsycake, and much else that was nice.

In the jar under the ale-tap she had drink enough, and the whole room was full of all kinds of dainties. They fed and lived well, and there was no end to the fell-mouse's greediness. Such fare she had never tasted. At last, she got thirsty, for the food was both strong and rich, and now she must have a drink of water.

"'It is not far off to the ale,' said the town-mouse; 'that's the drink for us;' and with that she jumped up on the edge of the jar, and drank her thirst out, but she drank no more than she could carry, for she knew the Yule ale and how strong it was. But as for the fell-mouse, she thought it famous drink, for she had never tasted anything but water, and now she took sip after sip; but she was no judge of strong drink, and so the end was she got drunk, for she tumbled down and got wild in her head, and felt her feet tingle, till she began to run and to jump about from one beer-barrel to the other, and to dance and cut capers on the shelves among the cups and jugs, and to whistle and whine, just as though she were tipsy and silly; and tipsy she was, there was no gainsaying it.

"'You mustn't behave as though you had just come from the hills,' said the town-mouse. 'Don't make such a noise, and don't lead us such a life; we have a hard master here.'

"But the fell-mouse said: 'She cared not a pin for man or master!'

"But all this while the cat sat up on the trap-door above the cellar, and listened and spied both to their talk and pranks. Just then, the goody came down to draw a mug of ale, and as she lifted the trap-door, the cat stole into the cellar and fixed her claws into the fell-mouse. Then there was another dance. The town-mouse crept into her hole, and sat safe looking on, but the fell-mouse got sober all at once as soon as she felt the cat's claws.

" 'Oh, my dear master, my dear master ; be merciful and spare my life, and I'll tell you a story.' That was what she said.

" 'Out with it then,' said the cat.

" 'Once on a time there were two small mice,' said the fell-mouse ; and she squeaked so pitifully and slowly, for she wanted to drag the story out as long as she could.

" 'Then they were not alone,' said the cat, both sharply and drily.

" ' And so we had a steak we were going to cook.'

" 'Then you were not starved,' said the cat.

" 'So we put it up on the roof that it might cool itself well,' said the fell-mouse.

" 'Then you didn't burn your tongues,' said the cat.

" 'So, then the fox and the crow came and gobbled it up,' said the fell-mouse.

" ' And so I'll gobble you up,' said the cat.

" But just then the goody slammed to the trap-door again, so that the cat got afraid and loosed her hold, and —pop—the fell-mouse was away in the town-mouse's hole, and from it there was a way out into the snow, and the fell-mouse was not slow in setting off home.

" ' This you call living well, and you say that you live best ? ' she said to the town-mouse. ' Heaven help me to a better mind, for with such a big house, and such a hawk for a master I could scarce get off with my life.

SILLY MATT.

" ONCE on a time there was a goody who had a son called Matthew, but he was so stupid that he had no sense for anything, nor would he do much either; and the little he did was always topsy-turvy and never right, and so they never called him anything but 'Silly Matt.'

" All this the goody thought bad; and it was still worse she thought that her son idled about and never turned his hand to anything else than yawning and stretching himself between the four walls.

" Now close to where they lived ran a great river, and the stream was strong and bad to cross. So, one day, the goody said to the lad, there was no lack of timber there, for it grew almost up to the cottage-wall; he must cut some down and drag it to the bank and try to build a bridge over the river and take toll, and then he would both have something to do and something to live upon besides.

" Yes! Matt thought so too, for his mother had said it; what she begged him do, he would do. That was safe and sure he said, for what she said must be so and not otherwise. So he hewed down timber and dragged it down and built a bridge. It didn't go so awfully fast with the work, but at any rate he had his hands full while it went on.

"When the bridge was ready, the lad was to stand down at its end and take toll of those who wanted to cross, and his mother bade him be sure not to let any one over unless they paid the toll. It was all the same, she said, if it were not always in money. Goods and wares were just as good pay.

"So the first day came three chaps with each his load of hay, and wanted to cross the bridge.

"'No! no!' said the lad; 'you can't go over till I've taken the toll.'

"'We've nothing to pay it with,' they said.

"'Well, then! you can't cross; but it's all the same, if it isn't money. Goods will do just as well.'

"So they gave him each a wisp of hay, and he had as much as would go on a little hand-sledge, and then they had leave to pass over the bridge.

"Next came a pedlar with his pack, who sold needles and thread, and such like small wares, and he wanted to cross.

"'You can't cross, till you have paid the toll,' said the lad.

"'I've nothing to pay it with,' said the pedlar.

"'You have wares, at any rate.'

"So the pedlar took out two needles and gave them him, and then he had leave to cross the bridge. As for the needles, the lad stuck them into the hay, and soon set off home.

"So when he got home, he said, 'Now, I have taken the toll, and got something to live on.'

" 'What did you get ?' asked the goody.

" 'Oh!' said he, 'there came three chaps, each with his load of hay. They each gave me a wisp of hay, so that I got a little sledge-load ; and next, I got two needles from a pedlar.'

" 'What did you do with the hay ?' asked the goody.

" 'I tried it between my teeth ; but it tasted only of grass, so I threw into the river.'

" 'You ought to have spread it out on the byre-floor,' said the goody.

" 'Well ! I'll do that next time, mother,' he said.

" 'And what then did you do with the needles ?' said the goody.

" 'I stuck them in the hay !'

" 'Ah !' said his mother. 'You *are* a born fool. You should have stuck them in and out of your cap.'

" 'Well ! don't say another word, mother, and I'll be sure to do so next time.'

"Next day, when the lad stood down at the foot of the bridge again, there came a man from the mill with a sack of meal, and wanted to cross.

" 'You can't cross till you pay the toll,' said the lad.

" 'I've no pence to pay it with,' said the man.

" 'Well ! You can't cross,' said the lad ; 'but goods are good pay.' So he got a pound of meal, and the man had leave to cross.

"Not long after came a smith, with a horse-pack of smith's work, and wanted to cross; but it was still the same.

"'You mustn't cross till you've paid the toll,' said the lad. But he too had no money either; so he gave the lad a gimlet, and then he had leave to cross.

"So when the lad got home to his mother, the toll was the first thing she asked about.

"'What did you take for toll to-day?'

"'Oh! there came a man from the mill with a sack of meal, and he gave me a pound of meal; and then came a smith, with a horse-load of smith's-work, and he gave me a gimlet.'

"'And pray what did you do with the gimlet?' asked the goody.

"'I did as you bade me, mother,' said the lad. 'I stuck it in and out of my cap.'

"'Oh! but that was silly,' said the goody; 'you oughtn't to have stuck it out and in your cap; but you should have stuck it up your shirt-sleeve.'

"'Ay! ay! only be still, mother; and I'll be sure to do it next time.'

"'And what did you do with the meal, I'd like to know?' said the goody.

"'Oh! I did as you bade me, mother. I spread it over the byre-floor.'

"'Never heard anything so silly in my born days,' said the goody; 'why, you ought to have gone home for a pail and put it into it.'

" ' Well! well! only be still, mother,' said the lad; ' and I'll be sure to do it next time.'

" Next day the lad was down at the foot of the bridge to take toll, and so there came a man with a horse-load of brandy, and wanted to cross.

" ' You can't cross till you pay the toll,' said the lad.

" ' I've got no money,' said the man.

" ' Well, then, you can't cross; but you have goods, of course;' said the lad. Yes; so he got half a quart of brandy, and that he poured up his shirt-sleeve.

" A while after came a man with a drove of goats, and wanted to cross the bridge.

" ' You can't cross till you pay the toll,' said the lad.

" Well! he was no richer than the rest. He had no money; but still he gave the lad a little billy-goat, and he got over with his drove. But the lad took the goat and trod it down into a bucket he had brought with him. So when he got home, the goody asked again—

" ' What did you take to-day?'

" ' Oh! there came a man with a load of brandy, and from him I got a pint of brandy.'

" ' And what did you do with it?'

" ' I did as you bade me, mother; I poured it up my shirt-sleeve.'

" ' Ay! but that was silly, my son; you should have come home to fetch a bottle and poured it into it.'

" ' Well! well! be still this time, mother, and I'll be sure to do what you say next time,' and then he went on—

" ' Next came a man with a drove of goats, and he gave

me a little billy-goat, and that I trod down into the bucket.'

"'Dear me!' said his mother, 'that was silly, and sillier than silly, my son; you should have twisted a withy round its neck, and led the billy-goat home by it.'

"'Well! be still, mother, and see if I don't do as you say next time.'

"Next day he set off for the bridge again to take toll, and so a man came with a load of butter, and wanted to cross. But the lad said 'he couldn't cross unless he paid toll.'

"'I've nothing to pay it with,' said the man.

"'Well! then you can't cross,' said the lad; 'but you have goods, and I'll take them instead of money.'

"So the man gave him a pat of butter, and then he had eave to cross the bridge, and the lad strode off to a grove of willows and twisted a withy, and twined it round the butter, and dragged it home along the road; but so long as he went he left some of the butter behind him, and when he got home there was none left.

"'And what did you take to-day?' asked his mother.

"'There came a man with a load of butter, and he gave a pat.'

"'Butter!' said the goody, 'where is it?'

"'I did as you bade me, mother,' said the lad. 'I tied a withy round the pat and led it home; but it was all lost by the way.'

"'Oh!' said the goody, 'you were born a fool, and you'll die a fool. Now you are not one bit better off for all your toil ; but had you been like other folk, you might have had both meat and brandy, and both hay and tools. If you don't know better how to behave, I don't know what's to be done with you. Maybe, you might be more like the rest of the world, and get some sense into you if you were married to some one who could settle things for you, and so I think you had better set off and see about finding a brave lass ; but you must be sure you know how to behave well on the way and to greet folk prettily when you meet them.'

" ' And pray what shall I say to them ?' asked the lad.

" ' To think of your asking that,' said his mother. ' Why, of course, you must bid them " God's Peace," Don't you know that ?'

" ' Yes ! yes ! I'll do as you bid,' said the lad ; and so he set off on his way to woo him a wife.

" So, when he had gone a bit of the way, he met Grey-legs, the wolf, with her seven cubs ; and when he got so far as to be alongside them, he stood still and greeted them with ' God's Peace !' and when he had said that, he went home again.

" ' I said it all as you bade me, mother,' said Matt.

" ' And what was that ?' asked his mother.

" ' God's Peace,' said Matt.

" ' And pray whom did you meet ?'

" ' A she wolf with seven cubs ; that was all I met,' said Matt.

" ' Ay ! ay ! You are like yourself,' said his mother. ' So it was, and so it will ever be. Why in the world did you say "God's Peace" to a wolf. You should have clapped your hands and said—"Huf! huf! you jade of a she-wolf!" That's what you ought to have said.'

"'Well! well! be still, mother,' he said. 'I'll be sure to say so another time;' and with that he strode off from the farm, and when he had gone a bit on the way, he met a bridal train. So he stood still when he had got well up to the bride and bridegroom, and clapped his hands and said: 'Huf! huf! you jade of a she-wolf!' After that he went home to his mother and said—

"'I did as you bade me mother; but I got a good thrashing for it, that I did.'

"'What was it you did?' she asked.

"'Oh! I clapped my hands and called out, "Huf! huf! you jade of a she-wolf!"'

"'And what was it you met?'

"'I met a bridal train.'

"'Ah! you are a fool, and always will be a fool,' said his mother. 'Why should you say such things to a bridal train. You should have said, "Ride happily, bride and bridegroom."'

"'Well! well! See if I don't say so next time,' said the lad, and off he went again.

"So he met a bear, who was taking a ride on a horse, and Matt waited till he came alongside him, and then he said 'A happy ride to you, bride and bridegroom,' and then he went back to his mother and told her how he had said what she bade him.

'And pray! what was it you said?' she asked.

"'I said, "A happy ride to you both, bride and bridegroom.'"

"'And whom did you meet?'

"'I met a bear taking a ride on a horse,' said Matt.

"'My goodness! what a fool you are,' said his mother. 'You ought to have said, "To the de'il with you." That's what you ought to have said.'

"'Well! well! mother. I'll be sure to say so next time.'

"So he set off again, and this time he met a funeral; and when he had come well up to the coffin, he greeted it and said, 'To the de'il with you!' and then he ran home to his mother, and told her he had said what she bade him.

"'And what was that?' she asked.

"'Oh! I said, "To the de'il with you."'

"'And what was it you met?'

"'I met a funeral,' said Matt; 'but I got more kicks than halfpence!'

"'You didn't get half enough,' said the goody. 'Why, of course, you ought to have said, "May your poor soul have mercy." That's what you ought to have said.'

"Ay! ay! mother! so I will next time, only be still,' said Matt, and off he went again.

"So when he had gone a bit of the way he fell on two ugly gipsies who were skinning a dog. So when he came up to them he greeted them and said, 'May your poor soul have mercy,' and when he had said so he went home and told his mother he had said what she bade him :

but all he got was such a drubbing he could scarce drag one leg after the other.

"'But what was it you said?' asked the goody.

"'May your poor soul have mercy; that was what I said.'

"'And whom did you meet?'

"'A pair of gipsies skinning a dog,' he said.

"'Well! well!' said the goody. 'There's no hope of your changing. You'll always be a shame and sorrow to us wherever you go. I never heard such shocking words. But now, you must set out and take no notice of any one you meet, for you must be off to woo a wife, and see if you can get some one who knows more of the ways of the world and has a better head on her shoulders than yours. And now you must behave like other folk, and if all goes well you may bless your stars, and bawl out, Hurrah!'

" Yes, the lad did all that his mother bade him. He set off and wooed a lass, and she thought he couldn't be so bad a fellow after all; and so she said, 'Yes, she would have him.'

" When the lad got home the goody wanted to know what his sweetheart's name was; but he did not know. So the goody got angry and said, he must just set off again, for she would know what the girl's name was. So when Matt was going home again he had sense enough to ask her what she was called. 'Well,' she said, 'my name is Solvy; but I thought you knew it already.'

"So Matt ran off home, and as he went he mumbled to himself,

> " 'Solvy, Solvy,
>   Is my darling!
>   Solvy, Solvy,
>   Is my darling?

" But just as he was running as hard as he could to reach home before he forgot it, he tripped over a tuft of grass, and forgot the name again. So when he got on his feet again he began to search all round the hillock, but all he could find was a spade. So he seized it and began to dig and search as hard as he could, and as he was hard at it up came an old man.

" ' What are you digging for ?' said the man. ' Have you lost anything here ?'

" 'Oh yes! oh yes! I have lost my sweetheart's name, and I can't find it again.'

" ' I think her name is Solvy,' said the man.

" 'Oh yes, that's it,' said Matt, and away he ran with the spade in his hand, bawling out,

> " 'Solvy, Solvy,
>   Is my darling !'

" But when he had gone a little way he called to mind that he had taken the spade, and so he threw it behind him, right on to the man's leg. Then the man began to roar and bemoan himself as though he had a knife stuck in him, and then Matt forgot the name again, and ran home as fast as he could, and when he got there, the first thing his mother asked was—

" ' What's your sweetheart's name ?'

" But Matt was just as wise as when he set out, for he

did not know the name any better the last than the first time.

"'You are the same big fool, that you are,' said the goody. 'You won't do any better this time either. But now I'll just set off myself and fetch the girl home, and get you married. Meanwhile you must fetch water up to the fifth plank all round the room, and wash it, and then you must take a little fat and a little lean, and the greenest thing you can find in the cabbage garden, and boil them all up together; and when you have done that you must put yourself into fine feather, and look smart when your lassie comes, and then you may sit down on the dresser.'

"Yes, all that Matt thought he could do very well. He fetched water and dashed it about the room in floods, but he couldn't get it to stand above the fourth plank, for when it rose higher it ran out. So he had to leave off that work. But now you must know, they had a dog whose name was 'Fat,' and a cat whose name was 'Lean;' both these he took and put into the soup-kettle. As for the greenest thing in the garden, it was a green gown which the goody had meant for her daughter-in-law; that he cut up into little bits, and away it went into the pot; but their little pig, which was called 'All,' he cooked by himself in the brewing tub. And when Matt had done all this he laid hands on a pot of treacle and and a feather pillow. Then he first of all rubbed himself all over with the treacle, and then he tore open the pillow and rolled himself in the feathers, and then he sat down on the dresser out in the kitchen, till his mother and the lassie came.

"Now the first thing the goody missed when she came to her house was the dog, for it always used to meet her out of doors. The next thing was the cat, for it always met her in the porch, and when the weather was right down good and the sun shone, she even came out into the yard, and met her at the garden gate. Nor could she see the green gown she had meant for her daughter-in-law either, and her piggy-wiggy, which followed her grunting wherever she went, he was not there either. So she went in to see about all this; but as soon as ever she lifted the latch, out poured the water through the doorway like a waterfall, so that they were almost borne away by the flood, both the goody and the lassie.

"So they had to go round by the back door, and when they got inside the kitchen there sat that figure of fun all befeathered.

"'What have you done?' said the goody.

"'I did just as you bade me, mother,' said Matt. 'I tried to get the water up to the fifth plank, but as fast as ever I poured it in it ran out again, and so I could only get up as high as the fourth plank.'

"'Well! well! but "Fat" and "Lean," said the goody, who wished to turn it off; 'what have you done with them?'

"'I did as you bade me, mother,' said Matt. 'I took and put them into the soup-kettle. They both scratched and bit, and they mewed and whined, and Fat was strong and kicked against it; but he had to go in at last all the same; and as for "All," he's cooking by himself in the brewing tub in the brew-house, for there wasn't room for him in the soup-kettle.'

"'But what have you done with that new green gowu I meant for my daughter-in-law?' said the goody, trying to hide his silliness.

"'Oh! I did as you bade me, mother. It hung out in the cabbage-garden, and as it was the greatest thing there, I took it and cut it up small, and yonder it boils in the soup.'

'Away ran the goody to the chimney-corner, tore off the pot and turned it upside down with all that was in it. Then she filled it anew and put it on to boil. But when she had time to look at Matt she was quite shocked.

"'Why is it you are such a figure?' she cried.

"'I did as you bade me, mother,' said Matt. 'First I rubbed myself all over with treacle to make myself sweet for my bride, and then I tore open the pillow and put myself into fine feathers.'

"Well, the goody turned it off as well as she could, and picked off the feathers from her son, and washed him clean, and put fresh clothes on him.

"So at last they were to have the wedding, but first Matt was to go to the town and sell a cow to buy things for the bridal. The goody had told him what he was to do, and the beginning and end of what she said was, he was to be sure to get something for the cow. So when he got to the market with the cow, and they asked what he was to have for her, they could get no other answer out of him than that he was to have *something* for her. So at last came a butcher, who begged him to take the cow and follow him home, and he'd be sure to give him *something* for her. Yes, Matt went off with the cow, and when he got to the butcher's house the butcher spat into the palm of Matt's hand, and said—

" 'There, you have something for your cow, but look sharp after it.'

" So off went Matt as carefully as if he trode on eggs, holding his hand shut; but when he had got about as far as the cross-road, which led to their farm, he met the parson, who came driving along.

" 'Open the gate for me, my lad,' said the parson.

" So the lad hastened to open the gate, but in doing so he forgot what he had in his palm, and took the gate by both hands, so that what he got for the cow was left sticking on the gate. So when he saw it was gone he got cross, and said, his reverence had taken *something* from him.

" But when the parson asked him if he had lost his wits, and said he had taken nothing from him, Matt got so wrath he killed the parson at a blow, and buried him in a bog by the wayside.

" So when he got home he told his mother all about it, and she slaughtered a billy-goat, and laid it where Matt had laid the parson, but she buried the parson in another place. And when she had done that she hung over the fire a pot of brose, and when it was cooked she made Matt sit down in the ingle and split matches. Meantime

she went up on the roof with the pot and poured the brose
down the chimney, so that it streamed over her son.

"Next day came the sheriff. So when the sheriff
asked him, Matt did not gainsay that he had slain the
parson, and more, he was quite ready to show the
sheriff where he had laid 'his reverence.' But when
the sheriff asked on what day it happened, Matt said 'it
was the day when it rained brose over the whole world.'

"So when he got to the spot where he had buried the
parson the sheriff pulled out the billy-goat, and asked—

"'Had your parson horns?'

"Now when the judges heard the story, they made up
their minds that the lad was quite out of his wits, and so
he got off scot free.

"So after all the bridal was to stand, and the goody had
a long talk with her son, and bade him be sure to behave
prettily when they sat at table. He was not to look too
much at the bride, but to cast an eye at her now and then.
Peas he might eat by himself, but he must share the eggs
with her, and he was not to lay the leg bones by his side
on the table, but to place them tidily on his plate.

"Yes, Matt would do all that, and he did it well; yes,
he did all that his mother bade him, and nothing else.
First, he stole out to the sheepfold, and plucked the eyes
out of all the sheep and goats he could find, and took them
with him. So when they went to dinner he sat with his
back to his bride; but all at once he cast a sheep's eye at
her so that it hit her full in her face; and a little while
after he cast another, and so he went on. As for the eggs

he ate them all up to his own cheek, so that the lassie did not get a taste, but when the peas came he shared them with her. And when they had eaten a while Matt put his feet together, and up on his plate went his legs.

"At night, when they were to go to bed, the lassie was tired and weary, for she thought it no good to have such a fool for her husband. So she said she had forgotten something and must go out a little ; but she could not get Matt's leave ; he would follow her, for to tell the truth, he was afraid she would never come back.

"'No! no! lie still, I say,' said the bride. 'See, here's a long hair-rope; tie it round me, and I'll leave the door ajar. So if you think I'm too long away you have only to pull the rope and then you'll drag me in again.'

"Yes, Matt was content with that ; but as soon as the lassie got out into the yard she caught a billy-goat and untied the rope and tied it round him.

"So when Matt thought she was too long out of doors he began to haul in the rope, and so he dragged the billy-goat up into bed to him. But when he had lain a while, he bawled out—

"'Mother! mother! my bride has horns like a billy-goat!'

"'Stuff! silly boy to lie and bewail yourself,' said his mother. 'It's only her hair-plaits, poor thing, I'm sure.'

"In a little while Matt called out again—

"'Mother! mother! my bride has a beard like a goat.'

"'Stuff! silly boy to lie there and rave,' said the goody.

"But there was no rest in that house that night, for in a

little while Matt screeched out that his bride was like a billy-goat all over. So when it grew towards morning the goody said—

" ' Jump up, my son, and make a fire.'

"So Matt climbed up to a shelf under the roof, and set fire to some straw and chips, and other rubbish that lay there. But then such a smoke rose, that he couldn't bear it any longer indoors. He was forced to go out, and just then the day broke. As for the goody, she too had to make a start of it, and when they got out the house was on fire, so that the flames came right out at the roof.

" ' Good luck ! good luck ! Hip, hip, hurrah !' roared out Matt, for he thought it fine fun to have such an ending to his bridal feast.

KING VALEMON, THE WHITE BEAR.

"NOW, once on a time there was, as there well might be, a king. He had two daughters who were ugly and bad, but the third was as fair and soft as the bright day, and the king and everyone was glad of her. So one day she dreamt of a golden wreath that was so lovely she couldn't live until she had it. But as she could not get it, she grew sullen and wouldn't so much as talk for grief, and when the king knew it was the wreath she sorrowed for, he sent out a pattern cut just like the one that the princess had dreamt of, and sent word to goldsmiths in every land to see if they could get the like of it. So the goldsmiths worked night and day; but some of the wreaths she tossed away from her, and the rest she would not so much as look at.

"But once when she was in the wood, she set her eyes upon a white bear, who had the very wreath she had dreamt of between his paws, and played with it. Then she wanted to buy it. No! it was not for sale for money, but she might have it, if he might have her. Yes! she said it was never worth living without it. It was all the same to her whither she went, and whom she got if she could only have that wreath; and so it was settled between them that he should fetch her when three days were up, and that day was a Thursday.

"So when she went home with the wreath every one was glad because she was glad again, and the king said, he thought it could never be so hard to stop a white bear. So the third day he turned out his whole army round the castle to withstand him. But when the white bear came there was no one who could stand before him, for no weapon would bite on his hide, and he hurled them down right and left, so that they lay in heaps on either side. All this the king thought right down scathe; so he sent out his eldest daughter, and the white bear took her upon his back and went off with her. And when they had gone far, and farther than far, the white bear asked,—

"'Have you ever sat softer, and have you ever seen clearer?'

"'Yes! on my mother's lap I sat softer, and in my father's hall I saw clearer,' she said.

"'Oh!' said the white bear, 'then you're not the right one;' and with that he hunted her home again.

"The next Thursday he came again, and it all went just the same. The army went out to withstand the white bear; but neither iron nor steel bit on his hide, and so he dashed them down like grass till the king begged him to hold hard, and then he sent out to him his next oldest daughter, and the white bear took her on his back and went off with her. So when they had travelled ar, and farther than far, the white bear asked,—

"'Have you ever seen clearer, and have you ever sat softer?'

"'Yes!' she said, 'in my father's hall I saw clearer, and on my mother's lap I sat softer.'

"'Oh! then you are not the right one,' said the white bear, and with that he hunted her home again.

"The third Thursday he came again, and then he smote the army harder than he had done before; so the king thought he couldn't let him slay his whole army like that, and he gave him his third daughter in God's name. So he took her up on his back and went away far, and farther than far, and when they had gone deep, deep, into the wood, he asked her as he had asked the others, whether she had ever sat softer or seen clearer?

"'No! never!' she said.

"'Ah!' he said, 'you are the right one.'

"So they came to a castle which was so grand, that the one her father had was like the poorest place when set against it. There she was to be and live happily, and she was to have nothing else to do but to see that the fire never went out. The bear was away by day, but at night he was with her, and then he was a man. So all went well for three years; but each year she had a baby, and he took it and carried it off as soon as ever it came into the world. Then she got more and more dull, and begged she might have leave to go home and see her parents. Well! there was nothing to stop that; but first, she had to give her word that she would listen to what her father said, but not do what her mother wished. So she went home, and when they were alone with her, and she had told how she was treated, her mother wanted to give her a light to take back that she might see what kind of man he was.

"But her father said, 'No! she mustn't do that, for it will lead to harm and not to gain.'

"But however it happened, so it happened; she got a bit of a candle-end to take with her when she started.

"So the first thing she did when he was sound asleep, was to light the candle-end and throw a light on him; and he was so lovely she never thought she could gaze enough at him; but as she held the candle over him, a hot drop of tallow dropped on his forehead, and he woke up.

"'What is this you have done?' he said. 'Now you have made us both unlucky; there was no more than a month left, and had you lasted it out, I should have been saved; for a hag of the trolls has bewitched me, and I am a white bear by day. But now it is all over between us, for now I must go to her and take her to wife.'

"She wept and bemoaned herself; but he must set off, and he would set off. Then she asked if she might not go with him. 'No!' he said, 'there was no way of doing that.' But for all that, when he set off in his bear-shape, she took hold of his shaggy hide and threw herself upon his back, and held on fast.

"So away they went over crags and hills, and through brakes and briars, till her clothes were torn off her back, and she was so dead tired, that she let go her hold and lost her wits. When she came to herself she was in a great wood, and then she set off again, but she could not tell whither she was going. So after a long, long, time she came to a hut, and there she saw two women, an old woman and a pretty little girl. Then the princess asked, had they seen anything of King Valemon, the white bear.

"'Yes!' they said. 'He passed by here this morning early, but he went so fast you'll never be able to catch him up.'

"As for the girl, she ran about clipping in the air and playing with a pair of golden scissors, which were of that kind, that silk and satin stuffs flew all about her if she only clipped the air with them. Where they were, there was never any want of clothes.

"'But this woman,' said the little lass, 'who is to go so far and on such bad ways, she will suffer much; she may well have more need of these scissors than I to cut out her clothes with.'

"And as she said this she begged her mother so hard, that at last she got leave to give her the scissors.

"So away travelled the princess through the wood, which seemed never to come to an end, both day and night, and next morning she came to another hut. In it there were also two women, an old wife and a young girl.

"'Good-day!" said the princess. 'Have you seen anything of King Valemon, the white bear?' That was what she asked them.

"'Was it you, maybe, who was to have him?' said the old wife.

"'Yes! it was.'

"'Well, he passed by yesterday, but he went so fast you'll never be able to catch him up.'

"This little girl played about on the floor with a flask, which was of that kind it poured out every drink any one wished to have.

"'But this poor wife,' said the girl, 'who has to go so far on such bad ways, I think she may well be thirsty and suffer much other ill. No doubt she needs this flask more than I;' and so she asked if she might have leave to give her the flask. Yes! that leave she might have.

"So the princess got the flask, and thanked them, and set off again away through the same wood, both that day and the next night too. The third morning she came to a hut, where there was also an old wife and a little girl.

"'Good-day!' said the princess.

"'Good-day to you,' said the old wife.

"'Have you seen anything of King Valemon, the white bear?' she asked.

"'Maybe it was you who was to have him?' said the old wife.

"'Yes! it was.'

"'Well he passed by here the day before yesterday; but he went so fast you'll never be able to catch him up,' she said.

"This little girl played about on the floor with a napkin, which was of that kind that when one said on it,

' Napkin, spread yourself out and be covered with all dainty dishes,' it did so, and where it was there was never any want of a good dinner.

"'But this poor wife,' said the little girl, 'who has to go so far over such bad ways, she may well be starving and suffering much other ill. I dare say she has far more need of this napkin than I;' and so she asked if she might have leave to give her the napkin, and she got it.

"So the princess took the napkin and thanked them, and set off again far and farther than far, away through the same murk wood all that day and night, and in the morning she came to a cross-fell which was as steep as a wall, and so high and broad, she could see no end to it. There was a hut there too, and as soon as she set her foot inside it, she said,—

"'Good-day! Have you seen if King Valemon, the white bear, has passed this way?'

"'Good-day to you,' said the old wife. 'It was you, maybe, who was to have him?'

"'Yes! it was.'

"'Well! he passed by and went up over the hill three days ago; but up that nothing can get that is wingless.'

"That hut, you must know, was all so full of small bairns, and they all hung round their mother's skirts and bawled for food. Then the goody put a pot on the fire full of small round pebbles. When the princess asked what that was for, the goody said they were so poor they had neither food nor clothing, and it went to her heart to hear the children screaming for a morsel of food ; but when she put the pot on the fire, and said—

" 'The potatoes will soon be ready,' the words dulled their hunger, and they were patient awhile.

" It was not long before the princess brought out the napkin and the flask, that you may be sure, and when the children were all full and glad, she cut them out clothes with her golden scissors.

" 'Well!' said the goody in the hut, 'since you have been so kind and good towards me and my bairns, it were a shame if I didn't do all in my power to try to help you over the hill. My husband is one of the best smiths in the world, and now you must lie down and rest till he comes home, and then I'll get him to forge you claws for your hands and feet, and then you can see if you can crawl and scramble up.'

" So when the smith came home, he set to work at once at the claws, and next morning they were ready. She had no time to stay, but said, ' Thank you,' and then clung close to the rock and crept and crawled with the steel claws all that day and the next night, and just as she felt so very very tired that she thought she could scarce lift hand or foot, but must slip down—there she was all right at the top. There she found a plain, with tilled fields and meads, so big and broad, she never thought there could be any land so wide and so flat, and close by was a castle full of workmen of all kinds, who swarmed like ants on an ant-hill.

" 'What is going on here ? ' asked the princess.

"Well! if she must know, there lived the old hag who had bewitched King Valemon, the white bear, and in three days she was to hold her wedding feast with him. Then she asked if she mightn't have a word with her. 'No! was it likely? It was quite impossible.' So she sat down under the window and began to clip in the air with her golden scissors, till the silks and satins flew about as thick as a snow-drift.

"But when the old hag saw that, she was all for buying the golden scissors, for she said, 'All our tailors can do is no good at all, we have too many to find clothes for.'

"So the princess said, 'It was not for sale for money, but she should have it, if she got leave to sleep with her sweetheart that night.'

"'Yes!' the old hag said, 'she might have that leave and welcome, but she herself must lull him off to sleep and wake him in the morning.'

"And, so when he went to bed she gave him a sleeping draught, so that he could not keep an eye open, for all that the princess cried and wept.

"Next day the princess went under the window again, and began to pour out drink from her flask. It frothed like a brook with ale and wine, and it was never empty. So when the old hag saw that, she was all for buying it, for she said,—

"'For all our brewing and stilling, it's no good, we have too many to find drink for.'

"But the princess said, 'It was not for sale for money,

but if she **might** have leave to sleep with her sweetheart that night, she might have it.'

" ' Well!' the old hag said, ' she might have that leave and welcome, but she must herself lull him off to sleep and wake him in the morning.'

" So when he went to bed she gave him another sleeping draught, so that it went no better that night than the first. He was not able to keep his eyes open, for all that the princess bawled and wept.

" But that night, there was one of the workmen who worked in a room next to theirs. He heard the weeping and knew how things stood, and next day he told the prince that she must be come, that princess who was to set him free.

" That day it was just the same story with the napkin as with the scissors and the flask. When it was about dinner-time the princess went outside the castle, took out the napkin and said, ' Napkin, spread yourself out and be covered with all dainty dishes,' and there was meat enough, and to spare, for hundreds of men ; but the princess sat down to table by herself.

So when the old hag set her eyes on the napkin, she wanted to buy it, ' For all their roasting and boiling is worth nothing, we have too many mouths to feed.'

" But the princess said, ' It was not for sale for money, but if she might have leave to sleep with her sweetheart that night, she might have it.

" ' Well ! she might do so and welcome,' said the old

hag; 'but she must first lull him off to sleep and wake him up in the morning.'

"So when he was going to bed, she came with the sleeping draught, but this time he was aware of her and made as though he slept. But the old hag did not trust him for all that, for she took a pin and stuck it into his arm to try if he were sound asleep, but for all the pain it gave him he did not stir a bit, and so the princess got leave to come into him.

"Then everything was soon set right between them, and if they could only get rid of the old hag, he would be free. So he got the carpenters to make him a trap-door on the bridge over which the bridal train had to pass, for it was the custom there that the bride rode at the head of the train with her friends.

"So when they got well on the bridge, the trap-door tipped up with the bride and all the other old hags who were her bridesmaids. But King Valemon and the princess, and all the rest of the train, turned back to the castle and took all they could carry away of the gold and goods of the old hag, and so they set off for his own land, and were to hold their real wedding.

"And on the way King Valemon picked up those three little girls in the three huts and took them with them, and now she saw why it was he had taken her babes away and put them out at nurse; it was, that they might help her to find him out. And so they drank their bridal ale both stiff and strong.

THE GOLDEN BIRD.

"ONCE on a time there was a king who had a garden, and in that garden stood an apple-tree, and on that apple-tree grew one golden apple every year. But when the time drew on for plucking it, away it went, and there was no one who could tell who took it or what became of it. It was gone, and that was all they knew.

"This king had three sons, and so he said to them one day that he of them who could get him his apple again or lay hold of the thief should have the kingdom after him, were he the eldest, or the youngest, or the midmost.

"So the eldest set out first on this quest, and sat him down under the tree, and was to watch for the thief; and when night drew near a golden bird came flying, and his feathers gleamed a long way off; but when the king's son saw the bird and his beams he got so afraid he daren't stay his watch out, but flew back into the palace as fast as ever he could.

"Next morning the apple was gone. By that time the king's son had got back his heart into his body, and so he fell to filling his scrip with food, and was all for setting out to try if he could find the bird. So the king fitted him out well, and spared neither money nor clothes, and when the king's son had gone a bit he got hungry and took out his scrip, and sat him down to eat his dinner by the wayside. Then out came a fox from a spruce clump and sat by him and looked on.

"'Do, dear friend, give me a morsel of food,' said the fox.

"'I'll give you burnt horn, that I will,' said the king's son. 'I'm like to need food myself, for no one knows how far and how long I may have to travel.'

"'Oh! that's your game, is it?' said the fox, and back he went into the wood.

"So when the king's son had eaten and rested awhile he set off on his way again. After a long, long time he came to a great town, and in that town was an inn, where there was always mirth and never sorrow; there he thought it would be good to be, and so he turned in there. But there was so much dancing and drinking, and fun and jollity, that he forgot the bird and its feathers, and his father, and his quest, and the whole kingdom. Away he was and away he stayed.

"The year after the midmost king's son was to watch for the apple thief in the garden. Yes, he too sat him down under the tree when it began to ripen. So all at once one night the golden bird came shining like the sun, and the lad got so afraid he put his tail between his legs and ran indoors as fast as ever he could.

"Next morning the apple was gone; but by that time

the king's son had taken heart again, and was all for setting off to see if he could find the bird. Yes, he began to put up his travelling fare, and the king fitted him out well, and spared neither clothes nor money. But just the same befell him as had befallen his brother. When he had travelled a bit he got hungry, and opened his scrip, and sat him down to eat his dinner by the wayside. So out came a fox from a spruce clump and sat up and looked on.

" ' Dear friend, give me a morsel of food, do ?' said the fox.

" ' I'll give you burnt horn, that I will,' said the king's son. ' I may come to need food myself, for no one knows how far and how long I may have to go.'

" ' Oh ! that's your game, is it ?' said the fox, and away he went into the wood again.

" So when the king's son had eaten and rested himself awhile he set off on his way again. And after a long, long time he came to the same town and the same inn where there was always mirth and never sorrow, and he too thought it would be good to turn in there, and the very first man he met was his brother, and so he too stayed there. His brother had feasted and drunk till he had scarce any clothes to his back ; but now they both begun anew, and there was such drinking and dancing, and fun and jollity, that the second brother also forgot the bird and its feathers, and his father, the quest, and the whole king-dom. Away he was and away he stayed, he too.

" So when the time drew on that the apple was getting ripe again the youngest king's son was to go out into the garden and watch for the apple thief. Now he took with him a comrade, who was to help him up into the tree, and they took with them a keg of ale and a pack of cards to while away the time, so that they should not fall asleep. All at once came a blaze as of the sun, and just as the golden bird pounced down and snapped up the apple the king's son tried to seize it, but he only got a feather out of his tail. So he went into the king's bedroom and when he came in with the feather the room was as bright as broad day.

"So he too would go out into the wide world to try if he could hear any tidings of his brothers and catch the bird, for after all he had been so near it that he had put his mark on it and got a feather out of his tail. Well, the king was long in making up his mind if he should let him go, for he thought it would not be better with him who was the youngest than with the eldest, who ought to have had more knowledge of the ways of the world, and he was afraid he might lose him too. But the king's son begged so prettily, that he had to give him leave at last.

"So he began to pack up his travelling fare, and the king fitted him out well both with clothes and money, and so he set off. So when he had travelled a bit he got hungry and opened his scrip, and sat him down to eat his dinner, and just as he put the first bit into his mouth a fox came out of a spruce clump, and sat down by him and looked on.

"'Oh! dear friend! give me a morsel of food, do,' said the fox.

"'I might very well come to need food for myself,' said the king's son; 'for, I'm sure, I can't tell how long I shall have to go; but so much I know, that I can just give you a little bit.'

"So when the fox had got a bit of meat to bite at, he asked the king's son whither he was bound. Well, he told him what he was trying to do.

"'If you will listen to me,' said the fox, 'I will help you, so that you shall take luck along with you.'

"Then the king's son gave his word to listen to him, and so they set off in company, and when they had travelled awhile they came to the self-same town and the self-same inn where there was always mirth and never sorrow.

"'Now I may just as well stay outside the town,' said the fox. 'Those dogs are such a bore.'

"And then he told him what his brothers had done, and what they were still doing, and he went on.

"'If you go in there you'll get no farther either. Do you hear?'

"So the king's son gave his word, and his hand into the bargain, that he wouldn't go in there, and they each went his way. But when the prince got to the inn and heard what music and jollity there was inside he could not help going in, there were not two words about that, and when he met his brothers, there was such a to-do, that he forgot both the fox and his quest, and the bird and his father. But when he had been there awhile the fox came —for he had ventured into the town after all—and peeped through the door, and winked at the king's son, and said now they must set off. So the prince came to his senses again, and away they started for the house.

"And when they had gone awhile they saw a big fell far, far off. Then the fox said :

"'Three hundred miles behind yon fell there grows a gilded linden tree with golden leaves, and in that linden roosts the golden bird whose feather that is.'

"So they travelled thither together, and when the king's son was going off to catch the bird, the fox gave him some fine feathers, which he was to wave with his hand to lure the bird down, and then it would come flying and perch on his hand. But the fox told him to mind and not touch the linden, for there was a big Troll who owned it, and if the king's son but touched the tiniest twig the Troll would come and slay him on the spot.

"Nay! the king's son would be sure not to touch it, he said ; but when he had got the bird on his fist, he thought he just would have a twig of the linden, that was past praying against, it was so bright and lovely. So, he took one, just one very tiny little one. But in a trice out came the Troll.

"'WHO IS IT THAT STEALS MY LINDEN AND MY BIRD?' he roared, and was so angry that sparks of fire flashed from him.

"'Thieves think every man a thief,' said the king's son ; 'but none are hanged but those who don't steal right.'

"But the Troll said it was all one, and was just going

to smite him ; but the lad said he must spare his life.

" ' Well ! well !' said the Troll, ' if you can get me again the horse which| my nearest neighbour has stolen from me, you shall get off with your life.'

" ' But where shall I find him ?' asked the king's son.

" ' Oh ! he lives three hundred miles beyond yon big fell that looks blue in the sky.'

" So the king's son gave his word to do his best. But when he met the fox, Reynard was not altogether in a soft temper.

" ' Now you have behaved badly,' he said. ' Had you done as I bade you, we should have been on our way home by this time.'

" So they had to make a fresh start, as life was at stake, and the prince had given his word, and after a long, long time they got to the spot. And when the prince was to go and take the horse, the fox said :

" ' When you come into the stable, you will see many bits hanging on the stalls, both of silver and gold ; them you shall not touch, for then the Troll will come out and slay you on the spot ; but the ugliest and poorest, that you shall take.'

" Yes ! the king's son gave his word to do that ; but when he got into the stable he thought it was all stuff, for there was enough and to spare of fine bits ; and so he took the brightest he could find, and it shone like gold ; but in a trice out came the Troll, so cross that sparks of fire flashed from him.

"'WHO IS IT WHO TRIES TO STEAL MY HORSE AND MY BIT?' he roared out.

"'Thieves think every man a thief,' said the king's son ; 'but none are hanged but those who don't steal right.'

"'Well! all the same,' said the Troll, 'I'll kill you on the spot.'

"But the king's son said he must spare his life.

"'Well! well!' said the Troll, 'if you can get me back the lovely maiden my nearest neighbour has stolen from me I'll spare your life.'

"'Where does he live, then?' said the king's son.

"'Oh! he lives three hundred miles behind that big fell that is blue, yonder in the sky,' said the Troll.

"Yes! the king's son gave his word to fetch the maiden, and then he had leave to go, and got off with his life. But when he came out of doors the fox was not in the very best temper, you may fancy.

"'Now you have behaved badly again. Had you done as I bade you, we might have been on our way home long ago. Do you know, I almost think now I won't stay with you any longer.'

"But the king's son begged and prayed so prettily from the bottom of his heart, and gave his word never to do anything but what the fox said, if he would only be his companion. At last the fox yielded, and they became fast friends again, and so they set off afresh, and after a long,

long time they came to the spot where the lovely maiden was.

"'Yes!' said the fox, 'you have given your word like a man, but for all that, I dare not let you go in to the Troll's house this time. I must go myself.'

"So he went in, and in a little while he came out with the maiden, and so they travelled back by the same way that they had come. And when they came back to the Troll who had the horse, they took both it and the grandest bit; and when they got to the Troll who owned the linden and the bird, they took both the linden and the bird, and set off with them.

"So when they had travelled awhile, they came to a field of rye, and the fox said:

"'I hear a noise; now you must ride on alone, and I will bide here awhile.'

"So he platted himself a dress of rye-straw, and it looked just like some one who stood there and preached. And he had scarcely done that before all three Trolls came flying along, thinking they would overtake them.

"'Have you seen any one riding by here with a lovely maiden, and a horse with a gold bit, and a golden bird and a gilded linden-tree?' they all roared out to him who stood there preaching.

"'Yes! I heard that from my grandmother's grandmother, that such a train passed by here, but Lord bless us, that was in the good old time, when my grandmother's grandmother baked cakes for a penny, and gave the penny back again.'

"Then all the three Trolls burst out into loud fits of laughter, 'HA ! HA ! HA ! HA !' they cried, and took hold of one another.

"'If we have slept so long, we may e'en just turn our noses home, and go bed,' they said; and so they went back by the way they had come.

"Then the fox started off after the king's son; but when they got to the town where the inn and his brothers were, he said :

"'I dare not go through the town for the dogs. I must take my own way round about; but now you must take good care that your brothers don't lay hold of you.'

" But when the king's son got into the town, he thought it very hard if he didn't look in on his brothers and have a word with them, and so he halted a little time. But as soon as his brothers set eyes on him, they came out and took from him both the maiden and the horse, and the bird and the linden, and everything; and himself they stuffed into a cask and cast him into the lake, and so they set off home to the king's palace, with the maiden and the horse, and the bird and linden, and everything. But the maiden wouldn't say a word; she got pale and wretched to look at. The horse got so thin and starved, all his bones scarce clung together. The bird moped and shone no more, and the linden withered away.

" Meanwhile the fox walked about outside the town, where the inn was with all its jollity, and he listened and waited for the king's son and the lovely maiden, and wondered why they did not come back. So he went hither and thither, and waited and longed, and at last he went down to the strand, and there he saw the cask which lay on the lake drifting, and called out :

"'Are you driven about there, you empty cask?'

"'Oh! it is I,' said the king's son inside the cask.

"Then the fox swam out into the lake as fast as he could, and got hold of the cask and drew it on shore. Then he began to gnaw at the hoops, and when he had got them off the cask, he called out to the king's son, 'Kick and stamp!'

"So the king's son struck out and stamped and kicked, till every stave burst asunder, and out he jumped from the cask. Then they went together to the king' palace, and when they got there the maiden grew lovely, and began to speak; the horse got so fat and sleek that every hair beamed; the bird shone and sang; the linden began to bloom and glitter with its leaves, and at last the maiden said :

"'Here he is who set us free!'

"So they planted the linden in the garden and the youngest prince was to have the princess, for she was one of course; but as for the two elder brothers, they put them each into his own cask full of nails, and rolled them down a steep hill.

"So they made ready for the bridal; but first the fox said to the prince he must lay him on the chopping-block, and cut his head off, and whether he thought it good or ill, there was no help for it, he must do it. But as he dealt the stroke, the fox became a lovely prince, and he was the princess's brother, whom they had set free from the Trolls.

" So the bridal came on, and it was so great and grand, that the story of that feasting spread far and wide, till it reached all the way to this very spot."

THE END.

BRADBURY, AGNEW, & CO., PRINTERS, WHITEFRIARS.